DOVLATOV
AND
SURROUNDINGS

DOVLATOV AND SURROUNDINGS

A Philological Novel

Alexander Genis

Translated by
Alexander Rojavin

BOSTON
2023

Library of Congress Cataloging-in-Publication Data

Names: Genis, Aleksandr, 1953- author. | Rojavin, Alexander, translator.
Title: Dovlatov and surroundings : a philological novel / Alexander Genis ;
    translated by Alexander Rojavin.
Other titles: Dovlatov i okrestnosti. English
Description: Boston : Academic Studies Press, 2023. | Includes
    bibliographical references.
Identifiers: LCCN 2022041676 (print) | LCCN 2022041677 (ebook) | ISBN
    9798887190518 (hardback) | ISBN 9798887190525 (paperback) | ISBN
    9798887190532 (adobe pdf) | ISBN 9798887190549 (epub)
Subjects: LCSH: 880-01 Dovlatov, Sergeĭ. | Authors, Russian--20th
    century--Biography. | Russian literature--20th century.
Classification: LCC PG3479.6.O85 Z63 2023 (print) | LCC PG3479.6.O85
    (ebook) | DDC 891.73/44 [B]--dc23/eng/20220901
LC record available at https://lccn.loc.gov/2022041676
LC ebook record available at https://lccn.loc.gov/2022041677

ISBN 9798887190518 (hardback)
ISBN 9798887190525 (paperback)
ISBN 9798887190532 (adobe pdf)
ISBN 9798887190549 (epub)

Book design by Kryon Publishing Services.
Cover design by Ivan Grave.
On the cover: a graffiti in St. Petersburg, by Misha Vert (2021). Reproduced by the
artist's permission.

Published by Cherry Orchard Books, an imprint of Academic Studies Press.
1577 Beacon Street
Brookline, MA 02446, USA
press@academicstudiespress.com
www.academicstudiespress.com

Contents

Foreword: Genis and Surroundings, or Twenty Years Later   1
Mark Lipovetsky

1. The Last Soviet Generation   15

2. Laughter and Trepidation   23

3. The Poetics of Prison   33

4. Do You Like Fish?   41

5. The Metaphysics of Error   51

6. Cabbage Soup from Borjomi   59

7. *Tere-Tere*   67

8. Poetry and Truth   77

9. None of Us Are Lookers   87

10. An Empty Mirror   95

11. A Dotted Novel   103

12. All That Jazz   113

13. Pushkin   121

14. A Concert for an Accented Voice   137

15. Halfway to the Homeland   147

16. A Matryoshka with Genitals   157

17. The Unwilling Son of the Ether   167

18. Death and Other Concerns   177

19. Without Dovlatov   185

20. A Brief History of *The New American*   187

21. Dovlatov as an Editor   199

22. Dovlatov on the Screen   207

23. Dovlatov and Death   209

Genis and Surroundings, or Twenty Years Later

Mark Lipovetsky

When Alexander Genis's book *Dovlatov and Surroundings* was released by the Moscow-based publisher Vagrius in 1999, for two months it held the place at the top of the most popular book charts and ceded its primacy (sliding down into second position) only to Pelevin's *Generation "P"*. For the first time in post-Soviet Russia, a critic's book became a literary fact and, as Tynyanov would have put it, became a phenomenon that changed the trajectory of literary evolution. In other words, without Genis's "philological novel," the biographies of Boris Pasternak and Venedikt Yerofeyev would have never won literary awards, Dmitry Bykov's literary lectures would have never reached so many readers (and now viewers), and we wouldn't have so many popular internet channels dedicated to the close reading of literary texts.

This is not entirely because of Dovlatov—though his mega-popularity certainly played a role—but because of Genis himself as well. A widely renowned literary critic, the author of many intellectual bestsellers (together with Pyotr Vail and without him), a longtime host for Radio Liberty, Genis wrote not a literary biography, not an analysis of poetics, not a philosophical commentary, and not a memoir—he wrote the former, the latter, and everything in between, calling the final result a "philological novel." In his own preface to one of his editions of *Surroundings*, titled "Coastal Navigation," Genis writes that,

> Before beginning its task, a philological novel must ward off all traces of a biographical one. The dubious hybrid of a novel with non-fiction, a biographical novel familiarizes the reader with the protagonist's life, relaying his thoughts, feelings, and creations in his own words. ('Pushkin came out onto the porch'). In order to achieve success in this strange domain, one must either be level with the hero or else be his superior, which is very rare. A philological novel is concerned with something

else—it unravels the tapestry that the author wove together with such artistry and diligence.

I don't quite agree with Genis. In my opinion, literary criticism is what concerns itself with "unraveling the tapestry." A philological novel, meanwhile, doesn't stop there: after unraveling Dovlatov's tapestry into the individual threads of the precise observations about devices that lurk behind his poetics, Genis weaves it together anew, but imbues the fabric with his own narratives and—more broadly—himself, his experience, and his understanding of his generation and diaspora. To put it into scientific language, a philological novel is a form of autofiction, where fiction is represented by philology, and everything stemming from the author is novelized. Novelized in the sense that Bakhtin put into the word: "The novel comes into contact with the spontaneity of the inconclusive present; that is what keeps the genre from congealing. The novelist is drawn to everything that is not yet completed. He may turn up on the field of representation in any authorial pose, he may depict real moments in his own life or make allusions to them, he may interfere in the conversation of his heroes."[1] All of this is applicable to Genis's book.

Let's begin with literary criticism. By painting a multifaceted portrait of Dovlatov in the foreground, Genis, as if in this portrait's shadow, casually constructs a theoretical model of his aesthetics. The book's loose structure itself resists such concepts as "a theoretical model" and "aesthetics." A certain effort is required in order to make it out. Meanwhile, not only does Genis not hide this concept—he, in fact, with a didactic insistence repeats the main ideas, slightly varying the terminology and constantly providing new examples. Per my calculations, in this way, Genis's formula for prose, which "lets in chaos/ emptiness," is repeated four times. This might irritate some people. But I find a particular attractiveness about this insistence: the spontaneity of *Dovlatov and Surroundings'* composition turns out to be conscious; the zigzags of authorial thought are actually subordinated to a strictly conceived trajectory. To use Genis's own metaphor, his essayist style constantly intersects with the theme of literary criticism rather than moving alongside it. If this theme were expressed directly, it would lose its complexity and devolve into an amalgam of ideas. But Genis proceeds from the assertion that "there *are* no ideas."[2]

---

1   M. M. Bakhtin, *The Dialogic Imagination: Four Essays*, ed. Michael Holquist, trans. Caryl Emerson and Michael Holquist (Austin: Texas University Press, 1981), 27.
2   Alexander Genis, *Dovlatov and His Surroundings* (Boston: Academic Studies Press, 2023), 6. From now on, quotes from this book will be marked in parentheses.

For Genis, this last conviction, which is easily integrated into the context of poststructuralist philosophy and aesthetics, is likely a function of psychology rather than philosophy. According to Genis, the principled absence of ideas—or rather, the clear-eyed understanding of the fictitiousness of any ideological constructions—becomes a lifelong principle of "the last Soviet generation" (to use Alexei Yurchak's catchphrase), among whose number he counts himself, the generation for which Dovlatov became its voice.

> Dovlatov de-conceptualized the Soviet regime. Strictly speaking, he vocalized what everyone already knew: the idea on which the country stood no longer existed. And he added something else: no other idea existed either, because there were no ideas at all.
> Cognition of this circumstance is what distinguishes the last Soviet generation from the preceding one. One juxtaposed just ideas to false ones—the other simply didn't believe in the existence of ideas. (6)

The situation, let's be honest, isn't particularly new: Chekhov's Nikolai Stepanovich worried about the lack of a "common idea," and Chekhov himself, as we all recall, was constantly hounded by criticism over his lack of ideology. Brodsky, whom Dovlatov loved so dearly, wrote about this as well:

> The truth is that there is
> no truth. This does not liberate
> from responsibility—it does the exact opposite:
> ethics are the very same vacuum that is filled by human
> behavior practically at all times;
> it's the very same cosmos, if you will.[3]

As we see, for Brodsky, just as for Chekhov, not only does the absence of truth not equate with moral relativism, but quite the opposite—it endows each personal ethical choice with a "cosmic" significance.

But today, Genis's deliberation on there not being any ideas "at all" rings somewhat different than it did at the end of the '90s. On the face of it, he and his

---

3   Iosif Brodsky. 1989. "A Lecture at the Sorbonne." Transcript of speech delivered at the Sorbonne, Paris, France, March, 1989, accessed August 4, 2022, https://izbrannoe.com/news/mysli/iosif-brodskiy-vystuplenie-v-sorbonne/.

generation were wrong: not only has the clash of ideologies not gone anywhere, it has, in fact, intensified—and not only in the Russian-speaking world, but across the globe. Genis—the political journalist—has more than once had the pleasure of ascertaining this: having once and for all assumed a liberal position, he is time and time again forced to counter the frenzied attacks of Trumpists both in Russian-speaking America and in Russia itself. But strange as it may seem, these last years most clearly demonstrate that it is Genis, together with Dovlatov, who are right. "There are no ideas," but this has not made ideologies disappear—it's just that today, it is more obvious than before that the ideologies heeded by the masses (including the hordes of Trumpists) aren't about ideas at all—they're about something else entirely. They're about powerful emotions, about precognitive affects, about fears and phantasms.

Which is to say they're about the very thing that literature deals with.

This is why, according to Genis, Dovlatov's aesthetics are his ethical—and I'll add, political—strategy: in every short story, in each scene from his notebooks, he searches for an answer to the question of how to present a whole picture of a world that has lost "the universal principle that united, justified, and enabled opposition to it." Paradoxically, in Genis's understanding, Dovlatov himself simultaneously embodies the freedom from ideas and surmounts it, denying it the ability to transform into the "pulp fiction" of contemporary affective ideologies. Because for Genis and his protagonist, "wholeness" and "integrity" aren't empty words: "The writer is the last guardian of coherence in a world of disintegrated knowledge," insists Genis. "He gathers what others scatter. In putting it together, he winds up with something greater than its parts." The question of integrity isn't answered even with such precise ethical, psychological, and philosophical determinations of Dovlatov's position like "underground amorality," which manifests itself as "a lack of commonly accepted criteria that would allow any kind of appraisal;" the ability "to hold on to one's moralistic verdicts, accepting the world as it is;" the discrediting of a "great" history and the "pathos of historical second-ratedness;" "indifference, which nurtured such hopeless modesty that it may as well have been called meekness."

Genis solves the question of Dovlatov's "worldview's" wholeness/integrity in the space of Dovlatov's poetics. Poetics that, despite its apparent simplicity, is founded on contradictions that cannot be called anything but philosophical.

In Genis's book, Dovlatov, on the one hand, comes across as a realist who depicted only what he knew and saw, and who reveled in the precision of detail. But on the other hand, unlike "normal" realists (like Solzhenitsyn, for example), Dovlatov is invariably fascinated with the atypical, the strange, the freakish: "Sergei told us that he would make his friends skip class to go to the square and look at the old man twitching his toe in a funny manner." Dovlatov absolutizes the precision of detail, and Genis proclaims an impassioned hymn to details, invoking the art of haikus and Kharms at the same time. And though it might seem that the absolutization of detail results in a fractured picture of the world, Genis reaches the opposite conclusion: "By equalizing all elements of creation, [Dovlatov's] peripheral vision made the fabric of reality whole".

The flight from the typical toward the bizarre and absurdist injects Dovlatov's "realism" with an unexpected element of documentality, but it is a documentality with a Vaginovian twist, since it presupposes the destruction of the boundary between life and fiction: "People comprised the alphabet of his poetics. That's how it was: a person as a unit of text." "Dovlatov understood that he surrounded himself with his own victims, but he couldn't do anything about it. Even substituting someone's name for a fake one was agonizing for him—he equated it with becoming a co-author of someone else's work."

Genis compares Dovlatov's method with impressionism. I feel like this comparison is nevertheless imprecise. It would be more accurate to speak of late modernist minimalism or postmodern hyperrealism—both involve an intensive examination of life's details, revealing their artificiality, unnaturality, even pretentiousness. For Dovlatov, a sign of such aestheticism has always been the absurd—the Dovlatovian narrator marvels at the absurdity of the world, finding in it the purely aesthetic joy of the unexpected, but Dovlatov's protagonist can never resist the pleasure of augmenting the world's absurdity. However, Genis insists on the opposite effect of Dovlatov's aestheticism as well: "Dovlatov knew the price of the 'wondrous power of the absurd,' but he dreamed of the norm, which also 'evokes the feeling of wonder.'"

As we see, all we are left with is traditional realism's outer layer, what Roland Barthes called "the reality effect," masking the unconventional structure of a fictional character and a fictional world as a whole. This isn't only or so much a way of deceiving or retaining the reader. It is an inbuilt mechanism of control over the organic nature of the entire fictional construction. Precise detail requires an organic context; otherwise, it is rejected as a foreign body. "Realism" writ so is what Dovlatov and subsequently Genis call an author's "shackles," discipline, a stick, a paranoid striving for order, in this case buttressed by the banal but no less effective determination of "like or unlike."

If "realism" is responsible for the style of Dovlatov's prose, then its "content" is described by Genis in terms of absurdity, chaos, emptiness: "By portraying socialism as a national manifestation of the absurd, Sergei denied it primacy among socialism's other forms. Dovlatov showed that all life was absurd, not just *Soviet* life. With that adjective out of the picture, the impression that there was something exceptional about our lot in life disappeared as well;" "The constancy of change, the Brownian motion of life, the incessant hum of chaos—working in the paper, Dovlatov found everything that made up his prose;" "... [*The Compromise*] is, like all of Dovlatov's books, about something else—it deals with the distribution of order and chaos in the universe."

I reproduce these passages of Genis's with pleasure both because they truly are accurate with regard to Dovlatov and because, in my opinion, it is exactly such a "dialogue with chaos" that is characteristic for postmodernism on the whole and for Russian postmodernism in particular. Genis discovered quite a significant turn that allows us to see the connection between this attention to chaos, absurdity, and emptiness with the characteristic Russian cultural tradition of longing for the organic wholeness of worldview. It is not accident that, as Genis puts it, Dovlatov inherits the central principle of his poetics directly from Pushkin: "the ability to reconcile contradictions without destroying them, but, in fact, highlighting them" (in my opinion, an excellent formula for postmodernist paralogism!). Genis formulates this principle while analyzing Dovlatov's *Pushkin Hills*, and now that this masterpiece is accessible in English thanks to an excellent translation by the writer's daughter,[4] I know what to give students to read about this book.

If the illusion of realism determines Dovlatov's style, and themes of absurdity, chaos, and emptiness dominate among his "signifieds," then how do we get the organic unity that is so tangible in each of Dovlatov's texts? Genis solves this problem particularly elegantly and convincingly. Per the logic of *Dovlatov and Surroundings*, Dovlatov's contradiction between "realism" and "chaos" is erased by the paradoxical nature of his prose's central character—the author himself. While the realist tradition bestows upon the author—typically situated beyond the text (endowed with "outsidedness")— knowledge of the truth, Dovlatov demonstratively embeds himself, with all his biographical viscera, into the very center of his own prose. At the same time, as Genis underlines, "Dovlatov turned out to be not only the strongest author of our generation, but the most beat up as well ... Sergei assiduously made sure not to become higher than the reader. Like no one else, he understood the advantage of such a position." Genis diligently explains that

---

4   Sergei Dovlatov, *The Pushkin Hills*, trans. Katherine Dovlatov (Berkeley: Counterpoint, 2014).

denying an author the right to judge his own characters means leaving him jobless ... By becoming a literary position, an author's inaction becomes paradoxical. On the one hand, Dovlatov is the inevitable hero of all his short stories. On the other hand, he's not a hero at all. He doesn't even have a reflection in the mirror. By equalizing himself with the characters, the storyteller steps aside in order to let his surroundings say their piece.

Genis and Dovlatov both consciously muddy the relationship between the narrator, the first-person character, and the biographic author—by mixing these different forms of expression of authorial consciousness (a simple example: the protagonist bears the same first and last name that is written on the front cover), they subvert the hierarchy of authorial knowledge that looms behind these categories: Dovlatov's omniscient author loses his "final say," and this is emphasized by the constant defeats of his intra-textual doppelganger.

It is also worth remembering that Russian modernism has already treaded such a path. We need only recall Olesha's Kavalerov or Babel's Lyutov: there are no doubts about the contiguity between these characters and their creators or about their defeats in the fictional worlds of *Envy* and *Red Cavalry* respectively. As for Russian postmodernism—it begins in *Moscow-Petushki*, where the author/protagonist is so much lower than his readers that next to him, Dovlatov's battered superman seems a veritable giant.

What makes Dovlatov's author-hero different from these literary "siblings" of his?

The thing that Genis calls "the metaphysics of error."

Dovlatov's author-hero thoroughly lacks a martyr's halo, and the reader does not pity him because Dovlatov's extra-textual author revels in his defeats, saturating his texts with the poetry of error and imperfection. In one of the best chapters, which is specifically titled "The Metaphysics of Error," Genis shows how Dovlatov, merciless outside the text when it came to the typos and blunders of others, treasured the blemishes and slip-ups of his own autobiographical hero. "Dovlatov despised only the mistakes of others. His own, he not only tolerated—he cherished them. And he hated typos too, because he wanted to be the author of his own mistakes ... For Dovlatov, a mistake is suffused in a halo of veracity . . . Any shortcoming—spiritual or physical—played the role of a mistake without which a person, as a character of fate and nature, would turn out unreal, false. Imperfection birthed personality. Error made it suitable for narrative." Doesn't this mean that there does exist some criterion of veracity? It would appear so. But it entails precisely the obvious deviation from the norm, imperfection, which is so much more interesting than protocol, because it is individual, although in defeat rather than in victory. In other words, in "incompleteness."

The combination of "humbleness" and "the poetics of error" in the author character allows us to connect "realism" with "absurdity." And to connect them through the insoluble contradiction between the textual and extra-textual depictions of the author—as Genis notes, though, an irreconcilable contradiction happens to be the most natural. This paradoxical logic of authorial behavior extends beyond the boundaries of the text: Genis's Dovlatov, while assiduously destroying the prerogatives of authorial knowledge and judgment in the text, behaves in the exact opposite manner in real life: "Dovlatov was sooner a plenipotentiary writer in life than in literature. Hence his love for intrigue. Sergei was a brilliant taunter-miniaturist. Where others resorted to a crowbar, he employed such a sharp scalpel that he left no seams in his wake." In this way, this complex game between the author-hero and the author-narrator is joined by the myth that the author creates around himself beyond the boundaries of the text (what Tynyanov called the "lyrical hero").

The inclusion of this layer in Dovlatov's aesthetics is justified by Genis's chosen method of analysis: when quotes from Dovlatov's texts enjoy the same status as personal recollections of how Dovlatov acted in this situation or that, how he carried out his intrigues, how he insulted others and was insulted himself. Moreover, Genis often prefers the latter kind of argument to arguments scooped out of Dovlatov's texts. It is illustrative how Genis shields from view his analysis of *The Émigrée* with his own tales of immigrant life in the '70s and '80s, limiting himself to a single miserly verdict: "As a whole, *The Émigrée*, Dovlatov's most immigrant-focused book, doesn't work—it resembles a comedy screenplay too much". And I'm ready to bet anything that any reader of *Surroundings* would more vividly remember the story of how Dovlatov, Vail, and Genis himself decided to publish the *Russian Playboy* than the analysis of sexual motifs in Dovlatov's works.

Nevertheless, the main argument in support of Dovlatov's aesthetic philosophy as proposed by Genis isn't the analysis of specific texts or recollections, but the philological novel itself as a whole. I don't mean the stylization, though specific fragments of Genis's book truly do read as if written by the book's subject. For example, I love the following "Dovlatovian" description birthed by Genis's quill: "The ride itself was captivating enough. The car didn't have any windshield wipers, and our new boss would intermittently remove his suede cap and use it to wipe off the windshield, resignedly stretching out the window."

But most importantly, Genis's book is written in accordance with the very principles that he discerns in Dovlatov's poetics. Two layers of Genis's text—one memorial, the other dealing with literary criticism—engage each other in a productive and irreconcilable contradiction. If we view the memorial layer as central to *Surroundings*, with its brilliant portraits and scenes, honed by the precise details to the biting sharpness of anecdote, then all the literary criticism performs the role of something foreign, thereby meaning chaotic— unorganized material. This is exactly how Tatiana Tolstaya read the book, after which she rebuked Genis for needlessly "diluting an engrossing novel about his own life with the philology of an experienced essayist."[5] Conversely, I consider the philological layer central to this book, and, in my view, all the funny stories about Dovlatov and his other acquaintances provide the necessary "noise," especially since at the heart of these stories—as in Dovlatov's texts—is always a scene featuring absurdity or the paradoxical mix of order and absurdity. But in any case, this recreates the dynamic balance—discovered by Genis in his analysis of Dovlatov and his prose—between "the cult of the detail" (achieved by Genis in the form of the conclusiveness of his critical analysis) and the chaotic, absurd image of human "surroundings" (substantiated by Genis's seemingly spontaneous manner of writing). These two layers are in constant contention with each other. In this way, the philological idea of the fictional world that for the sake of its wholeness has allowed into itself the complexity of chaos is seemingly contradicted by the discussion of "the mystery of Dovlatov's boozing: vodka made his world maximally straightforward." Genis the literary critic savors the precision of Dovlatovian details, while the memoirist recalls the relish with which Dovlatov wove his web of light intrigue. Genis deliberately inserts disorder into his well-balanced conception and in doing so, endows it not so much with an intellectual conviction, but an aesthetic one.

Like Dovlatov, Genis scrupulously makes sure not to stand taller than his characters, not to demonstrate knowledge to which they are not privy: "All events in my life have been contained. I cannot recall anything monumental. Which is what gives me the courage to remember . . . Likely my most significant metaphysical distress comes from the cognition of the insignificance of any experience." Genis refers to himself in the indirect way, first and foremost carefully fixating his congruence and incongruence with Dovlatov, but invariably pulling away from any judgment. The image of the author is formed in the intersecting reflections of myriad mirrors, be they Dovlatov, his characters, or Paramonov,

---

5   Tatiana Tolstaya, "A Cat and Surroundings," *Obshchaya gazeta*, July 28, 1999.

Sinyavsky, Brodsky, Vail, Naum Sagalovsky, or even the Jewish cowboy Shamir, about whom nobody knows anything. And, those rare moments that Genis talks about himself in the first person are the very episodes that most look like Dovlatov's own style.

The courage of such an experiment is remarkable: it is the same as testing a new medicine on yourself. If the conception is false, then Genis's book will disintegrate into bits, the surroundings will fall away from Dovlatov . . . but they don't. The construction is sound. As proof of the *organic nature* of *Surroundings*, I can quote Lev Losev:

> [Genis's book] has one more fascinating attribute that I cannot explain. When you read it from top to bottom, you are in constant disagreement with it: here is an imprecise observation, there an unconvincing comment, this is poorly worded, and this is said brilliantly, but unnecessarily, just for the sake of a pretty turn of phrase . . . But, however many times you sit down to read *Dovlatov and Surroundings*, regardless of where you start, even on a random page, you are immediately engrossed, and tearing yourself away is impossibly difficult.[6]

The experiment that Genis has conducted also has its own literary significance. It renews the tradition of modernist metafiction. In metafiction, the process of writing the book itself, its composition (as a rule, pointedly spontaneous and incomplete)—this is the most holistic model of creation, personality, and fate. Shklovsky's experiment of literary criticism fused with the novel is particularly relevant, especially such books as *Zoo, or Letters not about Love* and *The Third Factory*. Shklovsky, in turn, indisputably paid heed to Rozanov's experiments, which he had studied carefully. The only difference is that, per Shklovsky's interpretation, Rozanov departed from literature toward maximally concentrated autobiographical daily routine and the everyday "stuff." Shklovsky, meanwhile, took autobiographical "stuff" as ready material, but alienated it through literary criticism. But for both of them—as for Genis—the central artistic principle of metafiction is in full force, the principle explained by Shklovsky as *constructive oxymoron*.

---

6   L. Losev, "Alexander Genis. 'Dovlatov and Surroundings,'" *Znamya*, November 10, 1999.

In Rozanov's works, for example, the oxymoron is based "on the discrepancy between thought or experience and their circumstances."[7] In Shklovsky's own rendition, it is between the romantic type of the authorial identity[8] and the academism of the enunciated theory. Turning to closer models, one may be reminded of Sinyavsky's *Strolls with Pushkin* and Katayev's *My Diamond Wreath*. Characteristically, both books were severely criticized in various circles of the Soviet and post-Soviet *intelligentsia*, precisely because they disrupted the conventional relationship between the literary critic and the classic (Sinyavsky), and the memoirist and the great heroes of memoirs (Katayev). In other words, these relationships took on the form of an oxymoron: the literary critic cannot speak of the classic's emptiness and frivolity, and the memoirist does not have the right to place himself on a level with great martyrs. Meanwhile, in both cases, literariness was presented as the "substance of existence," to use Platonov's phrase, equalizing the author and the hero and abolishing any hierarchy that may have existed in the setting. In this way, literariness was presented as a specific version of the modernist utopia of freedom.

Genis relies on the "memory" of this genre and the "memory" of the modernist aesthetic, but he radically changes its semantics: his whole book is also about freedom, but freedom that is attainable by means contrary to the modernist transfiguration of life's husk into a self-reliant and individual literary mythology. Genis wrote a book about freedom from the individual project of fate and literature; freedom that is attainable through deliberate mistakes and conscious receptiveness to unorganized and chaotic material, which is produced from minute to minute by the long-indiscernible intertwining of life and literature. At the same time, the idea of literariness itself is transfigured as well: it ceases being proof of the power of authorial imagination and intellect, it emerges as the result of the author's refusal to assume a godlike position in the text and the subject's rejection of the pursuit of order in life; it creates not a limitless universe, but a thin film at the point where precise perception and the ordinary absurdity of existence intersect.

I wrote about *Dovlatov and Surroundings* exactly twenty years ago, but having reread it, I find that many of my judgments have aged well, and I have no desire to renounce them. Especially in the English translation. Curiously, though he was considered the most successful writer of the Russian

---

7   V. Shklovsky, *On the Theory of Prose* (Moscow: Federatsiia, 1929), 237.
8   On Shklovsky's Romanticism, see B. Paramonov's essay "Mozart in the Role of Salieri," in *The End of Style*, ed. B. Paramonov (Moscow: Agraf, 1997), 20–54.

Third Wave of immigration in life and was disassembled into quotes and aphorisms after his death like a new Griboyedov, Dovlatov hasn't evoked serious scholarly interest from Slavists. Dovlatov has found a place on Netflix, but not in dissertations and scholarly journals. Notably, Genis's book is only the second book about Dovlatov in English.[9] The explanation must lie in Dovlatov's in-betweenness—in the 1990s, he seemed an insufficiently critical realist, and in the 2000s, he was insufficiently postmodern. So Genis's book is very timely—the conception it explicates allows us to reconsider our ossified understanding of both postmodernist canon and of the place that the modernist tradition has in contemporary culture. It also organically folds into the "anthropological turn" in literary criticism, with the one caveat that the anthropology created by Genis bears a predominantly artistic character.

From the perspective of anthropology, the culture of the Third Wave of immigration is united by the figure of Dovlatov much more than by Brodsky (Brodsky was a deity, says Genis). As Genis recalls: "Sergei inserted his friends into every one of his texts, not just the ones in the paper. It is difficult to find an acquaintance of his about whom he didn't write anything. He tried to make the immigration intimate by making it his home. Purposefully framing the myth of the Third Wave as a family narrative, Dovlatov employed phantoms. He came up with a particular newspaper genre: 'Instances.' These tiny, unsigned notes were published as real-life events."

As in other cases, Genis takes an isomorphic path in relation to his protagonist, and, in Dovlatov's footsteps, he insistently blurs the border between reality and text. In justifying his title, he places portraits of the inhabitants of Dovlatov's surroundings next to the protagonist—characters who are not only real, but also quite famous. However, in Genis's rendition, they act like literary characters who have stepped out of their books' pages directly into the real world: Boris Paramonov "most resembles not Russian writers themselves, but their characters—all of them at once, in fact, from Gogol's old-world landowners to Svidrigailov, from Oblomov to the Karamazovs." Vagrich Bakhchanyan, "who is accompanying this book like old man Shchukar in *Virgin Soil Upturned*," had something to say on this matter too: "'A superfluous person—that sounds prideful.'" Lev Losev "scrupulously and ably cultivates the image and mannerisms of a pre-Revolutionary professor, which itself seems like a quote from an Andrei Bely memoir;" and Sinyavsky, "as the years went by . . .

---

9   The first was Jekaterina Young, *Sergei Dovlatov and His Narrative Masks* (Evanston: Northwestern University Press, 2009).

began more and more to resemble as creature out of Slavic mythology—a leshy, a domovoy, maybe a bannik. He fostered this resemblance, and he enjoyed it immensely. When he gifted me a copy of *Ivan the Fool*, one of his last books, he inscribed it: 'The leshy says hi.'"

I believe that in this way, Genis achieves the same effect that Dovlatov did: he simultaneously makes the Third Wave of immigration more intimate and more mythological. On the one hand, *Dovlatov and Surroundings* is the best possible memorial to a generation of immigrants who left the Soviet Union on a Jewish visa and created a new Russian literature abroad. On the other hand, it is a house, filled with joyful and dramatic life, whose doors are open to all who wish to enter. The fact that Genis's philological novel is coming out in English today is proof of this project's success.

When all is said and done, Genis's book is an inexhaustible source of *optimism,* which is in such deficit both in Russian and in immigrant culture. Describing the immigrant context of the '70s and '80s, he emphasizes: "Everything that happened here was a strictly private affair. Unsurprising, considering how few of us there were . . . Under such conditions, literature returned to its roots—an unprofessional, private activity. Books printed in tiny numbers were written for our own—both friends and enemies." Today, literature is going through a similar state of things both in Russia and in the diaspora, with the sole difference that today's private affair of literature is taking place on the fields of the internet, on Facebook, and its surroundings. And if many are wont to view this situation as the end of literature, Genis's book convinces us of the opposite: by returning to its private riverhead, literature does not die—on the contrary, it is born anew. And with time, it turns out that behind what initially seemed too simple actually lurks a hidden complexity, while what at first appeared too complex and esoteric has the possibility of becoming wildly popular. You just need to wait twenty years.

1

The Last Soviet Generation

1

These days, both young and old are trying their hand at writing memoirs. The hunt is on for a non-fictional reality. Memory fever is running rampant. Perhaps uncertainty about the past is a reaction to the death of a regime. In a single hour, everything important became unimportant. Words and job titles lost their value. Take the foremost Soviet poet, who became a chicken farmer in his new life. Just like the last Roman emperor, if we are to believe Dürrenmatt.

The black hole occupying the space formerly inhabited by an entire nation pulls in all of its surroundings. Those loath to share the government's fate write memoirs to distance themselves from it. Unsurprisingly, this is easier for those who never glued themselves to it in the first place. Taking pride in his marginality, the memoirist chronicles the history of the curb—the periphery. Previously, memoirs would be written to appraise the past; now, their purpose is to ascertain that the past happened at all. To confirm that we had a history—our own history, not one shared by all.

"A good memoir," wrote Dovlatov, "always has a second plot (beyond the author's own life)."

In my case, the second plot just happens to be the author's own life—my life. I was born in February of 1953. My birth certificate says March 5th. The registry offices were open that day—Stalin's death was announced later. The Soviet regime began thirty-six years before my birth and ended thirty-six years after—with the fall of the Berlin Wall. Born in the middle of the era, I feel myself less a witness of history than a refugee from it. All events in my life have been contained. I cannot recall anything monumental.

This does not bother more confident authors than me. John Cage—the one who made the audience listen to silence at his concerts—wrote, "I have nothing to say, and I am saying it, and that is poetry."

I can't make that lift. I enjoy the absurd, but only that of others. I myself am a slave to coherent narrative. I find it uncomfortable to dwell on details that don't have much significance even for me. Though these very details, as you find out sooner or later, are the threads that make up the tapestry of life.

Likely, my most significant metaphysical distress comes from the cognition of the insignificance of any experience. I was top of my class in university, which wasn't difficult—the women teaching us loved me. Also, there were only three representatives of the male sex, including me, in the entire group. One was a remarkably pimpled poet, and the other, conversely, became an officer after graduating from the philology department. I, meanwhile, was a hippie, a straight-A student, and a fireman. I came to exams in tarpaulin boots. My hair hung down from under my service cap all the way to my military shirt. In short, there were things far more entertaining than me in our somber little institution. Regardless, instead of accepting me into the graduate program, which had been the object of my dreams, they took in a lanky general's daughter who, like everyone else at the time, wrote in melancholic verse. There was nothing left for me to do in Riga, so I left for America. Many years have passed, and the whole story seems—and is—thoroughly unimportant. What is there for me to envy? A dissertation titled "Sholokhov in Latvia?" The general-father himself, who turned out to be an albatross in the newly independent Latvia?

But that's not my point. If the drama of my student years lost its significance the second that I happened to be on the other side of the ocean, then how insignificant will all our other affairs seem when we find ourselves on the other side of life—especially if there *is* no other side?

So, I decided to write a book about Dovlatov. You write books about other people when you have nothing to say about yourself. That's not exactly the case here. In fact, I'm writing this book fully expecting to talk about myself. It's just that Dovlatov is a massive character. Literally as well as figuratively.

Vail[1] and I once went over to Sharymova's,[2] who was renowned as a lightning-fast cook. Tired of bumbling around on an empty stomach, we came over with a block of frozen cod. We arrived just at the end of the festivities, which our appearance imbued with a second wind. Obliging the hostess to retreat to

---

1   Pyotr Vail (1949–2009) was Alexander Genis's longtime friend and coauthor.
2   Natalia Sharymova emigrated from the Soviet Union to New York, where she worked as a photographer.

the kitchen, we squeezed in behind the table, at which point the room filled with an acrid smoke. Succumbing to laziness, Natalia didn't bother unwrapping the fish and plopped it onto the frying pan still snug in its cardboard packaging. Dovlatov emerged from the bedroom to inspect the tumult. We hadn't even known that he was there. Sergei, whom we hadn't yet gotten used to, had a powerful look about him. Dressed in something with epaulettes, he struggled to squeeze through the doorway. I recalled a show in which the protagonist turned into a green monster when in danger, and I enthusiastically proclaimed in English: "Incredible Hulk!"

"The intolerable Hulk," translated a happy Dovlatov, incorrectly but fittingly.

This book began on a rainy day in May in St. Petersburg. I was sitting in the *Zvezda* editorial office, telling stories about Dovlatov. I had long since grown used to interrogations on the subject, but I still don't understand one thing: why is Dovlatov studied exclusively by tall, pretty young women in the Slavic department? Fine, there was a young woman from Canada once, and another from France, but when a Japanese girl tall enough to play basketball began interrogating me, I became thoroughly impressed with Sergei's masculine charm, which soars above his works.

One way or another, my interview in St. Petersburg was smoothly nearing its finish. The rain outside had been joined by hail and even flakes of snow. Out of nowhere appeared a drenched woman with a sturdy bag. She turned out to be a hawker. She visited local businesses, offering her wares: imported sunglasses. That moment was emblematic of the mundane absurdity that often served as the point of departure for Dovlatov's prose. I got the hint, returned to New York, and made myself comfortable behind my writing desk.

2

Dovlatov made his debut in print with a memoir. When I first read *The Invisible Book*, I felt like the literary field had gotten crowded from a surplus of undiscovered stars. Having grown up in the provincial Riga, where the literary field began and ended with the author of a lyrical novel on the adoption of leading manufacturing methods, I envied Dovlatov like d'Artagnan envied the three musketeers. The world that Dovlatov allowed me to glimpse was so full of literature, humor, and debauchery that it left no room for anything else. It was beautiful, because it seemed to be hand-tailored to fit me.

A year after Dovlatov's death, I took part in an evening in his honor in Leningrad. It seemed to me like everyone who was onstage had emerged directly out of *The Invisible Book*—the cubical Ariev, the double-jointed Uflyand, the medal-encrusted Popov, Sergei Wolf, who looked like he stepped out of an El Greco painting. Even the Mayakovsky Writers' Union House featured in Dovlatov's book. This last part stuck in my memory more than anything else— Mayakovsky's statue took up the entire coatroom.

Since then, many of Dovlatov's friends have become my friends. But rereading *The Invisible Book*, I can't shake the feeling that the only authentic thing in this memoir is the characters' last names.

Sergei's friends truly were wonderful people, but they resembled their literary portraits no more than cartoon characters resemble the angular protagonists of stop-motion films. In life, they lacked the hasty laconism with which Dovlatov's pen endowed them. In Dovlatov's rendition, all of them— dazzling, witty, devoted to artistic follies—seemed greater and more interesting than the author, perched on the sidelines.

Sergei intentionally let them all surpass him. By letting his friends take center stage, Dovlatov portrayed them in those extreme close-ups that destroy scale, warp perspective, and deform basic shape, thus making the ordinary strange. In this same way, in a Japanese print, the artist places an enormous butterfly next to the very edge in order to show in the distillation of its wings a tiny Mt. Fuji. Dovlatov similarly hovered in the memoir's background.

Dovlatov only provided an outline of himself, interspersing his own story with scenes of bohemian life that were as vivid as decals. This was less the product of humility so much as instinct. By mixing in with others, Dovlatov joined in a delicate pattern. He didn't sew his biography together—he wove it like a tapestry. When he entered the literary field, Dovlatov ensured himself good company.

Writers die in solitude, but they are born together. A generation is a quantum of literary history, which is capable of developing only in leaps and bounds. In wordcraft, succession is sporadic. A change in generations occurs suddenly. The accumulated contradictions in tone become so concentrated that there becomes nothing left to debate. However, because the fault lines are drawn in one environment (as Dovlatov wrote, they wouldn't have let any other onto a tram, let alone into literature), it is as difficult to recognize a given transition as it is to see yourself from all sides at the same time. To do so, you need other people. A generation is like a community clean-up. It needs a crowd to become reality. What changes isn't individual style, but collective values—ethical priorities, rituals, reactions to the surroundings, the surroundings themselves. But even that's not enough.

As with any child's revolt against their parents, the divide is not only agonizing but useless until it concludes with the birth of a new generation. In order for that to happen, you need a center of condensation. Like a magnet in a vortex of iron shavings, the center identifies the structure and order in the chaos of conversation among friends.

"Dovlatov," said Valery Popov many years later, "declared us a generation." Fortune and fate made it the last in Soviet history.

3

Nabokov writes that Gogol created his readers himself. Dovlatov's readers were created by the Soviet regime. Sergei became the voice of the generation with which the regime ended. It is unsurprising that it recognized him as its leader.

There was no one younger than me in émigré literature at the time, and Dovlatov only brought frowns to the faces of those who were older. Slavicists were especially astonished—they thought that it all seemed too easy.

Unlike the avant-gardists, Sergei disrupted the norm without scandal. He did not raise the plank—he lowered it. Common wisdom said that Dovlatov was walking a tightrope—a bit more, and he would tumble from literature into vaudeville. His works had a marked deficit of significance, which critics had a harder time processing than readers.

Even such enthusiastic fans like us wrote that Dovlatov got as a down payment the love of readers who appreciated his initial charming trifles, but were now waiting for something heftier and more important. Perplexed by this mysterious, hefty something, Sergei asked whether subscribers of our *New American* would think that we were talking about dicks.

Dovlatov's short stories did not house anything important. Other than life itself, of course, which innocently opened up to the reader in all its defenselessness. Hiding behind neither design nor purpose, life did not justify itself, and in doing so, shocked the reader. Dovlatov's characters lived neither well nor poorly, but merely as they could. And the author did not lay the blame for this at the regime's feet. In Dovlatov's works, the Soviet regime—so used to answering not only for its sins but for ours too—unnoticeably faded away. This was a regime that occupied a zone of adversity that was unavoidable, because it was an invariable condition of our existence.

Which isn't to say that Dovlatov made peace with the Soviet outrages. He simply did not believe in the possibility of ameliorating the human condition. By portraying socialism as a national manifestation of the absurd, Sergei denied it primacy among socialism's other forms. Dovlatov showed that all life was absurd, not just *Soviet* life. With that adjective out of the picture, the impression that there was something exceptional about our lot in life disappeared as well.

Dovlatov's books lay bare neither people nor regimes, but a powerful anti-Soviet complex that I would call the Stierlitz Myth.[3] What is most important in the famous TV series? A vanity-reinforcing justification of leading a dual life. Stierlitz is forced to hide from everyone the best part of his soul. Only exceptional circumstances—like living in the perpetual presence of enemies—deny him the chance to demonstrate grace, tenderness, sensitivity, and extraordinary talents like being able to write in French with his left hand. Admittedly, Stierlitz does demonstrate these qualities on occasion, but only while abroad. By all appearances, it wasn't even worth trying while at home.

Having been denied the demeaning status of victims of history, Dovlatov's characters similarly cease being surrounded by enemies on whom they can heap the blame for every little thing. Their political problems are replaced with existential, personal, and even intimate ones.

Any given regime is a manifestation of our being rather than someone else's rule. It is internal, not external. It has nowhere to be other than inside us, which means that nothing can be done about it.

Dovlatov's world has no soulless principles, but there are myriad unprincipled souls. His characters lack a common ideological denominator. Personal motives always take primacy over the common interest: his Armenian mother hates Stalin because he is Georgian, and his uncle joins the war effort because he liked to get into fights during peace time.

4

Dovlatov de-conceptualized the Soviet regime. Strictly speaking, he vocalized what everyone already knew: the idea on which the country stood no longer

---

3   The popular twelve-episode series *17 Moments of Spring* (1973) followed the adventures of Maksim Maksimovich Isayev, alias Standartenfuhrer Stierlitz, a Soviet double agent who masqueraded as a high-level Nazi intelligence officer.

existed. And he added something else: no other idea existed either, because there were no ideas at all.

Cognition of this circumstance is what distinguishes the last Soviet generation from the preceding one. One juxtaposed just ideas to false ones—the other simply didn't believe in the existence of ideas.

The fall of any empire abolishes the universal principle that united, justified, and enabled opposition to it. Reality untethered from design becomes too multifaceted to brook explanation—it permits only description. Unfiltered life demands an impartial perspective. Ideology is interpreted, but life should be regarded as it appears.

Writers of the previous generation discussed how ideas change the world. Dovlatov wrote about how ideas don't change the world—there are no ideas, and there's nothing to change.

Life without ideas compromised the previous system of ethics. Especially the moralistic rhetoric that both friends and enemies of the Soviet regime used to twist the others' arm.

From afar, heroism inspires admiration. From a medium distance, it evokes guilt. Up close, it arouses suspicion. One of my acquaintances who did time said that those who yearn to rule are those who don't know how to fix the problems waiting for them at home. Understandable: it is harder to save one's family than one's country. Plus, it's more fun to serve one's country than simply to serve.

Zhuangzi said: "To preach virtue, justice, and noble acts before an iron-hearted ruler means to show your beauty while laying bare another's ugliness. In truth, such a person should be called a walking misfortune."

Idealism is a constant source of underlying irritation, because it demands a response. Imagine living with a holy man or breaking bread with a martyr. However, the dissidents did not consider themselves holy. And they didn't even really show off their accomplishments all that often. And yet, the anti-Soviet beginning was nearly as concerning as the Soviet one.

"After communists," wrote Dovlatov, "I hate anti-communists the most."

I feel like dissidents were treated like priests: both are among the last whose sins are pardoned. Apparently, the presumption of virtue is too powerful a temptation for *schadenfreude*.

It was with good reason that the one time Dovlatov let loose his considerable physical attributes in my presence involved a dissident. In "The Branch Office," Dovlatov named him Akulich. As a veteran of the "uncompromising ideological battle," Akulich is nominated for president of a free Russia. But when a "pretty photographer" stands up and demands that he pay her sixty dollars for the slides she made, Akulich responds: "I'm waging a war against totalitarianism, and you're talking to me about debts?!"

I knew those involved in this story. I knew the photographer, Nina Alovert, and the veteran "Akulich," a loud Jew who introduced himself as a Georgian. I was present when he uttered the above phrase, which caused Dovlatov to toss this mighty warrior against totalitarianism down the editorial office's narrow stairs. A minute later, Dovlatov's victim stuck his head through the door, fussily mumbling: "It's winter, I forgot my coat in here."

Dovlatov didn't like dissidents. Rather, it's not that he didn't like them, but they made him scowl, he didn't trust them, he mocked them reservedly. Describing the crackdown on Estonian liberalism, he concludes the paragraph with a Shchedrin-esque[4] phrase: "The greatest among them—two young scholars—disappeared into the underground."

Inherent to Dovlatov's prose is an underground amorality. It manifests itself in a lack of commonly accepted criteria that would allow any kind of appraisal. The Dovlatovian character lives "on the other side of good and evil." However, not as a Nietzschean superhuman, but an under-human, a not-quite human—say, a cat.

I've always tied morality to animals, by the way. When I first heard my father say the word out loud, I launched a campaign to prove that morality is an herbivore. We even bet on it: lemonade and a pastry. And I won, pointing out in the *Children's Encyclopedia* the photo of a deer with branching antlers, beneath which it plainly said the Russian word *maral*—"elk."[5]

---

4   Mikhail Saltykov-Shchedrin (1826–1889) was a writer and satirist.
5   *Maral* sounds awfully close to *moral'*—"morality."

2

Laughter and Trepidation

1

Air is laughter's natural environment. There is something insubstantial, ephemeral, natural, and inconspicuous about laughter. Like the wind, a joke lifts you up and carries you through a conversation. Like flying in a dream, this movement has no purpose beyond enjoyment.

We used to joke a lot, joke all the time, even. It was like in an American show where laughter interrupts the action once every five–ten seconds. Such a manner of dialogue may seem mechanical, but only if you yourself are not taking part in the conversation, which consists of teasing, wordplay, and mangled quotes.

We used to call this illogical tongue-twister "the flow," believing that our generation invented it. But then I noticed the exact same dialogue in the first chapter of *Ulysses* and realized that the flow has always existed. It's a sort of literary school, bout-rimés, a philological protoplasm in which clots of artistic language are decocted.

As everybody knows, laughter is not subject to falsification. It is easier to fake a tear than a smile. It's like with the horse that you can lead to water but not force to drink. Laughter combines the directness and conspicuousness of physiological truth with the mystery of creation. After all, we enjoy only an indirect relationship with humor. Humor is dispersed throughout the atmosphere of a good conversation, when a joke flutters from one interlocutor to another, like an echo across a river.

Humor is a collective act, but even a choir has soloists. Greatest among them is the artist Bakhchanyan. (His own exotic last name provides the best categorization of the genre in which the multifaceted Vagrich works, and I call him an artist in the same way that people call a pickpocket an "artist").

Throughout twenty years of friendship, I've gotten a good look at Bakhchanyan's craft. His workshop is a gathering of friends at the kitchen table, a gathering in which he personally doesn't really even partake—unless his participation is that of a tiger lying in ambush. ("Vagrich" indeed means "tiger" in Armenian). Bakhchanyan tensely listens to the conversation, which serves as fecund ground for hitherto unknown inflorescences of humor. They are what Vagrich fishes out of the conversation. Slightly twisting the living, still trembling quip, he gives it a light makeover and reintroduces it into the conversation in a transfigured or disfigured form.

Unfortunately, tableside humor is too rooted in the situation that birthed it, which is why it is difficult to transpose it onto the page. Typically, all that's left on the page are Bakhchanyan's folklore-adjacent puns, like the epochal, "We were born to make Kafka real."[1]

2

Sergei loved Bakhchanyan very much. He drew him once, hanging in a wire noose. It was an illustration for a new humorous rubric in *The New American*, which Dovlatov also named—"Bakhchanyan on the Wire." Vagrich didn't like that. He liked being the master rather than the victim of circumstance, and they had to change the name. But the man with the long Armenian nose made out of commas stayed.

Unlike Bakhchanyan, Sergei was neither a joker, nor a brilliant improviser, nor even a particularly resourceful interlocutor. Like many others, he made do with "fleeting witticisms." When he met up with Brodsky after many years of separation, Dovlatov addressed him with an informal "you."

"I thought," the other noted, "that we used the formal 'you.'"

"With you, Iosif, I'm even willing to use 'them,'" Dovlatov replied—but only a day later, when he was telling everyone the story.

By the way, Sergei always happily recounted various awkward situations in which he found himself. By disarming others, he poked fun at himself, but he didn't particularly enjoy it when others did it.

---

1   This is an allusion to a line from a famous song called the "Air March" (1923), which served as the hymn of the Soviet Air Forces. The original line is: "We were born to make fairy tales real"—in Russian, *skazka*, "fairy tale," sounds very similar to "Kafka."

Vail and I once wrote a rather crude parody on Dovlatov's short story "The Milestone Boy" called "The Milestone Finger" ("boy" and "little finger" are merely one letter apart in Russian). As I recall, it took place in an Estonian bar called "Ukhnu." We pretended like the parody was a product of samizdat, and Dovlatov was outraged by the insult until he discovered that we were the authors, after which he uttered his favorite phrase: "It's easy to hurt Dovlatov, but difficult to understand him." As odd as it may seem, this unpretentious truism was the simple truth as far as he was concerned: he really is more difficult to understand than the majority of writers I know.

Sergei did not invent anything funny—he would find it. He had a remarkable ear and divined humor nowhere near where it was traditionally found. For example, Dovlatov insisted that Dostoevsky was the funniest writer of our literary heritage and challenged everyone to write dissertations on the subject. He was interested in those finds that hid beneath the surface like truffles.

And he would infect others with this contagious hunt. We would spend hours exchanging quotes from the classics in which we took such pride that you'd think they were our own. Dovlatov would bring up, say, Captain Lebyadkin's[2] monologue: "Were I to will that my skin cover a drum, let's say to the Akmolinsky infantry regiment . . . so that every day they would drum out the Russian national hymn before the regiment, it would be seen as liberalism, my skin would be forbidden . . ."

I would share a find from *The Government Inspector*:[3] "It seems to me," Khlestakov asks the regent of the charitable institutions, "that it is as if you were a little shorter yesterday, no?" To which Zemlyanika obediently replies: "It's very possible."

Vail liked to recall Pavel Petrovich Petukh, who says while treating Chichikov[4] to roast veal: "I raised him on milk for two years, took care of him as if he were my own son!"

Once, we spent so long in our favorite café, Borgia, that we tried everything on the menu. Eventually, the waitress couldn't resist any longer and asked, "What can you possibly talk about for four hours?" We honestly replied: "Gogol."

2   Captain Lebyadkin is a character in Dostoevsky's *Demons* (1872).
3   *The Government Inspector* (1836) is a renowned satirical play by Nikolai Gogol (1809–1852), who used the play to illustrate the Russian Empire's endemic culture of corruption.
4   Pavel Ivanovich Chichikov is the main character of Gogol's *Dead Souls* (1842).

3

Sergei didn't write in his *Notebooks* what people told him, but what he heard. For example, I don't remember ever telling Dovlatov a single one of the stories that invokes my name. It's not that he distorted the truth—all of these stories are, alas, fairly close to what actually happened—I simply struggle to understand how or why they were selected. I think Sergei knew better than me the building blocks of literature.

One winter, Dovlatov was planning to go abroad and asked where he was supposed to get the requisite papers. I provided him with a lengthy, tedious explanation. Frustrated by what he had to do, Sergei asked bitterly:

"And how am I supposed to find the right official in a sea of supplicants?"

"In the American office, where there's no coatroom, he'll be the only one without a coat," I said and earned Dovlatov's approval.

Another time, it was summer. Puffing on a cigarette (we both still smoked then), I complained that when it's hot, you don't have enough pockets, so there's nowhere to put your matches, but in winter, you have too many pockets, so you can never find the matches.

I don't know what Dovlatov saw in these straightforward quips, but Sergei knew how to put to good use what others took for lumps of coal. He was a guardian of words unaware of themselves. He was interested not in what people said, but in the things that they let slip.

Henri Bergson[5]—just about the only philosopher who said anything sensible about humor—wrote that we find amusing a person who behaves like a machine. For Dovlatov, the machine talks. He eavesdropped on his characters in those moments when they spoke mechanically, unthinkingly. In a world of deadened, clichéd language, what you say is unimportant. Speech performs a ritualistic role, the point of which isn't in what is said, but in who says the formulaic words and when they say them. Parts of these formulae are currently changing, but not their magical functions. Here's a recent example:

"The withdrawal of troops," says a talking head, "must be done in a civilized manner, which is to say that it must be done later than agreed upon."

The comical contradiction in content goes unnoticed because the speaker meets the formal requirement of using the word "civilized." Language operates senselessly. Nobody hears what is said because nobody is listening.

---

5   Henri Bergson (1850–1941) was a French philosopher known for advocating intuitivism.

Other than Dovlatov, who would make us drop everything to listen to him share what he had eavesdropped on. From one writer, he took away "a life-sized angel" and "a goat screaming in an inhuman voice." From another: "ringlets of hair peeking out from under a lace apron." And here's what his Major Afanasyev says: "It feels like he's already enjoying communism to the fullest. Don't like someone's mug? Punch him in the mouth!"

The best story from *The Zone* follows the same principle. In "The Performance," Dovlatov forces the reader—perhaps for the first time in his life—to listen to "The Internationale" as it is being performed for the inmates: "Stand up, ones who are branded by the curse, all the world's starving and enslaved!"

4

I once foolishly wound up in a New York night club called Tunnel. Lots of things were strange there: a mossy bar, walls overgrown with blue fur, models in scuba suits, a cart full of drinks next to the urinal. But most of all I was astounded by the optical orgy. For a fraction of a second, a blinding light flashes through the total darkness. The image changes with every flash, but no movement occurs in the room—it is hidden from us by the instants of darkness. The effect is disturbing. The continuous world we are accustomed to disintegrates into fragments, like on film taken out of a projector. The flickering light makes the dancers immobile, imbuing them with the expressiveness of wax figures. The living simulates the dead—frozen facial expressions, actions chopped off mid-motion.

Dovlatov made use of the same kind of freeze frame effect. Halting the flow of the senseless subconscious, he captured the instant. Not because it is beautiful, but because it is funny.

In theater, it is inappropriate to choke Desdemona onstage in full view of the audience. The side curtains of Dovlatov's stage filter out the boring, banal, and—most importantly—unfunny parts of life. Characters move through his stories in snatches. We see them only when they are saying or doing something funny. However, that is nowhere near the full extent of their role.

Sergei attributed his theory of comedy to Vail and me in a note once:

"Humor," he writes, seemingly paraphrasing our ideas, but in reality asserting his own, "is an instrument for learning the world. If you are researching some phenomenon, find what's funny about it, and the phenomenon will hide no more secrets from you. This has nothing at all in common with professional comedy or a desire to entertain the reading public."

Sergei believed that humor, like a flash of light, tears us from the usual flow of life in those moments when we most resemble ourselves. I didn't buy this theory, since I didn't recognize myself in Dovlatov's *Notebooks*, but then I realized: I don't resemble myself... but everyone else is a carbon copy.

5

Sergei taught that you must be frugal with humor. He once wrote a script for the radio—a two-page sketch of everyday immigrant life. It was precise yet boring—but at the very end, there is a dialogue to which the whole rest of the text conforms.

"Monya," Sergei asks the owner of a Russian grocery shop, "why are you selling bream with two 'e's?'"

"I sell whatever they deliver."

At first, I thought Dovlatov was simply being greedy. Especially since there wasn't some great secret to the method. I begin anything made-to-order from the ending too, from the very last sentence. But that works when you know what the final product needs to be. I hated algebra when I was in school, but I was decent at solving equations—huge equations that took up the whole class. I simply rushed the answer to a zero or a one, figuring that the textbook author's appreciation for aesthetic excellence would force him to make each example end in a clean, whole number. But therein lies the difference between belles-lettres and any other literature: the author of the former doesn't know the final product until the very end.

It wasn't economics, but philosophy that forced Dovlatov to scrimp with his jokes, which he placed only in strategically important—but not even remotely the most effective—spots. Sergei never began or concluded a story with a funny phrase. Dovlatov resorted to humor in situations where it was inappropriate. For him, laughter parasitizes off of violence; it feeds on fear and cruelty.

Dovlatov's comrade and adversary Valery Popov[6] noted in a short story that nowhere will you hear as much laughter as in an ICU. In Dovlatov's world, the funny is usually tied to the frightening. For example, one short story's protagonist finds out that while driving drunk, his brother hit a pedestrian. A phone call follows:

"'You must be in a terrible state?! You killed someone! You killed a person!'

---

6   Valery Popov (1939–present) is a Russian writer.

"'Stop screaming. Officers are made to be killed . . .'"

In Dovlatov's works, as in Tarantino's *Pulp Fiction*, laughter does not eliminate violence, but neutralizes it. Just as a banana counteracts a pepper's spiciness and milk drowns out the scent of garlic.

Humor and fear are external to one another, but in combining, they form a dynamic harmony whose individual parts are at peace with each other, neither losing itself in the union. By mixing bright red with dark blue, a painter will get a grey color. What differentiates this color from diluted soot or dirtied bleach is its extraordinary intensity. Greyness born of screaming contradiction holds on to the memory of its unusual genesis. The adjacency of the funny and the frightening in Dovlatov's world replaces a black-and-white world with a grey one. Everyday life in his stories is tinted with the greyness of surmounted terror and suppressed laughter.

6

You will rarely find someone who laughs easily among those who know how to make others laugh. Etiquette forbids them to laugh at their own jokes, and pride prevents them from laughing at the jokes of others. Dovlatov, however, loved both making others laugh and laughing himself, doing so in a way that flattered his conversation partner—howling and wiping away his tears with a fist.

Once, Vail and I put together funny stories from the newspapers and came up with our *Premature Memoirs*. We showed them to Dovlatov. We heard howling from the other room so often that we began blushing ahead of time in anticipation of the praise that was sure to follow. But Sergei's verdict was severe: having found neither form nor meaning in the text, he said we wasted the funny material. In prose, humor must not simply accumulate, but serve a purpose.

In those years, I was convinced that humor isn't a means, but the end. Fixated on the idea of craft mastery, I replaced all other characterizations with the word "funny" because it seemed laconic and precise. Length and ad-libbing are the enemies of a perfect joke. Like verse or music, something funny cannot be paraphrased—only quoted. Since humor is what remains after everything superfluous is removed, laughter is the prime literary environment in which wordcraft exists undiluted.

Dovlatov did not share this view and did everything in his power to change our minds. I found the following stern reprimand in his letters: "It is tragic if a writer lacks a sense of humor, but if he lacks a sense of drama (see Vail and Genis), that is also pretty bad."

In conversation, he expressed this thesis simpler: "If only you got a bad toothache!" Sometimes Sergei asked me hopefully: "Come on, admit it—have you and Petya even once gotten into a fight?"

His own sense of drama Sergei nurtured and cherished. Never forgetting himself, he would inject into any festivities that were getting too joyful an onset of the blues. Identifying the blues' source would be no easier than explaining Onegin's melancholy. Sergei could be hurt by an offhand comment, someone's careless tone, an unceremonious flourish. And then his mood would darken, and he would exit, leaving us to divine the cause of the grievance. Suspicion was his natural state. Sergei took bad news stoically, while good news enraged him. He waited for misfortune, anticipated and augured it.

Defending his right to worry—including his right to worry for no purpose— Dovlatov would rage at our semi-principled-semi-mindless carelessness. Once, I mechanically responded to another bout of his dolefulness: "You should try not worrying." Sergei never acknowledged meaningless quips, and he erupted in response: "Maybe I should try becoming blonde too?"

Dovlatov considered himself a gloomy man. "Most importantly," he wrote in one letter, "do not think that I am a joyful—let alone a happy—man." He repeated himself in another letter: "This fucking angst is like a personality trait—it isn't affected by circumstance."

I didn't believe him until I became acquainted with that angst myself. I feel like it is directly correlated with age. Only once you've reached the age when the next generation is repeating your mistakes do you realize the replicability of your existence. The source of angst is in the hopeless limitedness of your experience, which sarcastically contrasts with the inexhaustibility of being. Angst is distinguishable from tragedy in its hopelessness because it does not end in death.

"Sorrow and fear," writes Dovlatov, "are a response to time. Angst and terror are a response to eternity."

The problem isn't that life is short—more likely it's too long, because it allows itself to repeat. Looking to demonstrate the true magnitude of the abyss, Camus chose the undying Sisyphus as his protagonist, showing that eternal life is no better than a normal one. When we're dealing with life's most important questions, eternity is as mute as an instant.

Brodsky called this feeling boredom and advised others to trust in it more than anything else. Dovlatov wrote in agreement: "The petit bourgeois are those who are convinced that they should be happy."

For an artist, the beauty of angst lies in its ability to shine through life, like a primer through paint. Angst is the world's nadir, so the only place to go from there is up. And whoever ascends is not like those who never descended.

I used to be upset by the aftertaste of hypochondria in Dovlatov's laughter. But now I understand that without it, humor is like flat champagne: it packs the same punch, but it's not festive. Dovlatov does not surmount angst—that's impossible—but he accounts for it and utilizes it. This is why his gallows humor is so good. With death lurking around the corner, laughter becomes meaningful, because death sets the limits of inertia. Lacking the ability to repeat itself, death makes the moment unique. Death forces us to listen to ourselves. On the way to the graveyard, a person ceases being a babbling machine.

Dovlatov describes such an adventure in his short story "Someone's Death and Other Concerns":

"Bykover was silent the whole way there. But once they neared their destination, he noted philosophically: 'The man lived, lived, and then he died.'

"'How else would you have it?' I said."

3

The Poetics of Prison

1

Since the Soviet authorities' demise, the Alexandrian Greek Kavafis has become my favorite poet. I even made a copy of a map of Alexandria—not the one that used to be the center of the universe, but the one that became its marginalized outskirts. I've never been to Alexandria, but I can imagine it well enough in comparison with other Egyptian cities. Blinding dust, boys longingly poring over designs in women's magazines, a suspicious cognac named "Omar Khayyam" you buy from a stand hidden away in a side alley, and for a snack—dates with rubbed off newspaper print. "And the enduring stench of urine," adds the guide book.

I am enthralled by the pathos of Kavafis's historical second-ratedness. He called himself a poet-historian, but his was a strange kind of history. He was essentially interested only in the history of our blindness. Kavafis's verse has myriad forgotten emperors, defeated warlords, bad poets, foolish philosophers, and hypocritical saints. Kavafis was interested only in history's dead ends. By saving what others drowned in the Lethe and thereby filling in the lacunas emptied out by ennui, he made history whole. Kavafis restored justice with regard to the past. It is as full of mistakes, follies, and accidents as the present.

However, Kavafis did not in the least mean to replace the history of the victors with the history of the defeated. His project was more radical. He would discredit History as history, as something that is subject to a coherent retelling. For Kavafis, history does not fit neatly into the Procrustean bed of cause and effect. It splinters into separate pages, and even then, only the ink blots in the margins make it into the poems. These notes are valuable only for their veracity. The justification for each note's existence: its existence. Complacently living out their allotted times, Kavafis's characters are unable to go beyond their boundaries. Their worldviews are limited by the real. None of them are capable of divining fate. Which is what differentiates them from their author, who regards them by casting his gaze backwards: their future, his past.

In this way, Kavafis's measurement of history is ironic. And his irony takes the form of silence. By removing himself from the retelling, he lets others say their piece. The author does not intervene, he does not judge or indicate his preferences. He is silent because time speaks in his stead.

Why is this relevant to Dovlatov? Because Kavafis's original point of view is shared by Dovlatov's generation—the generation that grew up on the curb, the generation with whose voice spoke Dovlatov. The thing is that the Soviet regime disappeared from the horizons in Dovlatov's prose long before its actual demise. Without even noticing it himself, Dovlatov looked on things as a historian—in Kavafis's meaning of the word.

Most important to this perspective isn't wisdom, but humility: we see not what we know but what we are watching. No less, but under no circumstances any more. This isn't so simple. After all, we were taught that history, like life, has a beginning and an end. That it always has meaning, which imbues our own days with significance. Looking at things directly meant abandoning the presumption that we can understand their interrelation. We once again found ourselves in a world that we could not explain—not through governmental schemes, not through the whims of wicked fate.

Like Kavafis, Dovlatov did not correct or provoke reality, forcing it to speak on its own at those points when its voice sounds clearest—in the Zone:[1] "I looked around the barracks. It all looked familiar. Life with its covers torn off. A simple and singular meaning of things."

2

The Japanese rarely speak of war. Discussing war means either bragging or complaining, and neither is compatible with the rules of propriety. Something similar occurs with the Zone's inhabitants. They discuss the past mainly through jokes. The stories of people doing time are often humorous, occasionally touching, rarely deep, but never tragic. They never speak of anything frightening—fear is a backdrop, dark as a blackboard on which cartoonish faces scribbled in chalk turn out all the more amusing.

---

1   The "Zone" was the slang term for the Soviet penitentiary labor camps and colonies.

Sinyavsky,[2] for example, spoke even of Mordovia with a degree of warmth. He told of how after returning to Moscow, he couldn't shake the habit of greeting strangers on the street, as was customary in the labor camps. As for why he despised kasha and always covered his mouth with his hand when eating—I can only guess.

The subject of labor camps figured prominently in the circles that I ran in. Dovlatov himself used to be an overseer, and our mutual acquaintances included renowned prisoners, famous snitches, and even an investigator. When taking part in their conversations, Sergei liked to listen more than speak. Maybe because he valued his own experience in the camps too much.

Dovlatov was biased toward inmates and spoke with delight about their language, their imagination, their gait. Sergei also accepted his popularity among former *zeks*[3] with a degree of pride. Despite all this, Dovlatov did not delude himself—he did not see *zeks* as his "little brothers." Naturally, he also didn't experience that envy towards street rats that often causes various complexes among members of the intelligentsia.

In Dovlatov's coordinate system, the *zek* functions as an alarm bell. The criminal is as inextricable a part of the world as the academic and the ballerina. Life is not subject to editing—it is total, whole, indivisible. Either you accept creation as it is, or you petition the Creator for a refund.

3

I once got my hands on the letters Dovlatov sent while in the army. Sergei wrote them to his father from the camps where he was stationed. Just about every one featured some verse. The verse is noteworthy for its mix of banality and grotesque, vulgarity and precision—Oberiutys[4] to the tune of a harmonica. But the characters are recognizably Dovlatovian:

> At a metro station, two braves
> Are drinking jars of after-shave,

---

2   Andrei Sinyavsky (1925–1997) was a Soviet writer who immigrated to France in 1973. He was also known by his pseudonym Abram Terts.

3   A *zek* is someone who is doing or has done time in the Zone. *Zek* is short for *zakliuchionny*, which means "prisoner."

4   The OBERIU stood for *Obyedineniye real'nogo iskusstva*, meaning the "Union of real art." This was a group of writers in the late 1920s and early 1930s who employed the grotesque, alogisms, and the absurd in their works.

And a lone fish tail is a sore
On the marble-lined and shining floor.

Sometimes you can almost make out the author that you'll meet for real in Dovlatov's short stories:

I thought about the past,
And savored it like a snack;
Not only did I love women,
But they loved me right back.
The days went by,
Some better and some worse they'd be,
But they were all alike—
All quite partial toward me.
Once in a field I stood,
Amidst a grassy bed,
And in the end, I understood
That I was their common thread.

Most often, of course, Sergei would describe the Zone:

In my mind, the taiga was strong,
Simple, mighty, wide, and long.
But it was somber and quite dirty.
And crowded, like inside a throng.
"The sturdy taiga, shrouded in a fog,
Unknowable and wild like a mire."
A group of thieves around the fire
Is finishing the last boiled dog,
I used to read some Kant and Hagel,
But here, the situation's dire.
No wonder that I'm wan and tired—
It's me that always gets finagled.

I most liked a poem in which Sergei starts feeling his way towards the central idea of *The Zone*. It is called "In Memoriam of N. Zhabin."

Zhabin was one of the kulaks,
A toady and a cheapskate.

They buried him by the river bank,
Nikolai Zhabin, that reprobate.
My story here comes to an end,
There's nothing more to tell.
As he is now, would that he had lived then,
Before Nikolai Arkadyevich fell.

4

If *The Zone* wasn't Sergei's favorite book, it was definitely the most important. He didn't assemble it—he built it, deliberately, obstinately, and pedantically. By combining tales from the labor camps into what he called a novella, Dovlatov constructed a commentary of himself. It was the first time he had tried to explain what he had to offer the word of literature. He would not have been able to do this without dealing with his predecessors—Shalamov and Solzhenitsyn. Sergei liked one and respected the other.

Other than Paramonov, none of us had ever seen Solzhenitsyn. This unapproachability provoked spiteful barbs. They said that Solzhenitsyn's children locked themselves in the bathroom and read Limonov.[5] They passed around a photo of Alexander Isayevich in short shorts on a tennis court. Worst of all was the unavoidable Bakhchanyan, who put together a photo album titled "One Hundred of Solzhenitsyn's Namesakes." In short, Solzhenitsyn was treated like a member of the Politburo—anything you'd say about him was funny. Poking fun at the situation, Dovlatov wrote: "The world is round because it spins, and roosters lug their balls around, as do we all, including Solzhenitsyn."

None of this stopped Sergei from sending Solzhenitsyn each new book of his that came out. He accompanied each with a note that preempted any possible contempt: "I'd consider it an honor if the book were to find a spot in your library." While Sergei was alive, Solzhenitsyn never responded. After, they say, he read the books and praised them. Turned out they had a lot in common. Repeating Solzhenitsyn, Sergei said that it was prison that turned him into a writer. As in Solzhenitsyn's case, the camps became Dovlatov's "pilgrimage into the masses."

Prison opened Sergei up to what he would call twenty years later "the truth": "I was stunned by the depth and variety of life . . . I realized for the first

---

5   Eduard Limonov (1943–2020) was a controversial writer, publicist, and political figure.

time what is freedom, ruthlessness, violence . . . I witnessed freedom behind bars. Cruelty, meaningless like poetry . . . I saw man, fully reduced to an animal state. I saw what could cause him joy. And I believe I began to see clearly."

Prison is like an abbreviation of life: by stripping away all social layers, it flays life down to its meat, to its essence, to pure existence.

"The moment of truth" hit Dovlatov not when he was a *zek*, but an overseer. His position didn't change the subject, but it did alter his attitude toward it. Seeing that it wasn't any sweeter to be on one side of the prison bars than the other, Dovlatov refused to acknowledge their existence: "There unfolded a singular soulless world on either side of the bars." The Zone is either ubiquitous or nonexistent—that's the conclusion that Dovlatov brought with him from his life in camp security. And this is where he diverges from Solzhenitsyn: "According to Solzhenitsyn, the Zone is hell. I, however, think that we ourselves are hell."

Solzhenitsyn's prison takes on a providential significance: the GULAG is where the top and bottom melded; the GULAG is where the *intelligentsia* and the masses mixed into one; the GULAG is a spiritual experience of conciliarity, paid for by pointless suffering; the GULAG is the instrument of Russian fate that unites a country disjointed by the centuries.

According to Solzhenitsyn, having passed through the crucible of labor camps, Russian literature can finish its eternal task—not only go into the masses, but even reach its goal. Solzhenitsyn's moral imperative is to give meaning to the GULAG experience within the framework of national history, to find it a spot in the greater picture of creation.

This is exactly where Shalamov rejected prison. For him, the Zone was a minefield of metaphysics where, under the unbearable weight of hardships, reality itself begins to flow, like metal under extreme pressure. This is where reality becomes unstable, grotesque, absurd. Shalamov's prison takes mankind outside of the world's parentheses—his prison is absolute, meaningless evil.

Dovlatov disagreed with this also. "I knew Varlam Tikhonovich a little. He was an astonishing man. And yet, I disagree. Shalamov despised prison. But I think that's not enough. It doesn't presuppose the love of freedom. Or even the hatred of tyranny."

Dovlatov and Shalamov's conversation never ended—Sergei polished his own principles in his arguments with him. One such dialogue is exactly where he plopped me in:

"A rabid Genis told me:

"'You're still afraid that it'll turn out like it did for Shalamov. Don't be afraid. It won't be the same . . .'

"I understand that this is nothing, just some friendly irony. But still, what's the point of rewriting Shalamov? . . . I'm interested in life, not prison. And people, not monsters."

Sergei couldn't accept Shalamov's verdict towards prison, because the Zone was exactly where he realized that the world contained nothing that was purely black-and-white. Sergei even hated chess.

5

The Zone has a plot the story behind which Sergei loved to tell. The story involved a *zek* refusenik who chopped his own fingers off so he wouldn't have to work. In the text, he mutilated himself silently: "Kuptsov stepped to the side. Then he slowly knelt next to a stump. He placed his left hand on the scintillating, rough, yellow stub. Then he swung his axe and lowered it down to the final thud."

But as Sergei told it, Kuptsov first uttered a dreadful phrase: "Look how the sausages fly."

I didn't understand then why Dovlatov sacrificed this precise detail. Now I think I understand. The story is told as a battle of two strong men—the overseer and the criminal. The duel follows a Romantic scenario: Mérimée, Hugo, Jack London, even Gorky. But Dovlatov intentionally ruined the finale—he erased the obvious period at the end of the phrase. By eliminating the effective ending, Sergei dimmed the story, as if spitting on a cigarette butt.

He did this to switch out the protagonist. Just like Tolstoy did in his dearly beloved "Master and Man," in a single instant, Dovlatov shifted the reader's sympathies from the overseer to the criminal.

Dovlatov's security guard has too strong a will, which is why he enacts violence against nature, forcing the hereditary criminal to work. In our eyes, he is a pitiful blind man looking to fix the world at any cost, having bound it with the muzzle of universal law. It isn't truth, but life that is on the side of the prisoner, who, to the very end, defends his nature from attempts to pervert it.

4

Do You Like Fish?

1

I knew Dovlatov well. Not at first, but our relationship continued after his death. Perhaps I became closer to the dead him than I was with the living one. No necrotic phenomena at work here—just age. He died when he was forty-eight, and I'm forty-five as I'm writing this. The difference is determinedly growing smaller. And the more quickly I close the distance, the more I understand and sometimes even discover.

My friends were always older. Older enough that I cheerfully joked: "I'll have to write obituaries for all of you." Paramonov would respond meaningfully with a quote: "Four old men carry the coffin of a youth."

Boris does not like infernal implications. He once batted away my accusations of avarice. "You can't take it all with you!" I said. "We'll see about that," he replied haughtily. Paramonov likes to praise capitalism, conservatism, and most of all that petit bourgeois brand of happiness. However, there is also something in him from the revolutionary democrats like Pisarev[1] or Belinsky.[2] Only Boris can call at eight in the morning to ask your opinion on the soul's immortality. Then again, he most resembles not Russian writers themselves, but their characters—all of them at once, in fact, from Gogol's old-world

---

1   Dmitry Pisarev (1840–1868) was a Russian literary critic and leading member of the nineteenth-century Sixtiers—visible members of the intelligentsia who were energized by Alexander II's reforms.
2   Vissarion Belinsky (1811–1848) was a Russian literary critic and a leading Westernizer—adherents to the school of thought that Russia needed to become more like the West; they stood in opposition to the Russophiles.

landowners to Svidrigailov,[3] from Oblomov[4] to the Karamazovs—all of them, including the devil.

Paramonov knew (this was his hobby) how to drive anyone up a wall. In his letters, Sergei told how he was often ready to throttle Boris while simultaneously delighting in "a rare quality of his—intellectual generosity." And it's true: on the path to a debatable, even outrageous, conclusion, Paramonov's train of thought executes such flourishes that you gape at them, forgetting all about the dangers of the route itself. Obsessed with philosophemes as Russians can be, Boris throws about "grainy thoughts," each of which would equip a diligent owner with enough material for a dissertation.

On one talk show on Radio Liberty, Paramonov threw out a proposition explaining Dovlatov's popularity in Russia: his lyrical hero—the positive prison overseer—reconciled the half of the populace that sat behind bars with the other half, which put them there.

Though I was younger than my friends, I was no more foolish, but more decisive than them. I loved to argue, victoriously, of course. You don't listen to your interlocutor's arguments—you wait them out as you would a warm rain. In the meantime, the best mode of conversation is the mutual sharpening of expression. An exchange of opinions is only useful when you can change your own opinion rather than someone else's.

From this point of view, Dovlatov was the worst of all possible conversation partners. He didn't engage in discourse himself, and he didn't let others do it either: in his presence, any concept froze on the lips like lamb fat.

Sergei acknowledged a single genre of conversation: turn-based solo performances. That being said, Dovlatov was a professional not only at storytelling, but at listening. Which is exactly why talking to him was torture. By imposing his own manner of conversation, he sucked others into a storytelling mode, forcing everyone to compete with him.

Dovlatov's cunning also lay in the fact that he knew his own tales by heart, but he performed them with a false innocence and pretend naiveté. As if he were reading off a sheet, he would artfully choke up, mumble, bleat, and stutter as if searching for the right word, which would make the most gullible trip over each other in a rush to help him out.

The measure of success—laughter, which is how every Dovlatovian sketch would end—was achieved by such seemingly straightforward means

---

3 Arkady Svidrigailov is a character in Dostoevsky's *Crime and Punishment* (1866).
4 Ilya Oblomov is the titular character of Goncharov's *Oblomov* (1859).

that it seduced others. Preemptively dying from laughter, the storyteller would enter the arena. But having stepped onto the Coliseum's sands, he would find that his introduction was too long, he didn't have a vivid enough vocabulary, his characters were dull, the situation was incoherent, and instead of a victorious culmination, the ending was unremarkable: "Yeah, so that's how it was."

Accompanying the unfriendly silence that would then engulf the speaker, Dovlatov himself would make the killing blow. Curiously, with sadistic deliberation, he would ask:

"Now, why don't you explain to us why you felt the need to tell that story?"

This cruel operation was undoubtedly useful for young writers (experienced writers relish listening to themselves so much that they don't notice their audience's reactions). Sergei's mockery trained a respect for reality. Per Dovlatov, a story cannot be retold, but only quoted so as to preserve the picturesque unrefined material, that raw meat that only Mandelstam valued in poetry.

2

The other thing is that everyone loved him. In Dovlatov's presence, everyone behaved as if they were with a model—they joked more often, laughed louder, were more exaggerated in their movements. Once, while reading a feature story about Dovlatov, I mixed up the author's sex—men rarely write like that about other men.

People's love of Dovlatov was jealous, envious, earnest, and, as any other, short-sighted. Sergei capriciously went from favorite to favorite, acting upon a monstrously tangled emotional logic.

At first, I thought that it was difficult only for me to speak with Dovlatov, but that turned out not to be the case. Vagrich Bakhchanyan—that émigré Nasreddin Hodja whom everyone follows around obediently—admitted that any time he spoke to Dovlatov, he was deathly afraid of saying something silly.

I had it worse. Sergei learned that I had a son half a year after he was born. Even though we saw each other almost every day, I could never figure out the right genre within which to frame this news.

Imagine a drinking buddy whom you are permitted to address only in verse. This wouldn't even have disturbed Sergei. He could write rhymes by the kilometer. His notes were usually written in verse. Once, when handing his short stories off to me and Vail (we were writing an article on them), he accompanied them with two quatrains:

> In dispersing my lingering hangover,
> The Golgotha of work I will scale,
> With the purpose of leaving my work
> At the valiant end of this trail,
> Where they'll respect me and won't judge me bitterly,
> They'll pick up everything I'm laying down,
> Because your two sad, sorry asses
> Have also been fooling around!

Once, Dovlatov promised Edik Stein, who passionately loved poetry, to accompany every shot with a quatrain. By morning, when he had enough verses for several epic poems, we made for a waterfall in the woods. Dovlatov squeamishly refused to swim, saying that he had already brushed his teeth. Then, the indefatigable Stein organized a soccer match. Edik chose my athletic brother to join his two-man team, and even though there were three of us on the other team, our forces were unevenly matched from the start: from the first hit, Vail fell to the ground, and Dovlatov stepped off to the side to have a smoke.

Sergei loathed everything that wasn't literature. When we met for the first time, I asked him if he liked fish. It's hard to believe that such an innocent question could kick up such a storm.

"You madman!" he thundered. "*Faulkner* is something you can like!"

The man who liked fish was his father, who had the rare last name Mechik (which means "little sword"). He believed that he was the reason why that last name found a spot in Fadeyev's *The Rout*, since he went to school with Fadeyev in Vladivostok.

"Fish," wrote Dovlatov, "played the same role in my father's life that religion played in Tolstoy's."

Donat Isaakovich didn't argue. He respected literature more than himself or his relatives. I make this judgment because unlike his son's other victims, when he came across his name in Dovlatov's books, he never tried to explain what actually happened.

Also, Donat Isaakovich truly did love to eat. In his stories, he resembled Hemingway—he always mentioned what he ate and where he ate it. At parties, Mechik was tireless and elegant. In the eighteen years I knew him, not once did

I see the top button of his shirt. He would even don a suit when coming out to greet the mailman. Donat Isaakovich wrote a lot and with satisfaction, but I like his last will most of all: he ordered that no one mourn him at his funeral and that nobody waste their time by going to the graveyard.

Dovlatov liked meat, not fish, and he especially liked meat patties. He assured me that he once ate half a bucket's worth. He liked, as he wrote, "technically simple dishes. Something roughly formed, dry, and easily broken apart. Like meat chops."

Or—I'll add this myself—dumplings, which he taught me to make out of petals of Korean dough. He also knew how to make pea soup, and once, in order to convince his wife Lena of his sobriety—and as compensation for the pot of soup he just overturned—he made cabbage soup out of the salad that he mistook for cabbage. Anyway, Dovlatov exaggerated his culinary indifference, because it was part and parcel of his belief system: "If you're a declassified poet, classy wallpaper isn't going to be your priority."

Writing leaves no leisure time. It must be attended to with astronomical constancy. The author and the book are bonded by particular cause-and-effect ties—like a wardrobe and the floor on which it stands. The indent it leaves on the carpet is the result of constant pressure. Under such pressure bends not only the floor, but reality itself. It is, after all, elastic, even if no more so than the hood of a car.

Then again, I most often imagine a trail through a damp meadow: your footsteps sink through the ground, letting in rivulets of water, turning the trail into a gully. Thus changes the topography of the patches of reality we often visit. The writer pushes against reality until he leaves his mark on it. If he is successful, we note with surprise that life resembles literature. Words—literally—acquire physical form.

Kharms[5] dreamed of writing such verse that could break a window like a rock. The trick here is in the constancy. The writer is always focused on one thing: he waits until literature grows through like a bamboo shoot in a Chinese torture chamber.

In becoming a writer, the author squeezes out to the last drop everything from life that isn't literature. But even then, his efforts are rewarded not with an entry ticket, but a lottery ticket.

---

5   Daniil Kharms (1905–1942) was a Russian writer famous for his humorous, absurdist stories and literary anecdotes.

3

Dovlatov's life in literature was so long that, like a marriage, it needed to be officially formalized—in print. Not with a manuscript, like in Bulgakov's case, but a book—Dovlatov's primary heroine.

Today's printing press is no different from the one that prints money: it's all paper and ink. But in the past, a book would change things. And not only because it could be exchanged for "classy wallpaper." Like any rite, a book was an empty and indispensable formality. Its publication was an initiation that allowed entry into literature for the author not on his, but on its terms.

This was difficult for me to grasp. The magic of typography didn't enrapture me—I worked there as a *metteur en pages* in a Russian newspaper. The floor below housed the book stand of the ninety-year-old socialist revolutionary Martyanov, who was famous for missing when he shot at Lenin. His store had everything: from a tome titled "Gogol in the KGB" to a monograph that began: "As everybody well knows, Atlantis is located in the sunken continent of Lemuria." In the diaspora, getting published costs nothing. Or rather, it costs something, but so little that there are as many books as there are sunflower seeds.

Dovlatov had a different attitude toward publication. There were, of course, enough idiotic books in Russia, but they didn't prevent him from valuing the ritualistic nature of literature.

The virtual book of samizdat exists in the world of ideas along with other abstractions. It has a phantom quality to it, an arbitrariness, a certain optionality. A manuscript is like fingernails: an intimate part of the author that begins to weigh him down with time. Living too long with a manuscript is unhygienic, spiritually slovenly. The unprinted manuscript infects the author and begins to rot, inhibiting new growth. The liquid text, not yet frozen through the typographic process, provokes futile changes. It's like with childish adults—their shortcomings are indisputable, but it's too late to fix them. Only by burying the manuscript between two covers is the author freed from the sensation of the text's inconclusivity. By publishing it, the author can at least temporarily be rid of imperfection.

A manuscript that does not become a book is the nightmare of an entire generation. Dovlatov was the generation's voice, having made his debut with a publisher's phantasmagoria titled *The Invisible Book*. After Ardis brought his first phantom into the sun, Dovlatov never grew tired of being published. Rein, who stayed at his place, told his friends in Moscow that "Dovlatov created two meters of literature."

Sergei liked the rough materiality of a book, its indisputable weightiness, its assured rootedness in time. A book is a pass into the library of the future. Constantly fussing over his literary last will, Dovlatov treated this future with a sense of responsibility that to this day baffles me.

Sergei believed in the indispensability of literary succession. In his mind, there were no books that formally differed from those written by the classics. Sergei emphatically expressed this thought at a Los Angeles conference of the Third Wave[6]: "Every person in this room can find their double in Russian literature."

The tragedy of any "invisible book" is that it continues literature through a warped method. Dovlatov didn't desire the normal. This is why even in Perestroika-era Russia, he preferred official government publishing houses to avant-gardists and private ones.

"I want to get my change," said Sergei, "in the same place that they shorted me."

He was governed not by a thirst for revenge, but for order—which, then again, are the same thing. Dovlatov was so irritated by the typical Russian contradiction between the formal and the factual that when—in yet another internal squabble at the newspaper—he was given the choice to formally give up his title as editor in chief but retain control over *The New American*, he decidedly preferred the former to the latter.

He safeguarded his position as a writer with fastidious decisiveness. A year before his death, he wrote to Leningrad: "I would like to come for a visit not simply as a Jew from New York, but as a writer. I've grown used to this status, and I wouldn't want to shed it even temporarily."

I think it was superstition rather than arrogance. He hoped—vainly, like all authors—that the status of writer would rid him of the "usual fear of a blank page." Consequently, Dovlatov spent time proving to himself something that nobody doubted. He spent his whole life fighting for the right to do what he did his whole life. This fight became the drama and the plot of his literature.

It seems that this tautological chain eventually tired him out too. In his last interview, Dovlatov lamented that he treated literature "with extraordinary seriousness."

---

6   There were multiple roughly demarcated waves of immigration from the Soviet Union to the United States. Genis was part of the Third Wave, which went over in the 1970s.

Now I think that the subject of disappointment in literature might have captured Dovlatov's interest no less than being enraptured by it. He told me something along these lines too, but I didn't listen. At the time, I even thought it was base foolishness—just noise. Nietzsche asserted that we can only read something that we already know.

4

Between life and books, Dovlatov made room for newspapers—he spent his whole life in editorial offices. Without the paper, Sergei would get bored, at which point he wouldn't shy away from the basest periodicals—women's journals, comic journals; once he even patronized a one-off gazette incredibly titled "Masya."

And yet, Sergei didn't like journalism—genuinely, I think. He didn't value others' opinions any more than he did his own, which were either accidental or banal. Numbers irritated him, as did facts—especially accurate ones. That left only the literary details, which he played with within the bounds of the opinion column. This isn't to say that everything that Dovlatov came up with here was garbage. And yet, there was truth to his assertion, "When I create for the paper, my handwriting changes."

He valued the paper for something different—"the typical atmosphere of the editorial office, with its strained, feverish unproductiveness."

Dovlatov was more confident in journalism than in literature because there, he had a reserve of imposing might, like a car with six cylinders. Sergei viewed the paper as an arena of others' literary ambitions rather than his own.

In an editorial office, people are particularly vulnerable, because they aim at a higher target than the paper is capable of providing. Though it seems that a newspaper eternalizes a passing instant, it actually merely decorates the instant's corpse. However, a newspaper's ephemerality is elegantly seductive—there is nobility in a sand castle's perfection.

Inherent to a newspaper is a tuberculoid beauty. A newspaper's transience endows it with an—also tuberculoid—intensity. With a morbid swiftness, the newspaper kick-starts romances, births and kills reputations, forms alliances, weaves intrigue. The constancy of change, the Brownian motion of life, the incessant hum of chaos—working in the paper, Dovlatov found everything that made up his prose. It's why even in The New American, he behaved not as an editor but as a stage director. Sergei paid attention to the ambitions he frustrated and the prides he wounded, and he defended the rights he himself violated.

The paper was his notebook, his rough draft, his novel. Maybe this is why Dovlatov didn't succeed with a novella titled *The Invisible Newspaper*—it would have been merely a copy of the original.

5

The Metaphysics of Error

1

Both Dovlatov's mother and his wife were proofreaders. It is unsurprising that he was obsessed with typos. His family constantly waged a war against errors. And no allowances were made for oral speech. Those incensed by Dovlatov's eloquence repeatedly accused him for speaking exactly like he wrote. His speech really was devoid of trip-ups, disagreeing conjugations, or abandoned, aborted phrases. As for word stress, he could stun listeners mute. I, for example, rehearsed complex words ahead of time. But even this didn't help: in his presence, I made either idiotic or refined mistakes. I mean, who other than Dovlatov knew that in the word "*poslushnik*,"[1] the first syllable was stressed?

But in written text, every typo was a tragedy. When he got a book fresh off the press and found an error like the one that turned Sergei Wolf from the "grandfather of Russian literature" into the "young woman of Russian literature,"[2] Dovlatov personally fixed the typo in every single author's copy.

I do the same thing now, but back then, my attitude toward typos was much more lenient. Especially toward my own: in university, I was famous for writing "boatter" with two t's.

Typos aren't always evil. According to Karel Čapek, they're the one thing in newspapers that amuses the reader. People only read the Soviet press, for example, because of typos. Some gloated that the only truths in *Pravda* were

---

1   A *poslushnik* is an initiate in Orthodox monasteries. Most Russian speakers stress the second syllable.
2   In Russian, "grandfather"—*dedushka*—and "young woman"—*devushka*—are only one letter apart.

the typos, like Dovlatov's favorite "commander in shit."[3] Others—sadistic veterans—harassed editors with litanies of accumulated mistakes. Yet others collected typos as tableside conversation starters.

The thing is that a typo shares a most mysterious attribute with jokes: it has no author. An intentional mistake is rarely funny. We are amused specifically by the unintentionality of the mix-up. The mistake mocks not only the spoiled word, but speech writ large. The typo demonstrates the vulnerability of writing, the imperfection of speech, the defenselessness of language before chaos, which, playing and messing around, tears open the deathly seriousness of the printed page. Laughter represents our applause for liberated happenstance that has managed to break through to meaning.

Once, when I was editing a television program in my youth, an errant "y" got dropped from a film title. We were left with a historico-cultural gem: "Ulyanov's Famil." That seems tame compared to what's put out these days.

Much like anyone, Sergei loved stories about funny typos. Like how Aleshkovsky[4] released a book dedicated to his "dear frionds," like how Glezer[5] published his memoirs with the semi-Ukrainian title "The Mahn with the False Bottom." But worst of all was one of his own misses.

In preparation for Brodsky's fortieth anniversary, Dovlatov got one of his poems for *The New American*. Trusting no one, Sergei locked himself in a room alone with the typeset text. He spent nearly the whole night with it, but that didn't save him. The poem was missing a few letters—it came out as "the tomb of the unknown soler." Armed with the anniversary edition full of that "soler energy," a horrified Dovlatov went to Brodsky, who merely grunted and said that maybe it was better this way.

Sergei would eagerly harness his purism to become a pain in the ass. When appraising his colleagues' articles in strategy sessions at *The New American*, he would always explain that he wasn't judging the content of the materials, but the cleanliness of the language. At the same time, Sergei—the only one of the editorial staff without a higher education—would often demonstrate an unexpected erudition. Admittedly, his ignorance was equally unexpected. He once tried to turn the Old Testament into the Ancient Testament.

---

3   In Russian, "commander in chief"—*glavnokomanduiushchiy*—and "commander in shit"— *gavnokomanduiushchiy*—are only one letter apart.
4   Yuz Aleshkovsky (1929–2022) was a writer and lyricist who became famous after penning a mocking quatrain, which began "Comrade Stalin, you are a great scientist . . ."
5   Aleksandr Glezer (1946–2016) was a member of the Third Wave and a writer, poet, and publicist.

Dovlatov had, as he used to say, "an ethical sense of spelling." True to form, the strongest of Sergei's reactions would be caused not by political outrages, but grammatical ones. With feeling bordering on civic indignation, he would write, for example, that in Veller's book, he found that it said "enlengthens instead of lengthens."

Sergei's own relationship with the Russian language was solemn and intimate. His exclamation, "What joy! I know the Russian alphabet!" didn't have a hint of showiness.

Any writer who spends years toiling over each sentence grows to love and respect the raw material's resistance. The journey from the first letter to the last period resembles a brain teaser. Lengthy manipulations are rewarded with a silent click, indicating that the solution has been found: the same taut inflexibility of the language that got in the author's way now holds down the page, spreading it out with invisible force fields.

Dovlatov despised only the mistakes of others. His own, he not only tolerated—he cherished them. And he hated typos too, because he wanted to be the author of his own mistakes.

We once fixed a typo in one of Dovlatov's manuscripts. Sergei flew into a rage, and no number of dictionaries could calm him. In the end, he reprinted—because of one error!—the whole page, having forced us to make a footnote in the newspaper: "The typo was published with the author's permission."

Similar notes exist in Dovlatov's books. Having intentionally made a mistake, Dovlatov boastfully brings the reader's attention to it. For example, in one of his short stories, a magnificent quote by Goethe is accompanied by a footnote: "An example of authorial fancy. Goethe never wrote this." Another of his short stories opens with a warning: "Stylistic defects follow."

Sergei was also intrigued by the mistakes of classics. Why, he asked, did Gogol refuse to fix "paster," and why did Dostoevsky let slide the "round table, oval in shape?"

"It would seem," he muses, "mistakes, imprecisions are somehow dear to the writer. And are therefore dear to the reader."

For Dovlatov, a mistake is suffused in a halo of veracity. A mistake is a sign of life in literature. It unites fiction with reality, like a part with its whole. A mistake brings the wind of freedom to a zone encased in a narrative logic. It is a sign of the natural, just as faultlessness is an invariably artificial—and therefore lifeless—phenomenon.

A world without mistakes is—like any utopia—a dangerous totalitarian fantasy. By fixing, we improve. By improving, we destroy.

2

Brecht said that only the happy are loved. Dovlatov exclusively loved the unhappy. He accepted any handicap with joy, even triumph. Any shortcoming—spiritual or physical—played the role of a mistake without which a person, as a character of fate and nature, would turn out unreal, false. Imperfection birthed personality. Error made it suitable for narrative. It is why Chinese artists left the corner of a landscape unfinished. Through cracks in one's armor—sins, crimes, or even just bad habits—a person melds with the amoral world from which they stepped forth.

Dovlatov's passion for human weakness was devoid of schadenfreude and seemed pure. Sergei was obsessed not with sin, but with forgiveness. Which wasn't all too sweet a characteristic, as he forgave the weak everything and the strong nothing. When he met someone strong, he wouldn't rest until he could view them as weak.

The simplest way to do this was with the help of money. Sergei would lie in wait for everyone around him to display signs of avarice, and if his hunt proved unsuccessful, he would provoke or imagine them. Dovlatov's generosity was quite burdensome. Going to restaurants with him was pure torture. He would fight over the check viciously, but woe befall anyone who ceded the privilege of paying.

The thing is that nothing disfigures someone quite as easily as greed. Miserliness is like a skin condition. Since nobody dies from it, it evokes not sympathy, but squeamishness. Because it is not seen as a serious disorder, it is not deserving even of forgiveness—only mockery.

At the same time, Dovlatov was enraptured by the magic of money. Sergei talked about it constantly, and wrote about it too, like Dostoevsky. He wanted to become rich too, like the characters from Fyodor Mikhailovich's books: an instant passes, and bam, you're rich.

Dovlatov was astounded by the connection—indirect, of course—between money and love. He was surprised by the affection of money for its owners. Sergei religiously believed that some are destined for wealth at birth, while others are similarly condemned to poverty, and no external circumstances could ever undo this predetermined arrangement. But most important for him was the ability of money to make any person funny.

Sergei himself had an ambivalent attitude toward money, because however you spin it, money is the most direct equivalent of success. Meanwhile, all of Dovlatov's characters are unlucky. I wanted to change "characters" to "favorite characters," but I realized that Dovlatov didn't have any others. An unfortunate lot in life makes negative characters if not positive, then at least tolerable. The aura of failure reconciles the author with everybody. With the editor-functionary whose pants ripped accidentally, with the KGB major who drinks warm vodka, with the snitching classmate whom none of the girls like, and of course, the countless alcoholics, people of "blinding nobility."

What does all of this mean? Benevolence? I'm not so sure. I think that Dovlatov savored failure. For his vision of the world, any perfection was ruinous. It's essentially a religion of the luckless. Its foundational dogma is the world's helplessness before our success in it. And the greater our success, the more frightful the consequences. Absolute infallibility would make life impossible. Imagine the effects of a completely successful collectivization, of absolute ethnic cleansing, of a flawlessly working secret police. A Ford factory reprocessing the surrounding environment into shiny new cars with 100% efficiency would be more effective than an atomic bomb.

The world's only defense against our indomitable pursuit of success is the imperfection of human nature itself. Our capacity for error is a built-in insurance policy. Mistakes do not take away from the universe—they add to it. And therein lies the metaphysical justification for misfortune. Delinquency, sloth, drunkenness—these are all destructive, which means that in them lies salvation, because when we eliminate our faults, we are left alone with our virtues, from which we can expect no mercy.

3

Dovlatov was excellent at drawing. I never saw him absentmindedly doodling something—even on a napkin. Possibly because he didn't trust his subconscious. His caricatures were his best work—incisive and accurate. He finished everything he started, carefully fitting the drawing into the allotted space. The paper itself seemed to discipline him (Sergei made rough drafts not only of letters, but of short, two-word-long notes).

Dovlatov's drawings are no different from his prose, which is exactly why they cannot serve as excellent illustrations for it. The best accompaniment for Sergei's books are the drawings of the *mityok* "hippy artist" Alexander Florensky, who illustrated a four-volume collection of Dovlatov's works. They are so on-point because of a delicate contrast between form and content: the drawings look like they could've been drawn not by the author, but by his characters. The external contradiction of strictness and laxness is dispelled by a congruence of worldview: the *mityoks* sprouted from the same soil.

Florensky agreed to accept the order only after he learned that he and Dovlatov frequented the same beer stall. Florensky's style resembles Sergei's algorithm for drawing Karl Marx: liberally smear an ordinary ink blot, and you're more than halfway there. The main hero of Florensky's drawings is the line. A fat, lazy line—the kind you get when drawing with a cigarette butt. It seems a miraculous coincidence that we can recognize in each of these inky blotches Dovlatov and his characters, from Pushkin to the dachshund. Each of them radiates an unsightly charm, evoking in the reader that condescending sympathy that one is used to experiencing when reading Dovlatov's prose.

The *mityoks'* works were absolutely not naïve art. Were we to search them for traces of any infantile ingenuousness, we would do so in vain. These drawings' primitive nature is the result of surmounted complexity. A *mityok* isn't a simpleton, but a clown surreptitiously walking along a tightrope. A *mityok's* preferred style is a *pas de deux* with a bottle of cheap, fortified red wine. Which, we might note, requires the ability to dance.

The *mityoks'* art is the aestheticization of misfortune—the artistic manifestation of error. Their philosophy is a meditation on defeat. The *mityoks* are the national response to progress: not a fair-haired knight in shining armor, but a bum in an oversized, padded coat. He is invincible, because he has already been vanquished.

I developed an appreciation for the *mityoks* after buying a specific picture off of their ideologue, Vladimir Shinkarev. Out of a venomous green cloud emerges a bewildered cow. Its eyes are full not of fear, but of the hopelessness of a creature that isn't sure of anything. It isn't waiting for help—it is simply waiting, preemptively ready to exchange the familiar hardships of life for some new, unfamiliar ones.

Showing the new acquisition to my American acquaintances, I translated the title of the drawing: "A Little Cow Got Lost." Which prompted the practical question: "But where's the udder?" Only then did I realize that I bought an animal without sexual identifiers. At first, I wanted to demand that the artist send me the udder separately, but I gradually grew to like the sexless cow.

Shinkarev, who appreciated all things eastern, also gave me an anecdote by Zhuangzi to go with the picture. It tells of an unrivaled horse expert who couldn't tell the difference between a stallion and a mare, because he judged things by their essence rather than their appearance. A cow with no udder is like a soul with no body—the manifested emanation of fear and trepidation. By tearing the animal out of its natural environment, the artist depicted not a cow, but that existential state of "abandonment in the world" that unites us and it.

Then again, like a true *mityok*, Shinkarev probably just forgot to draw the udder. And it was this very mistake that made the picture complete.

4

Like any movement, the *mityoks* have their own creation myth. Theirs is the Icarus myth. In opposition to the Promethean version of things, which lauds the daring of human genius, the *mityoks* created the image of a tragicomic schlemiel. Having found such a hero in one of Breughel's paintings, they came up with a *mityok*-style haiku about him:

Poor Icarus's feet
were all that was left sticking
from the cold water.

It is widely accepted that "Landscape with the Fall of Icarus" is a parable about an unnoticed tragedy. An unrecognized genius, Icarus, dies a heroic death, surrounded by the indifference of the very people whom he wanted to bless with the gift of flight.

The artist really does demonstrate to us how NOBODY notices Icarus's fall. Among those NOT looking at his body aren't just people—the shepherd, the fisherman, the sailors, and the plowman—but animals too: a horse, a dog, four birds, and twenty sheep. But that doesn't mean that they didn't notice what was happening—merely that they didn't care. There is no way that the people in the painting could have failed to notice the splash and the scream. However, Icarus's unfortunate fate—hurtling out of the sky to his death—did not strike them as important enough to stop plowing, shepherding, and adjusting their tackles.

Breughel's characters ignore not only Icarus. They're not even looking at each other. In all of Breughel's paintings, people avoid each other's gaze—at parties, at dances. Even the empty eye sockets of the blind are directed elsewhere. They have nothing in common. Including a common cause. Likewise, Breughel's characters are unable to fully see the world that they inhabit.

Only the viewer is capable of perceiving the entire landscape—the author presents him with the highest vantage point. By endowing us with the bird's-eye view, he allows us to discern everything—from the individual blades of grass to the mountains melting into the horizon. Similarly, only the viewer can grasp the meaning of the unfolding tragedy, which he is powerless to prevent. By placing the viewers above the world, by allowing them to comprehend the causes and effects of everything happening in it, Breughel has placed us in the same position as God, whose omnipotence is rivaled only by His helplessness. God is unable to aid Icarus, for, by fixing mistakes, He only multiplies them.

Breughel's rendition of Icarus's fall occurs during the spring. The same sun that melted the wax of Icarus's wings awoke nature. What can be done? Should we cancel spring to save Icarus?

Good always becomes evil when a willful or miraculous intervention alters the normal flow of events. Neither wisdom nor love holds the answer—only the indifference of nature is capable of solving this ethical equation. Icarus cannot be saved. His failure isn't an accident of fate—it is the tragic conformity to the laws of nature. Icarus's death is a mistake, not a sacrifice—a critical miss, not a heroic deed. And Icarus himself is a screw-up, not a martyr. By depicting Icarus's pitiful end in the "cold green water," Breughel issues a call not for sympathy, but for humility. Courage and strength of will are necessary not to attempt to change the world, but to refrain from doing so.

It's impossible to help anyone anyway. This is something that I've been repeating since Dovlatov died.

6

Cabbage Soup from Borjomi

1

"I am the son of an Armenian and a Jew," complained Dovlatov, forced to explain himself publicly, "and yet I was sweepingly branded as an 'Estonian nationalist' in the papers!"

It must be said that not only did he not look like the latter—he didn't even look like the former two. By calling himself "a relatively white man," Sergei described his inarguably exotic appearance in broad terms, sans details—he would vaguely indicate some Mediterranean influence, indirectly emphasizing a resemblance to Omar Sharif.

Ethnicity itself—especially his own—actually didn't interest him at all. It's not that Dovlatov ignored this issue, which is so torturous for most of my friends and acquaintances. He just did with the issue of ethnicity what he did with everything else—he transported it into literature. Dovlatov tied ethnicity not to one's blood, but to one's accent. From his early prose to his semifinal short story "The Grape," which features the vaguely Eastern con man Bala, non-Russians always helped Dovlatov solve his literary problems.

Nabokov used to say that only the oblique grammatical case made words and things interesting.

"Any truly new tendency," he taught, "is a knight's move, a shift in the shadows, a change, dislocating the mirror."

A person's accent was the very oblique case that made Dovlatov's Russian "interesting." Sergei wrote so cleanly that the language became unnoticeable. It's the same thing with Absolut: we know that the vodka is there only because of the weight of the bottle. And just as when you add pepper to the Absolut, accents in Dovlatov's prose highlight its transparence rather than clouding it. Success is dependent on the precision of the dose. In order to highlight rather than erase the language's correctness, any shift must be minimal. Sergei loved examples of a successful injection of accents.

"The reader," he assured us, "will never forget that the short story's protagonist is Georgian if just once, he says 'overcot' instead of 'overcoat.'"

But when I asked Sergei how to depict rhotacism on paper, he had no advice to give. Apparently, he found it too meaninglessly simple to depict a Jewish speaker with such a device. As the Soviet writer and poet Valery Popov wrote, it's not a good sign if the sight of a mailbox makes you think of mail. However, one of Dovlatov's Armenian characters actually did have trouble making "r" sounds:

"'Drhat,' said the younger one, Levan, rolling his r's, 'forhgive me. I left our rhifle in the trhunk.'"

The reader expects a guttural accent from the characters of the short story "We Once Lived in the Mountains." But Dovlatov teases the reader, depicting not an accent, but a speech defect. The essence of the Caucasus is hidden deeper within. The Eastern tone is achieved not with phonetics, but with syntax: "Come to the birthday. I was born tomorrow." Plus a light touch of the absurd:

"'Of course all people are equal. White, yellow, red . . . And those . . . What do you call them? Well? White and black mixes?'

"'Mules, mules,' said the scholarly Ashot."

By the way, this short story is an exception. To the chagrin of both the journal and the author, it was published in *The Crocodile*. This prompted an open letter from Yerevan. A group of academics took umbrage at the depiction of Armenians as a wild people, grilling shish kebab on hardwood floorboards.

Bakhchanyan, who was well acquainted with the Caucasian brand of touchiness, came up with the idea of publishing a resplendent journal that exclusively featured Southern authors. Other than Vagrich himself and Dovlatov, it would have featured Okudzhava, Iskander, Akhmadulina, Olzhas Suleimenov. The journal's title was supposed to be a pejorative slang term for someone from central Asia—"Chuchmek."

2

In America, as in the kingdom beyond the grave, people atone for the sins of their past lives. Which is why we learn so acutely what it's like to speak with an accent here.

Once, a large group of us—including Dovlatov—was returning from Boston to New York. On the way, we stopped for a bite at some roadside restaurant. Despite the late hour, I wanted some soup, which is what I told the waiter, who flinched. It quickly became apparent that everybody wanted soup. So I ordered four more. The waiter flinched again and conveyed his confusion with a helpless gesture. But I assuaged him: Russians love soup so much that they'll eat it even in the dead of night. He shrugged a little squeamishly and disappeared, as I thought, into the kitchen.

He returned some twenty minutes later. He carried a tray of five paper cups with a thick pink liquid that smelled of soap. After inspecting the drink a little more closely, I ascertained that it was, in fact, liquid soap, which our waiter patiently poured into the cups from the bathroom dispensers.

Only then did we comprehend the horror of what had happened. The Russian *mylo* becomes "soap" in English, while *soop* is still just "soup." What could be simpler? But instead of just doing the straightforward thing and ordering "soop," we pronounced the word in a way that we thought sounded English: "se-oop." Which led to us getting exactly what we asked for: some one and a half liters of liquid soap.

They say that you can only completely ditch your accent in prison. Those who have never been behind bars have it worse.

3

Sergei never went to either of his ancestral homes, but the Caucasus concerned him way more than Israel. After all, he was never long separated from his mother, who grew up in Tbilisi. Sergei loved telling how in an American supermarket, she would helplessly start speaking Georgian.

Nora Sergeyevna spoke with us in Russian, and there was nothing eastern about her. Maybe other than the fact that everyone was a little afraid of her. Especially guests. Sergei warned everyone that his mother loathed those who did not wash their hands after using the restroom. Which is why, when guests felt nature's call, they would mumble anxiously, "Guess I should wash my hands . . ." Any time I myself left the bathroom, I would energetically shake the water from my hands so that it would be impossible to miss.

Dovlatov's short stories have many of Nora Sergeyevna's tales, including some with a Caucasian entourage. Sergei held it particularly near and dear to his heart, but again, out of literary considerations. Dovlatov preferred to replace the traditional Soviet oppositional duality of "East-West" with an antithesis out of the Russian classics: "North-South." For him, the Caucasus functioned as it did in Lermontov's *Mtsiri*—it was a school of feelings, a reservoir of open emotions, a reproach aimed at the wan Northerners.

"It's better in Georgia. Everything is different there," he writes almost in verse in "Blues for Natella," a short story that resembles a toast.

It is important to note, however, that Dovlatov's South, like the south depicted on the globe, exists only in relation to the North. Their inextricability allowed Sergei to simultaneously continue and parody the tradition of a romantic Caucasus:

"Two shots rang out simultaneously. A loud bang, smoke, and a thunderous echo. Then, Natella's sad and reproachful voice cut through:

"'I'm begging you, stop fighting. Be friends, Gigo and Archil!'

"'She's got a point,' said Piradze. 'Why all the bloodshed? Wouldn't it be better to drink a bottle of good wine?!'

"'You're right,' agreed Zandukeli.

"Piradze took a 'small one' out of his pocket."

Dovlatov's South needs the North simply because without one, the other cannot be. With their help, Dovlatov achieved his favorite effect—the combination of pathos and humor. In his works, these seemingly mutually exclusive elements neither oppose nor inhibit each other—they galvanize each other. This dynamic balance of high and low is what holds Dovlatov's prose together. Geography only makes this structural principle all the more vivid:

"'I want to go home," said Chikvaidze. 'I cannot live without Georgia!'

"'You've never been to Georgia.'

"'But my entire life, I've made cabbage soup out of Borjomi!'"

The cardinal directions served Dovlatov only as a symptom of difficulty. As a phony Caucasian, he nevertheless still felt himself a secret agent—variably of the South or the North. His detective novella even features a spy—a sheep in wolf's clothing.

In another work, Dovlatov can be recognized in the fighter named Julesverne Khachaturian, who, "at the Melbourne Olympics, managed to secure himself the nickname 'Russian Lion.'"

Dovlatov's mix of pathos and humor resembles a pair mentioned in *Fiesta*—irony and pity. I always knew that Dovlatov read Hemingway more carefully than others. It is exactly because the funny cannot be grandiloquent that this pairing cannot be disentwined—just like a magnet, that blue-and-red horseshoe that I so desperately wanted to saw in half in my childhood. I tried to convince Dovlatov that he should undertake a similar operation. I was always irritated by the "sad" spots that regularly popped up in his funniest short stories. Dovlatov bore my broadsides without explaining a thing.

Chekhov helped me understand Dovlatov. Or rather, one of the characters in *The Cherry Orchard*—Gayev. His monologues are deeper than the others. By entrusting the play's most critical thoughts to a comical character, Chekhov doesn't compromise them—he instead tests their durability. We can laugh at Gayev, but his pompous declamation holds the key to the play: "Oh, nature, miraculous nature, you shine with an eternal radiance, beautiful and indifferent, you whom we call mother, unite creation and death, you live and destroy . . ."

That, by the way, was a very intimate issue for Dovlatov, who would ask: "Who would call a swamp amoral?" And he would answer himself with a Shakespeare quote: "Thou, Nature, art my goddess." And he would add immediately: "Then again, who said that? Edmund! A rare villain . . . "

4

Dovlatov found it more interesting to be an Armenian than a Jew. Russian Jews aren't all that exotic. However, immigration forced Dovlatov to clarify his relationship with his Jewishness.

Typically, the opposite happens. For example, I take note of my ethnicity only when I visit Russia. It's still relevant there. And not because they don't like Jews. Once, a taxi driver in Moscow closely inspected me and said:

"Still, though, we have a criminal government. How many Jews have left because of it! How are we going to deal with the Chinese now?"

"And how would Jews deal with them?"

"How am I supposed to know?" sighed the taxi driver. "*I'm* not a Jew."

Another time, I went to a market. I asked an old lady there where the milk was from. She said it's from Ryazan. I felt moved and said it's my hometown. "You don't look like it," the grandma shot back.

It is simpler to be a Jew in Russia than in America. Across the ocean, the question of ethnicity loses relevance. In my town, for example, there are many Armenians and Turks. I often see them crowding in the same Middle Eastern shop—I've heard that the dried meat there is something else. Meanwhile, there's a good soccer team in the neighboring town, and it consists entirely of Yugoslavs: Serbs, Croats, Bosnians—they're all there.

Jews also don't really concern anyone here. Other than our immigrants, who are the exception. For Russian America, the subject of Jews is always in vogue. In fact, for many, if the subject isn't Jews, then there is no subject at all. I have one acquaintance who always walks away if people aren't talking about Jews. I personally heard how he once defended a theory that the Jewish tribes are descended from aliens. In one of his letters, Dovlatov describes him with a degree of astonishment.

"He," writes Sergei, "is almost uncharacteristically foolish for a Jew."

In America, Dovlatov initially tried if not to become a Jew, then at least to seem Jewish. He used to explain murkily that he belonged to "a cute ethnic minority," but he later began to confidently mention both sides of his heritage. He even tried to act out some ethnic pride:

"I very much liked the soccer team Zenit," he would sweet-talk the reader, "because it had Levin-Kogan. He would often play with his head."

In reality, Dovlatov didn't care.

"Antisemitism is simply a special case of evil," he wrote. "I have never met someone who was an anti-Semite but didn't deviate from normal people in everything else."

Dovlatov's ethnic indifference didn't prevent him from heading up *The New American*, which, in light of categorically misplaced commercial hopes, boasted the outlandish subheading "A Jewish paper in Russian."

To this day, I have no idea what that means. Sergei didn't know either, but he explained it in an editorial like this: "We are the Third Wave of immigration. And we are read by members of the Third Wave. Their problems are our problems. We understand their attitudes. We share their interests. And that is why we are a Jewish paper."

The syllogism clearly didn't work. Especially since Soviet Jews missed some of the finer points of what it means to be a Jew.

"They've turned from God," Brightonians would say about their neighbors who didn't fast during Yom Kippur.

For the longest of times, *The New American* was no more Jewish than any other paper. *The New Russian Word*, for example, had only one ethnic Russian working there—Svetlana the proofreader, whose husband's last name still managed to be Shapiro. The Dovlatovs were friends with them.

The situation changed dramatically only when *The New American* changed ownership to an American. The new boss—when he wasn't sitting in prison—was a practicing Orthodox Jew and demanded that everyone who worked there also observed every rite. Since he didn't know Russian himself, he assigned a commissar to watch over us. In one article, the guy crossed out the last name of André Gide.[1] Dovlatov never even wrote about this—it sounds *too* absurd.

---

1 Since in Russian *zhid* means "kike."

But another instance did make it into Dovlatov's *Notebooks*. We once published a map of medieval Jerusalem on the front page. In the morning, I crossed paths with our enraged owner. He demanded to know who put all the churches in the Jewish capital. I told him it was the crusaders.

Sergei didn't mention me in the retelling of this story. Vail and I are absent from Dovlatov's story about *The New American* too. Sergei left the newspaper almost immediately after the change in leadership, but we stayed a while longer. Dovlatov didn't like that at all, and we grew close again only after the Jewish subject was exhausted.

Having bid farewell to *The New American*, Dovlatov returned to the philosophy of ethnic indifference with a sense of relief. Sergei generally didn't believe in the possibility of an ethnic literature.

"Russians consider Babel a Russian writer," he wrote. "Jews consider Babel a Jewish writer. Both consider Babel an outstanding writer. And that's what truly matters."

He batted away objections by bringing up the cosmopolite Brodsky, who, according to Dovlatov, "successfully dragged Russian wordcraft out of the provincial swamp."

As for Jews, Dovlatov once more turned them into a literary device:

"An opulent black limo pulled up to Marusya's building. Out clambered fourteen Spaniards with the last name Gonzalez . . . there was even an Aaron Gonzalez among them."

"There's no avoiding it."

Sergei valued the explosive power of a Jewish name alone. He viewed it as a hieroglyph of the comedic. He had no need for Jews themselves, and in places where there were none, he got on just fine.

"'Let's get to know each other,' said the lieutenant-colonel in a civil tone. 'These are our stars. Sergeant Tkhapsaev, Sergeant Gafitulin, Sergeant Chichiashvili, Corporal Shakhmatyev, PFC Lauri, Privates Kemoklidze and Ovsepyan . . .'"

Which spurs the following peculiar reaction from the Estonian guard:

"'*Perkele*,' thought Gustav, 'kikes as far as the eye can see . . .'"

7

Tere-Tere

1

In the spring of 1997, I came to Estonia. Not because of Dovlatov, no—some publishers invited me. Fate slightly mixed up the address when sending me to the Baltics. I arrived not in Riga, my hometown, but in its cousin, Tallinn.

Many people have a murky understanding of Baltic geography. Not only in New York—Muscovites often forget that Lithuanians and Latvians are close in language, while Latvia and Estonia are close in architecture: Catholic ochre is replaced with the Protestant carmine of brick.

I have no doubt that Riga's gothic architecture saved my health. It was our wont to drink out in the fresh air, hopping from one urban panorama to another. Every new drink was accompanied by a unique view—say, from the roof of a warehouse at the Riga Cathedral. To this day, I associate organ music with fruity wine.

In Estonia, I felt like I was abroad—which is to say, I felt myself at home. Everything there is like in the West—only better, or at least newer. The nation underwent a turnkey European-style renovation. The scaffolding was gone, but the plaster was still clean. Russians in Estonia drive Western cars, speak Estonian well, and incessantly criticize the government. In short, they behave the same way that our people do in America. And their attitude toward Estonians is the same as it is toward Americans: overt condescension mixed with grudging respect. Immigrants seem alike everywhere.

But Estonians are different. When entering a train car, a Russian border guard yells "No sleeping!" An Estonian, meanwhile, offers a polite greeting, "*Tere-tere.*" A waiter in Tallinn apologized that there would be a short wait before the coffee was ready. I asked, "How long?" "Fo-our minutes." He was telling the truth—it really did take only four minutes.

A new joke cropped up after Gagarin did his thing. An Estonian is out fishing. A buddy comes up to him and says, "Jaan, did you hear, the Russians have gone to space?" "All of them?" asks the fisherman without turning around.

I learned later that the joke existed in all the Soviet republics, but it seems most appropriate for Estonians. Phlegmatics and melancholics, they embody that which we sanguinics and cholerics don't have enough of. First and foremost, a mute imperturbability. In Estonia, they didn't forgive or forget the Soviet regime—they overwhelmed it with silenced.

"Silence," wrote Dovlatov, having observed Estonians for a good long time, "is a mighty power. It should be banned as a biological weapon."

2

In Estonia, Dovlatov is no hero. And not only because everyone knew him, but also because he knew everyone. In Tallinn, they read Dovlatov's *Compromise* as if it were Khlestakov's[1] letter in *The Government Inspector*.

There is nothing generic about Dovlatov's Estonian characters, each of whom is uniquely recognizable and, moreover, as they explained to me, completely unblemished. They are all, regardless of what Dovlatov wrote about them, decent people. Only the Russian photographer Zhbankov turned out as depicted: an alcoholic's alcoholic, and he himself knew it for the truth.

However, taking offense at something is also a form of acknowledgement. Sergei is remembered like a tsunami: people point out all the destruction while secretly taking pride in the damage he wreaked. Honestly, I even felt like Dovlatov left a greater mark on Tallinn than the entire Soviet regime. Tallinn is too small a city not to notice Sergei's footprint. There was so much Dovlatov that he was referred to in the plural.

"I went over his place," one lady said, retelling me how she met Dovlatov, "and there were many dangerous Caucasians there. And each shoe in the entryway was large enough for two men!"

It very well might be that Sergei came up with the story himself and injected it into the local folklore. He liked deterring ill gossip by preemptively dictating its form, though not its content.

---

1   Ivan Khlestakov is a seminal character in Gogol's *The Government Inspector* (1836).

Tamara, Dovlatov's Estonian wife, recalls how he described himself over the phone when scheduling their first date: "I look like a dried apricot merchant. Large and dark—you'll immediately be scared of me."

Sergei simultaneously took pride in his threatening appearance and shied away from it. He had one quip in the newspaper in which he aggrievedly reminded everyone that Tolstoy was "quite a sizeable man" and that Chekhov was a "large individual"—which is why, he explained, only idiots think that "large people should write only about athletes."

In his search for compromise between brawn and brains, Sergei came up with a suitable costume for himself: "something military-athletic-bohemian, a cross between a marine and an abstract painter." In reality, it was a leather jacket that shone like well-polished boots. I enraged him something dreadful when I told him it made him look like a traffic cop.

Taking advantage of his imposing appearance, Dovlatov once put on a voice like Karabas Barabas and asked my little son, "Well, are you afraid of me?" However, in America, kids are like cats or dogs or squirrels—they're not afraid of anything, which is why Daniel firmly took Sergei by the hand and told him all about his favorite toy machine gun. I think we still have it lying around somewhere.

For Dovlatov, Estonia was a rehearsal immigration. In Russia, Estonia seemed like a pocket West that got stuck in the East by accident. Ignoring the political map of the world, Dovlatov placed Estonia in the space nominally known as "abroad." Having clambered out of the window, the protagonists of the fantastical short story "Chirkov and Berendeyev" chart a distinctly unfathomable route, flying over "the gothic spires of Tallinn, the domes of the Vatican, and the Aegean Sea."

That's the geography of an ad agency, not a school atlas. But Dovlatov needed the other, foreign world to begin right above St. Petersburg's "sleepy Fontanka River." It's so foreign, so strange that not only does space bend around it—time joins in as well. On the other side of the border, everything changes—both the structure, and the seasons. This is the source of the surreal nostalgia that plagues Dovlatov's Bunin, who yearned for Russia while sitting in his Provencal Grasse: "That Bunin kept wanting to go to back. In the winter, he'd look out the window, sigh, and utter: 'Meanwhile, on Orlovshchina, it's June right now. The robins are singing, the flowers are aromatic.'"

Being well acquainted with the black market, Sergei liked signaling that something was Western by applying sartorial labels: "a Moulin shirt," "Oxford cuff links," "Stetson shoes." Even once in America, he still delighted in brand names and told everyone that they should write down the story of the Parker pen and the Borsalino hat. The things weren't what mattered—the *sounds* did. Russia ended where strange phonetics began.

"There lies beauty," he wrote, "in foreign last names themselves."

There was more than enough of them in Estonia, which Dovlatov gladly put to good use. His short stories that take place in Tallinn have whole paragraphs that could belong in a Graham Greene novel: "He was forced into a closed car and driven to Pagari Street. Three minutes later, Bush was being interrogated by General Pork himself."

Previously, Pagari Street housed the KGB, since replaced by a KGB museum. The good baroque building—like all in Tallinn—has been renovated. Strange as it seems, this was the very building in which they ruined Dovlatov's life, having blacklisted his book. It is unsurprising that the Estonia-based *The Compromise* is the single most anti-Soviet work Dovlatov ever wrote. It really does have a lot of straightforward attacks on the regime, but it is, like all of Dovlatov's books, about something else—it deals with the distribution of order and chaos in the universe.

3

Like many who drink, Dovlatov was a neurotic defender of order. He was obsessed with punctuality, he worshipped the postal service. He would write down the day's agenda in a spreadsheet. He reminded people about their debts every minute of every day—or else he never did.

"The basis for all of my activities," he wrote, "is a love of order. A passion for order. In other words—a loathing of chaos."

But being the chief disturber of the peace, Sergei understood full well the fragility of any reasonably organized life. He treated order as an invariably unattainable ideal. By constantly resisting the temptation to betray it, he did what he could.

In his attempt to solve the main contradiction of his life, Dovlatov perceived Estonia as a sanctuary from chaos: "The landscape changed beyond the Narva River. Nature now seemed less disorderly."

Admittedly, in the Baltics, order isn't the antithesis to chaos, but rather a particular case of chaos—chaos is artificially self-restrained. Ulmanis, the president of a bourgeois Latvia, put forth a slogan: *Kas ir tas ir*—"it is as it is." It was a very popular turn of phrase—they even hung it up in schools. As I understand it, the beauty of this chumpish existentialism lies in the rejection of attempts to explain or change the world.

In his search for a more straightforward life, Sergei came face-to-face with the sincere Baltic simplicity. The local variant of the Soviet governing organs allowed Dovlatov to transpose his own conflict with the regime into the philological sphere. Sergei's Estonia became a nation of literalism, where everything, like in math, means only exactly what it means. Just like, for example, the "Introduction" in the book titled *The Technology of Sex*, which Dovlatov loans his Estonian girlfriend.

The Estonian government interpreted too literally the flowery rhetoric of its higher-ups. As a result, the usual Party-line metaphors took root in a soil that yielded such outlandish crops that they frightened *themselves*. It wasn't freedom that Estonia had more of—it was common sense, which made the most steadfast loyalty seem like frondeur-like criticism of the powers that be. The Estonian Communist Party district committee tries so hard to resemble the one in Moscow that it turns into a caricature:

"The first floor housed a towering, bronze Lenin. The second floor's Lenin was also bronze, but slightly smaller. The third floor was guarded by Karl Marx with his funeral wreath of a beard.

"'I'm curious, who's standing vigil on the fourth floor?' asked Zhbankov, snickering.

"Turned out that the fourth floor was home to yet another Lenin—but this one was made of plaster."

Nowhere did the Soviet regime seem quite so laughable as it did in Estonia. Its senility became particularly loquacious against the backdrop of "groundedness and responsibility," those boring Estonian virtues that enter into a graphic conflict with the Soviet paradigm of nomenclature. Untranslatable and invisible Party idioms, like a headline that reads "Proletariat of the world, unite," acquires a lexical tangibility in Dovlatov's Estonia. The second that meaningless words begin to mean something, the cliché dissipates, setting free an impressive dose of cretinism:

"Next to speak was some responsible worker from 'Ykhtu lekht.' I caught one phrase: 'His father and grandfather fought against Estonian absolutism.'

"'Excuse me, against Estonian what now?' asked an astounded Altmyae. 'There has never been absolutism in Estonia.'

"'He meant against tsarism,' said Bykover.

"'And there's never been an Estonian tsarism either. There was Russian tsarism.'"

Estonian literalism had no less a destructive effect on anti-Soviet stereotypes. Having made the acquaintance of an amiable Estonian doctor ("Show me a *Russian* who would do gymnastics all by himself!"), Dovlatov automatically categorizes him as a dissident. After learning that the doctor's son is under investigation, he asks:

"'Is it the Soldatov case?'

"'Excuse me?' asked the doctor, not understanding.

"'Your son—is he involved with the Estonian Restoration?'

"'My son,' explained Teppe, "is a black market dealer and a drunk. And I don't worry about him only when he is safely tucked away in prison.'"

4

In "The Milestone Boy," Sergei described the 400,000th inhabitant of Tallinn. Confronted with its reflection, the city became smaller than it was. As in medieval times, beyond the castle walls are lilacs, fields full of crops. In the fifteen minutes it takes us to go to the store, it takes them to get to their summer houses.

However, *The Compromise* does not make it seem like Dovlatov finds Estonia particularly cramped. Like a cat on a balcony, Sergei liked to sense the boundaries of his territory, be it the Zone, the Russian Tallinn ("an enormous house, a coworker in every window"), or 106th Street in Queens. As in Joyce's Dublin, hyperlocality gave Dovlatov the chance to dig deep enough to get to the very foundation.

By decreasing the scale, we not only zoom in on the details, we also destroy the illusory seamlessness and simplicity. You can't see out of an airplane that the forest is made up of trees.

Sergei liked to live among his characters. Dovlatov liked the feeling of intimacy, since it allowed him to mingle with his characters. This is why Dovlatov's Estonia does not seem provincial.

In Sergei's vocabulary, the word "provincial" was a justification, if not an obscenity. Blaming us for not appreciating an author that he loved, he would justify the deficit in taste with our non-metropolitan "Riga background." He had nothing against Riga, of course—he was criticizing our inability to see the grand in the small. Dovlatov found the roots of provincialism in one's oversized grievances. Short people become laughable only when they stand on their tiptoes. A textbook example: the leading article of a newspaper in Melitopol' begins with, "We have repeatedly warned the Entente . . ."

Sergei despised pretentious monumentalism and was audaciously consistent in his convictions: "Next to Chekhov, even Tolstoy seems provincial."

Content with its place under the sun, Estonia doesn't seem to Dovlatov a backwoods until it begins to draw it itself up on its tiptoes: "I went to the theater in the evening. They were doing Hemingway's *Bell*. The show was terrible: a mix of *The Magnificent Seven* and *The Young Guard*. In the second act, for example, Robert Jordan shaved with his dagger. And he was wearing Polish jeans."

By the way, Estonians, like Dovlatov himself, have a particular opinion of Hemingway. Every single person here knows one specific phrase from *To Have and Have Not*: "No well-run yacht basin in Southern waters is complete without at least two sunburned, salt bleached-headed Estonians." Estonia is such a small nation that, like Gogol's Dobchinsky, it is grateful to anyone merely for knowing that it exists.

5

The Compromise is the first book Sergei published himself in the West. In a rush and trying to spend as little as possible, he didn't even nurse the text as he usually would—he compiled everything from the various journals that published the novellas that ultimately comprised the book.

Sergei was persuaded at the time that it's possible to break through in America only with a novel, which is why he tried to pass off as a single work what was obviously a collection of short stories. Sergei did the same thing—though much more successfully—with *The Zone*. For *The Compromise*, he came up with a special device. He leads with an excerpt from the *Soviet Estonia* newspaper, then follows it up with the novella that explains how everything happened in real life. I don't know for sure how authentic the excerpts are—some philologists in Tartu are currently ascertaining them with fiendish delight. But that's beside the point. The idea of compromises quietly dried out, and Sergei himself became disillusioned with various generic trickeries.

He prepared for his unreached fiftieth birthday by taking apart his old books to compile a collection of the best short stories: "The Show," "The Milestone Boy," "Moving to a New Apartment"—these are some of the choice ones. He decided to call the whole thing *Short Stories*. We tried to dissuade him, believing that such an imposing title was good only for posthumous publication. This is called "jinxing it."

The Compromise was Dovlatov's first self-publication, and he kept tinkering with it with great satisfaction. Sergei placed on the cover a severely magnified goose feather and accompanied each chapter with a drawing in the style of the Soviet and post-Soviet literary journal *Youth*.

Despite the profound feather and a shade of blue reminiscent of long johns, Sergei took pride in the book and generously gifted it to everyone he knew—albeit with hurtful notes. In the book he gave as a present to our graphic designer Dlugy, he wrote: "Vitaly, I love you, from your balls to your hairdo." My book came with the backhanded compliment, "As if I don't know which of you is the truly talented one." Vail's book, naturally, had the same note.

But that's nothing! At a literary evening, one lady decided to buy Alexander Glezer's verse with his autograph. Dovlatov, who was standing nearby, introduced himself as the author. After asking for the lady's name, Sergei, without batting an eye, wrote on the title page, "To the glittering Sara from the glitzy Glezer."

Like the majority of immigrant publications, *The Compromise* was an act of friendship, not of commerce. The book was released by the Silver Century publishing house, whose founder, owner, and everything else was Grisha Polyak, a man uniquely devoted to Dovlatov and his family.

Polyak was Sergei's constant confidant. They lived close to each other, they went out together for walks with Glasha the fox terrier, then with Yasha the dachshund, and they talked about books that Grisha valued even more than elegant wordcraft. Dovlatov called him a "literary madman" and wrote about Grisha's passion with respect: "He loved books—physically. He marveled at the texture of old printed covers. The coarse density of glazed paper. The calligraphy of the font."

All the more incongruous that the content of Silver Century's publications absolutely didn't want to mesh with the form. Grisha's books bled from the slightest touch and disintegrated like aspens in October.

One of Polyak's important virtues was the boundless amiability with which he shouldered Dovlatov's bullying. Maybe because a significant percentage of the bullying was deserved. Grisha was notable for his breathtaking irresponsibility. He would forget and mix up everything, and most importantly, he couldn't stand mailing his published books to customers or even to the authors themselves. When we, working as a team, released the first issue of a pretty good almanac titled *A Part of Speech*, Dovlatov physically dragged Grisha to the post office, showering him with reprimands the whole way there.

It must be noted that Polyak hasn't changed one bit. He still tenderly collects everything Dovlatov ever wrote, he is still friends with Lena, he touchingly looks after Nora Sergeyevna, and he still hates the postal office. He recently asked my permission to reprint something. Naturally, I gave it. I told him there was no need for money—I just wanted the almanac. "I make no promises," replied Grisha and hung up the phone.

Polyak dreamed big. He intended to publish Brodsky's collected works, issue a library of modern poetry, ameliorate bookselling in the immigrant community, and open his own store in New York. Carl Proffer, head of the legendary Ardis publishing house, asked him not to discuss any of those things with him: Carl had stomach cancer, and it hurt to laugh.

Despite everything, Sergei always stood up for Grisha. Polyak was a readymade character for Dovlatov's prose, and Sergei loved him like Flaubert loved Madame Bovary.

8

Poetry and Truth

1

In *The Invisible Book*, everybody's name was real. And this didn't bother anyone, because Sergei only wrote good things about everyone: "I could recall something bad about these people. But I categorically have no desire to do so. I don't want to be objective. I like my friends."

In *The Compromise*, the names were also real, but this time, Dovlatov didn't write a single good thing about his acquaintances. Sergei dished the dirt on everybody, much to the delight of his readers. First of all, it really was very funny. Secondly, it is gratifying to join Dovlatov in a group of ironic individuals who so acutely understood and identified human weaknesses. Thirdly, the feeling of exclusivity warmed you: only the closed circle giggling around Sergei was cured of arrogance, foolishness, and materialism. Accidental witnesses were satisfied with these three reasons, but the more experienced knew of another, fourth reason that allowed them to laugh at those close to them with a clean conscience. They knew that as soon as they got up and left the table, they would immediately join the ranks of fodder.

The Compromise didn't compromise anyone in the immigrant community. In America, Estonian functionaries, like "the timid son of a bitch, Turonok," seemed as fictional as Nozdryov and Manilov.[1] Things got worse when it became clear that Dovlatov only painted from life, and *we* were the life. We are the very things that make up the landscape that he depicts on the canvas with broad, unceremonious strokes.

---

1   Nozdryov and Manilov are two of the characters in Gogol's *Dead Souls* whose dead souls Chichikov attempts to purchase.

Popovsky was the butt of it probably more than anyone else. Mark Aleksandrovich was an experienced and prolific writer. The Soviets blacklisted many of his books, but they released many more. In *The New American*, he made his debut with a scorched earth article titled "Kindness." Then, fighting against malpractice, he put out of business the only active organization in the immigrant community—the Veterans' Association. A recklessly principled man, he was run out of fourteen editorial teams. However, his difficult character hid one particularly rare and noble trait: he was rude exclusively to his higher-ups. Popovsky fearlessly told editors-in-chief nothing but the truth. At his very first strategy session at *The New American*, he recognized in Dovlatov's contribution a quote from Kafka and was indescribably amazed.

"I am pleasantly surprised," he exclaimed, "I would have never thought that you read books!"

It got even worse: Popovsky chided everyone for lacking principles. We responded with typos. In the list of editorial staff, he was listed either as Mrak[2] or Marx Popovsky. Popovsky instilled such fear in the owners of *The New American* that in one difficult moment, the owners named him Dovlatov's deputy. Popovsky was assigned the role that Furmanov held under Chapayev[3]—he was to compensate our cavalier flippancy.

Nothing came of it, but Sergei never forgot the unasked-for deputy and portrayed him in *The Foreign Girl* as the author of a book titled "Sex under Totalitarianism." While collecting material for his monograph and simultaneously flirting with the novella's titular heroine, he asks "when she was subject to defloration":

"'Before or after the events in Hungary?'

"'What do you mean by the events in Hungary?'

"'Before or after the denunciation of the cult of personality?'

"'Probably after.'"

Most amazingly, it wasn't only Dovlatov's victims who bore his insults with difficulty—Dovlatov himself couldn't live with them either. Five years after Sergei's death, Popovsky published a letter Dovlatov wrote him: "The ignominy I feel with regard to what I did to you hasn't given me peace for quite some time. I believe that you had every right to sock me directly in the mouth ... In short, I am not asking you for forgiveness, and I am not expecting

---

2   *Mrak* means "darkness" in Russian.

3   Vasily Chapayev (1887–1919) was a Red Army commander during the revolution. He became popularized as a hero of the revolution and eventually became an easy target for mockery and a recurring figure in Russian jokes.

a response to this message, I merely wish to inform you that I consider myself with regard to you an immeasurable swine."

There is no reason to doubt the letter's earnestness—Sergei atoned with the same ambition with which he sinned. But, characteristically, when he admitted his folly, by no means did he make any promise to change. Maybe that's why he didn't ask for any forgiveness. It seems like Dovlatov didn't have a way out. The literature that he wrote was neither fiction, nor documentary. Sergei torturously searched for a third path—his own.

One of Dovlatov's rare admissions speaks to the intentionality of this search. It is unique, because it is made under the guise of a letter to the editor. By putting on the mask of a fictitious professor at a teachers' college in Minsk, Sergei said about himself what he wanted to hear from others:

"Dovlatov-as-storyteller creates a new literary genre. The documentary manner of his short stories is merely a misleading imitation. He does not use real documents. He creates them through fictional methods. That is, the documentary appearance is the fruit of the solution to the aesthetic problem. And the result is twofold. The credibility of the underlying facts is augmented by the artistic effect."

2

I could never understand how a writer can sit at a desk and write on the paper: "Ivanov (or Petrov, Johnson, Pushkin, a poodle, whatever) came out onto the creaky porch and gazed at the low-hanging clouds." The carefree and haphazard nature of these and similar phrases compromises the grand design. Gorky forbade young writers to write that someone "took off his boots," because that had already been written before them. The hopeless banality of the removed boots and the creaking porch makes literature impossible.

The classics were unbothered by this, because they knew how to effect a sprawling sense of reality. The reader was willing to believe in it right up until the device, exhausted by myriad uses, stopped working. Today, it isn't a narrative or the characters that seem plagiarized, but the very method of artistic reproduction of reality, straightforward and conditional, like a cross-stitched painting.

Tolstoy complained to Leskov: "You feel ashamed writing about people who never existed and who didn't do any of the things you wrote. Something is off. Either the literary form has lived out its time, or else I am living out mine."

Recognizing how worn out the path was, Dovlatov parodied it beautifully. Without pausing once, he could imitate for pages at a time novels written by Vera Panova,[4] whom he held in the highest regard. This sort of pseudo-quote had everything that comprises an ordinary novel: exhaustingly detailed landscapes, minute descriptions of the characters' clothes, their complicated inner lives.

Sergei earnestly believed that royalties were to blame for everything. The Soviet Union was the only nation where they paid by the page rather than by the book or by one's talent. Of course, he said, Soviet novels were the thickest in the world. Every subordinate clause was worth another half-kilo of beef sausages.

Sensing the exhaustiveness of normal fiction, a writer either waves it off, exchanging "the creaky porch" for a half-kilo of sausages, or else he writes something unusual.

Sergei tried to write strange prose. Sometimes, he succeeded: "I froze off the fingers of my hand and the ears of my head." (Platonov had clearly replaced Hemingway by that point). But more often, his attempts didn't work, as was the case with the occasionally cute, but mostly incoherent detective novella *A Donkey Should Be Skinny*.

In essence, avant-gardist fads disgusted Dovlatov. And understandably so. Someone once correctly noted that unsuccessful literature is called experimental. Successful literature has no need for labels.

I didn't believe this at the time and was excited for anything strange. But Dovlatov's attitude toward such affections was cooler. He didn't like the esoteric journal *Echo*, which Maramzin and Khvostenko published in Paris. Zinovyev left him bored, Mamleyev—gloomily confused. Dovlatov gave away Sasha Sokolov's book to us having barely opened it.

Sergei didn't believe in the incomprehensible and didn't forgive even his friends for engaging in it. Kuzminsky, who collected avant-garde poetry, heatedly sought to defend one of them, but it was too late—there was already a spot for him in *The Compromise*:

"'Who is that squirrely, redheaded beanpole? I saw you two together out of the bus this morning.'

"'That's not a squirrely, redheaded beanpole. That's the poet-metaphysicist Vladimir Erl'.'"

---

4   Vera Panova (1905–1973) was a Soviet writer.

Dovlatov never led literary discussions, he couldn't stand smart words, and he eagerly made fun of people who did. For example, me:

"Genis wrote a script for Radio Liberty. It had a lot of scientific words—'allusion,' 'caesura,' 'consequentive.' The editor told Genis:

"'There's no need even to mute such segments. The only people who understand them are professors from Moscow State.'"

I have no memory of this whatsoever, and as for "consequentive," I still don't know what it means and have no desire to. But I understand that Dovlatov was rightly incensed by anything that couldn't be translated into normal, accessible language. Sergei found a mutual understanding with Vonnegut, who decreed that anyone incapable of explaining to a six-year-old what their job entails is a charlatan. Most of all, Sergei hated the word "hypostasis," but "metaphysics" could make him get up and leave the table too.

Dovlatov tried not only combating banality, but occasionally ceding to it. He assured us that he ghost-wrote a book titled *Bolsheviks Subdue the Tundra*. Dovlatov signed his name and even attached a headshot when he published in the journal *Youth* a short story about the working class. An epigram about the short story made its rounds, and many suspected Dovlatov himself was the author:

The headshot's great, could be a big hit,
But the text itself is a pile of shit.

The publication made Sergei 400 rubles, part of which got him a new watch. Tamara Zibunova recalls that she got the watch engraved with the phrase "Lost in a drunken stupor by Dovlatov" so that it would never actually happen. The engraving didn't help, but the plan itself was emblematic of the era's idiosyncrasies. Salinger's *Raise High the Roof Beam, Carpenters* features matches that are branded with the phrase: "These matches were stolen from Bob and Edie Berwick's house."

I feel like the idea of sellout literature didn't offend Sergei too much. He used to say that incorruptibility is of greatest concern to those whom nobody is attempting to corrupt. At any rate, he had a fairly good opinion of Soviet writers, and he wrote about them with touching gratitude. Above all else, he considered literature a profession, and poor language angered him more than Party language. He didn't so much fear commissioned work as much as he didn't believe in its possibility: "In reality, hackwork doesn't exist. Alas, what does exist is our artistic helplessness."

The Soviet regime's foolishness wasn't in its ideological jealousy, but in its purely practical shortsightedness. No other regime had ever been so condescending toward idleness and so merciless toward action. Sergei wanted to write well. The regime only tolerated those who wrote however they could.

3

Having seen my fill of the rusted pipes of New York galleries, I decided to gain a new appreciation for the Russian Itinerant movement in painting. In a nostalgic bout, I was ready to forgive them everything: school compositions about paintings, Narodism, all the candy wrappers.[5]

A questionable object of love gains from separation and loses from proximity. After a fifteen-year break, I once again wandered the halls of the Russian Museum, and I realized that it wasn't the same when I was right next to those paintings, which were as familiar as my wallpaper at home. Previously, I thought the problem was the soul-rending banality of Perov's immortal *Last Tavern*. As Dostoevsky said, give Russians the most lyrical painting in the world, they'll toss it aside and hang up another that depicts someone getting whipped.

Like matryoshkas, the Itinerants seem like a purely Russian phenomenon. Their wandering subjects can be encountered in any second-rate European museum. But here's the thing: the Itinerants' paintings seem as anemic as the ones made by their rivals. The academics' lifelessness can be explained by an unnecessarily detailed knowledge of anatomy. Not wanting to sacrifice all that they had learned in the morgue, they tightly wrapped each drawn carcass in leather, like cabinet makers. As a result, what was left on the canvas was a corpse, not a person.

When you make your way through a museum and get to the Impressionists, you get the feeling that their paintings are burning through the walls. As if you, the viewer, put on a pair of glasses to deal with your hitherto unnoticed nearsightedness. By depicting grapes in a thick light that makes them seem shaggy, the Impressionists show us what we could see without their help if only we saw the world as directly as they did.

---

5 There is a series of popular Russian candies whose wrappers feature images from Itinerant paintings; the image on the wrappers of Clubfooted Bear candies, for example, is the bears from Ivan Shishkin's *Morning in a Pine Forest*.

This directness is what eluded the Itinerants. They didn't paint portraits of reality—they blocked it like set pieces in an amateur theater. These paintings boast no more verisimilitude than the horn of plenty. The more assiduously they copied life, the farther they trekked away from it: a portrait isn't waxwork.

In a museum like Madame Tussauds, they often place a fake ticket collector among all the figures of kings, presidents, and murderers. Out of all the figures, this is the only one that truly looks like a real person.

Sergei usually called his short stories short stories, but in his youth, he added the epithet, "Impressionist short stories." This was odd, because Dovlatov was never really interested in painting. He made excellent drawings, he had a taste for design, but I don't recall his ever making even glancing mention of paintings. He swore that he had never been to the Hermitage, and I believe him, because imagining Sergei in a museum is as difficult as imagining him opening a savings account. I think that Dovlatov appreciated the Impressionists only as far as they could teach him something: not the result, but the method.

"They," notes Sergei, "prefer the fleeting to the eternal."

The same can be said of Dovlatov's prose. If the Itinerants loaded up their paintings with significance up until the artistic illusion became artless convention, the Impressionists placed their trust in ephemerality. By depicting the world through a particular lens, they trusted that reality is like cervelat: any small bit of it contains the full range of life's qualities. An ant crawling along a railroad will never comprehend the railroad's full setup. To do that, it would need to cross it—at any point along its length.

Dovlatov didn't go along a subject—he crossed it. Like the Impressionists, he didn't insist on his subject's exclusivity. In order to depict a portrait of the world, all Dovlatov needed—much like the Impressionists—was any old landscape.

People—real people—were his landscape. This is why Dovlatov had no need for imaginary characters—he had to work *en plein air*. After all, only living people retain a fidelity to nature. They *are* nature. A person is a product of nature. Nature lives in people just as in trees or rocks. By making it visible, art gives birth to the universe: the artificial creates the real and returns it whence it came.

Marienhof, the author of the famous memoir *The Novel without Lies*, described this process with a rare insider's knowledge: "Good writers do this: they take living people and insert them into their books. Then, they clamber out of the books and roam the world anew, but in a slightly different guise, I would say a less mortal one."

It is as impossible to come up with a person as it is to wish a cloud into existence. Nature will always outdo our imaginations. Thus, unable to contend with nature, an artist can only simplify it. For example, draw a square cloud, as the surrealists did. However, a square cloud isn't a cloud at all. It is an inversion of nature.

In this way, we can derive character types in literature. By turning Oblomov into "an oblomov," we transition from the living concreteness of arithmetic into the deadened abstraction of algebra—from the endless diversity of numbers to the limitations of the alphabet, each letter of which carries conditional, not absolute, significance. Stubbornly retaining its inimitable individuality, a number, like a person, can only be equal to itself.

Dovlatov liked one of Leonid Andreyev's[6] characters, who said that because of his moral defects, he was unworthy of carrying a human name and therefore asked to be called a single letter, or, better yet, a digit.

4

Dovlatov understood that he surrounded himself with his own victims, but he couldn't do anything about it. Even substituting someone's name for a fake one was agonizing for him—he equated it with becoming a co-author of someone else's work.

Fake names, like paper flowers, can neither take root nor grow. The substitution might escape the reader, but not the author. The fake name will bother him, since it does not so much replace the real as combat it: the false character pushes aside the real one. Even when working for the paper, Sergei preferred to make do without pseudonyms. If he really had to, he used his initials, "S.D."

The danger of pseudonyms is that they replace the author's identity with phantoms. It's no coincidence that they so rarely resemble an author's real name. I did know one Katz, a journalist who signed his name "Levin" as a

---

6 Leonid Andreyev (1871–1919) was a Russian writer active during the Silver Age of Russian literature.

matter of principle. But usually, pseudonyms are extravagant, like Severianin, or melodramatic, like "Gorky."[7]

Only Limonov has a pseudonym that matches his personality more than his real last name, but only thanks to Bakhchanyan, who came up with the "bombastic and trashy" surname for Eduard Savenko. Proud of his invention, Vagrich demanded that every one of Limonov's signatures be accompanied by the words "copyright Bakhchanyan." This didn't inhibit their friendship. At least, not until Limonov added a homosexual scene into his autobiographical novel, which prompted Vagrich to react with an announcement in the newspaper: "Open season on my ass. Limonov."

Out of all the New Yorkers, other than Bakhchanyan, only Dovlatov tolerated Limonov. Sergei not only read his scandalous novel *It Is I, Edichka* with interest, like everyone else, but—unlike the others—he publicly defended Limonov, whom our crowd ultimately pushed out of New York into France. The same Vagrich saw him off. Before he left, he helped Limonov find some sneakers with good heels.

---

7   *Sever* means "north," and *gorky* means "bitter."

9

None of Us Are Lookers

1

Sergei didn't like too many things—not the opera, not the ballet. The only thing he liked in theaters was the buffet. Even nature irritated him. During one of our lunch breaks, we dragged him outside to eat some sandwiches on the spring grass. First Sergei squinted, then he scowled, and finally he declared that he wasn't capable of functioning when not surrounded by cigarette smoke. Admittedly, over the years, he grew to like going to his summer house in the Catskills. But even there, he still preferred the interior, leaving the house only to get the Russian paper.

"Passion for inanimate objects irritates me," wrote Dovlatov. "I think that love for beeches comes at the expense of love for people."

I feel like Sergei simply lacked a curiosity for anything that didn't directly have to do with him. He had absolutely no respect for knowledge, especially the knowledge that Paramonov labels "optional." He thought the exchange of facts a foolish activity. Information that wasn't funny was superfluous. Dovlatov couldn't stand antiquated allusions. He even loathed historical novels, believing them to be the sole genre in which erudition can masquerade as talent.

Sergei generally didn't strive to learn new things. He preferred not to read books, but to reread them. He avoided travel, attended conferences unwillingly, and all he did at the one in Lisbon was drink. His impressions while traveling would result in just a few lines of text, and even these only dealt with appetizers: "Portugal . . . There was some unprecedented fish dish with vegetables. I remember I wanted to ask: 'Who's the artist?'"

I found everything interesting at the time, and comprehending Dovlatov's indifference was beyond me. I not only took out a dozen books every month, I even read them. A history of Carthage, Nansen's diaries, a culinary dictionary.

I understood the mechanics of a rock crusher, I could list the peaks of the Himalayas and the emperors of Rome. Moreover, I reread Jules Verne on the down-low, and I resembled Captain Nemo, who responded to the question "how deep is the world's ocean?" with forty pages of densely packed text. As for adventures—I was *dying* to travel. I went to thirty-eight countries. And I liked it everywhere. I didn't tell Dovlatov—wanderlust was foreign to him. And not just foreign—unpleasant.

"Vail and Genis," wrote Sergei during a cooling period in our relationship, "are still doing talented work. They're on par with Zikmund and Hanzelka. For them, literature is Africa. And nothing but Africa surrounds us. The images are so vivid that they make one's blood vessels pop . . ."

Maybe Sergei was right. Paris has a museum of undelivered packages. A fan once suggested that Beckett go there: things without owners, anonymous, abandoned—each exhibit was an absurdist drama. Beckett, however, politely declined:

"You see, madam," he said, "I haven't left my house since 1958."

Beckett was a highly educated man. He knew many languages, traveled across half of Europe by foot. He was the best student at Dublin's Trinity College, he was erudite, he loved pure, aimless knowledge, he dreamed of being left alone with the Encyclopedia Britannica. I couldn't even make heads or tails of the title of the poem about Descartes he wrote as a youth. The thing has more footnotes than body text. But at some point, it hit Beckett that there is more incognizable in the world than that which we can comprehend. After that, the footnotes disappeared from his books, while he himself rarely left his house. Everything that Beckett needed for literature he found in himself. Sergei found it in others.

Dovlatov was interested only in people, their complex inner endlessness, the thin "cosmetics of human connections." Sometimes, I felt like Sergei was more interested in people than in anything else in the world, even more than in literature. Incidentally, Dovlatov never made a clear dividing line between a person and the corresponding character. People comprised the alphabet of his poetics. That's how it was: a person as a unit of text.

Sergei compassionately recalled the lessons of Boris Vakhtin, who advised his younger colleagues to write with letters, not with ideas. But Dovlatov himself wrote with people.

2

Modern thought has it that culture has lost the universal, one-size-fits-all myth that answered all of an artist's questions. This is why the great writers of the twentieth century who were forced to worry about themselves—Joyce, Elliot, Platonov—came into literature with their own myths. The myths ended with our generation. Dovlatov understood this, and instead of making fruitless attempts to find life's common denominator, he simply stopped in triumphant bewilderment before a gallery of notable faces that was borne of the Soviet regime's indefatigable love for the grotesque. Having stopped on the curb of humanity, it spawned so many inexplicable individuals, that a document cataloguing them would be enough to birth a whole new movement.

I've always thought that the crackpot was the socialist economy's only worthwhile product. The authors of *samizdat* journals, the directors of various avant-garde theaters, artist-nonconformists, inventors, poets, witch doctors, wanderers, icon collectors, Hittite translators—they were all possible because the regime hid them away from an indifferent world. The regime didn't like them, of course, but it always noticed them, imbuing their work with significance through its persecution.

Only in a nation indifferent to its economy could these oddballs find their niche in society, a niche in which they were free from society— incoherent research institutes, obscure laboratories, hazy businesses, a guard booth, an elevator operator's room, finally that boiler room that Dovlatov immortalized: "We have a peculiar crowd here. Olezhka, for example, is a Buddhist. A follower of zen. He searches for serenity in the monastery of his own soul. Hood is an artist, the left wing of the global avant- garde. He works in the tradition of metaphysical synthetism. He primarily depicts packaging material—boxes, cans, covers . . . As for me, I am a simple man. In my spare time, I work on music theory. Speaking of, how do you feel about Britten's polytonal layering?"

The Soviet oddball is as vivid an archetype as the medieval monk or the Renaissance painter. It's readymade material for the wordcraft that no longer really qualifies as literature. Rather, it is writing from nature, *en plein air*, a cabinet of curiosities, a freak show.

This is a strictly Russian tradition that stems not from Pushkin, but from Gogol. The more predictable West births types, but we give rise to insane individualities, cranks and crackpots all.

This is why Sergei loved Shukshin more than any other Soviet author. In one of the first shots of one of his films, right after the intro titles, a man stumbles along uncertainly. The camera slowly pans across his trembling, straining legs, his withdrawn figure, his rigid neck—and then it freezes before reaching his chin. Nothing else makes it into the shot. The point is that a full glass of vodka is balancing on his head. The film doesn't do anything with the scene—it is irrelevant to the narrative, but this episode is far from unnecessary—it is the most important sequence in the film. Like a good epigraph, it not only sets the tone, but it serves as a mute declaration of the film's intentions—to show life's passions, not explain them.

Another scene that Sergei often retold was from the film *When the Trees Were Tall*. A character is asked:

"Why did you lie?"

"I don't know," he replies, "I thought, what if I just lie? And I did."

The tone is close to Dostoevsky's. In *Notes from the House of the Dead*, one of the inmates repeats over and over: "They won't steal any of my own things, probably, but I'm afraid maybe that I'll steal something myself."

In life and in art, Sergei valued neither strict alogisms à la absurdist literature, nor high-minded sophistry that simulated nonsense, nor the direct antithesis of reason—he valued the circumvention of reason, which is to say a circuitous and ailing train of thought. Each of its inelegant instances bears witness to the fact that the person is greater than their words and actions. The person simply doesn't fit neatly inside the lines. Because of a person's confusion in themselves, they limit our ability to analyze them. A person, like the atom of the ancient Greeks, possesses that same indivisible wholeness that cannot be disaggregated into the elemental particles of fears and passions.

Dovlatov was enthralled by that remnant of personality that cannot be translated into the language of debate. Sergei derived great pleasure from that semantic haziness that, like champagne, made the room spin lightly. He lay in wait for those barely noticeable shifts in rationality that insidiously throw the soul out of balance.

Since his youth, Dovlatov collected the oddities of reality, which, like Alice said in Wonderland, provoke certain thoughts, only it's unclear what kind. Sergei told us that he would make his friends skip class to go to the square and look at the old man twitching his toe in a funny manner.

It's not surprising that Dovlatov didn't stay in university for long. Sergei wrote that he went to take his German exam knowing only two words in German: Marx and Engels.

3

Admiring the mysteriousness of our nature, Dovlatov acknowledged only the mysteries that were closest to him. He never heard of the Bermuda Triangle, he didn't read science fiction, he wasn't interested in the transfer of souls, and he simply ignored the horoscope section in the paper, though he did come up with a name for it: "The stars look down on us." Dovlatov shrugged when I wrote an article about a yeti. What genuinely caught Sergei's interest wasn't snow men, but ordinary ones. Take, for example, his neighbor, whom he described as the "mysterious religious agent Lemkus."

Truth be told, I didn't see anything mysterious about him. An ordinary person, affable, quiet, accommodating. He got Dovlatov's daughter Katya into a Baptist summer camp. When we made kebab and came to visit, he asked us, out of respect for the religion, to hide behind a tree if we wanted to drink. But Dovlatov couldn't find a suitable trunk.

Lemkus was an energetic writer. Along with the rest of us, he was published in Victor Perelman's journal *Time and Us*. His short stories weren't all that unique, but they caused immense bewilderment in Dovlatov. (He probably wasn't used to it. I immigrated before him and had already spent some time working for the paper, where nuke-carrying planes were called "atomic bomb carriers"). Sergei couldn't fathom what he meant by "the pink sunrise of dawn was reminiscent of a young woman's breast." I, on the other hand, was much more disconcerted by the title of another short story: "The Backside that Doomed Us All."

Aside from engaging in elegant wordcraft, Lemkus also partook in journalism. He issued a paper called *The Literary Courier*. In it, he published an interview with Aksenov, who had only just come to the West. According to Lemkus, Vasily Pavlovich's first words were, "I miss for Moscow, I miss for my friends."

Lemkus was distinguished not by his literary success, but by his religious pursuits, which, it must be said, aren't much beloved in the immigrant community. It was believed that neophytes sought material advantage rather than spiritual achievement. At the kosher *New American*, our science editor carried around two Old Testaments in his pockets—one in the left pocket, one in the right. Bakhchanyan provided the following commentary on the subject: "He runs around the agora, an idiot with his Torah." The Torahs didn't prevent him from being fired, so he abandoned Judaism and took up Esperantism instead. Faith yielded dubious dividends at best. True, the Baptists did provide free meals on Sundays, but only for those who genuflected.

Nevertheless, Lemkus prevailed. During Perestroika, he published in the *Literary Gazette* an opinion piece in defense of Christ, signing off as "an editor of the trans-universal radio." I didn't really understand whether he was boasting an interplanetary connection or a transcendental one, but I immediately thought of Dovlatov's perceptiveness, since he considered

Lemkus mysterious even back when he simply picked up the phone and "called to confirm Lermontov's patronymic."

4

As Lyosha Losev accurately noted, people in Dovlatov's world are "larger than in life."

I call Losev "Lyosha" not out of a sense of familiarity (in twenty years of knowing each other, we still haven't made the transition to the informal "you"), but to avoid any unnecessary confusion. The thing is, he used to sign his name as either Lev Losev or as Aleksei Livschitz. This annoyed his readers. Forced to explain why he switched between Lev and Aleksei, Losev wrote that there was nothing special about it—Tolstoy did the same thing.

Losev was generally unlucky with his readers. When we published a poem about the war in Afghanistan, the newspaper became a forum for discussion about the limits of what was permissible in contemporary poetic language. Subscribers from the old diaspora managed to find something indecent about the word "muezzin," which made a solitary appearance in the poem.

Dovlatov, like all of us, paid careful attention to and was delicately interested in Losev. Sergei wrote about him respectfully: "His courteous, quiet voice was almost always decisive." This harbors undercurrents of a choleric's envy. Dovlatov was the antipode to Losev. Lyosha scrupulously and ably cultivates the image and mannerisms of a pre-Revolutionary professor, which itself seems like a quote from an Andrei Bely memoir. People who see Losev for the first time might think that poems like the wonderful "Memories of Vodka" cycle were written by his namesake.

Normally, the Dr. Jekyll in Losev has quite an easy time with Mr. Hyde. But once, at a conference in Honolulu, Losev jumped out of the tour bus packed with some hundred Slavicists and clambered up a palm tree with such agility and speed that I just barely managed to take a photo. I vigilantly keep the photo in my archive, waiting for the time when Losev becomes an academic or a classic.

So, Lyosha Losev wrote that people in Sergei's works are larger than in life. And it's true: in comparison with other characters, Dovlatov's seem naked in a sea of the clothed. Maybe it's because Sergei crafted the portraits of his characters via subtraction rather than addition.

The paradox of art is that, like Achilles with the turtle, the artist will never catch up to the original he seeks to depict. How old is a person? Two? A hundred? A living person changes, a dead person isn't a person at all. Which is why any portrait is the artificial combination of the eternal with the immediate. By adding details, we only diminish the likeness.

Sergei did the opposite. In transferring the likeness to paper, he removed everything superfluous. Sometimes, Dovlatov made do with a simple participle: "'It's six exactly,' said Tsurikov and, without stooping, scratched his knee."

"A person," wrote Sergei, "is born, suffers, and dies—unchanged, like the formula for water, H_2O." Searching for such formulae, Dovlatov divined for each of his characters the minimal combination of elements whose bonds makes the accidental inevitable. In this way, Dovlatov's portraits resemble Japanese tercets:

> She cut her hair short,
> Read Tsvetayeva's prose,
> And wasn't fond of Georgians.

5

Haikus are fascinating in their indecipherability. These poems don't "sprout from refuse," [as Akhmatova wrote—A.R.]—they stay in it. Haikus don't care what the subject is, because what's important isn't the picture, but the perspective. Haikus do not communicate what the poet sees—they force us to see what is visible without him. We see the world not as we imagine it and not as it could be and not as it should be. We see the world as it would be without us.

Haikus do not photograph the moment—they chisel it out in stone. They halt the flow of time like a clock that has stopped but not broken.

Haikus aren't laconic—they are self-sufficient. Reticence would be excessive. This is the final result of subtraction. They resemble the pyramids, whose grandeur is not a function of their size.

The narrative of a haiku unfolds outside of the text. We see its result: life, the indisputable presence of things, the uncompromising reality of their existence. A haiku is interested in things not because they symbolize something, but because they, the things, *are*.

The words of a haiku must stagger with their precision—as if you thrust your hand into boiling water.

6

Dovlatov considered precision to be the greatest virtue. Which is why I take pride in the fact that he found in our work "first and foremost—precision, my beloved, forgotten, wasted precision, lost in modern Russian literature; precision, which Daniil Kharms said is the first indicator of genius."

Only let's not confuse precision with pedantic faultlessness. Its criteria are internal, not external. Precision is the intimate affair of the author, who is obligated to say only what he or she wants to say—not almost, not kind of, not sort of, but specifically and only.

Precision is the happy conjunction of means and ends. Or, as Dovlatov said, "unity of effort and result," which, he added unexpectedly, is easiest to achieve at a shooting range.

In literature, Dovlatov saw only one unforgiveable sin: approximation. In *The Invisible Book*, he notes: "I wanted to write: 'This is a complex man . . .' If he is, then don't write it down." But the vast majority, lamentably, write—at great length, prettily, and irrelevantly. Reading something like that is like conversing with a garrulous stutterer.

Most often, precision is replaced with good intentions. It is believed that good can be defended with any words—the first on the left, in accordance with the right-hand rule of physics.

Precision, by the way, is not at all the same thing as simplicity. But by combining in itself both darkness and complexity, it makes even the incomprehensible crystal clear. This is why precision is an integral aspect of nonsense and the absurd. It wasn't coincidence that Dovlatov referenced Kharms.

In essence, the antithesis of literature isn't silence—it is imprecise language.

10

An Empty Mirror

1

Although Dovlatov said that he didn't understand how you could write not about yourself, he earnestly tried. He has short stories written from a woman's point of view. In the best of them—"The Road to a New Apartment"—a certain phrase from the speaker's diary serves as a refrain: "The thing we most feared happened."

But still, the thing that makes Dovlatov's prose unmistakably Dovlatovian is Dovlatov himself. With his presence, he glues the surroundings into a single whole. Dovlatov the character is even alike in appearance to Dovlatov the author—we always remember that he is afraid of hitting the chandelier with his head. This outsider's perspective is consciously built into his prose—Sergei constantly sees himself through the eyes of another.

We see ourselves as transparent, which is why we so quickly forget that we are wreathed in opaqueness. In order to constantly be the focus of another's attention, stronger shocks are needed, like an open fly or a hole in your pants. Which is exactly how one of Dovlatov's short stories begins: "The editor Turonok's pants tore open on his ass."

Sergei loved to depict himself in a situation painful as a hangnail. I didn't understand it until I tried it on myself. Turns out that the best way to exorcise yourself of any permitted or experienced awkwardness is to share it. By recounting your miss, you surround yourself with sympathizing companions rather than gloating onlookers. Unlike sorrow or joy, shame *is* subject to division, and public disclosure diminishes the remainder.

Sergei understood such nuances well. Calculatedly demeaning himself in the eyes of the onlookers, he understood that they'll give him their love in spades. Once again retelling the first time he met his wife, Dovlatov begins the tale with an unflattering intimacy: "I was embarrassed by my legs sticking out from under my bathrobe. They are my family's least expressive body part."

Truth be told, I always thought that only a woman could have a nice pair of legs. But Sergei, with his lively interest in his anatomy, never wore shorts, and when he saw me wearing them once, he thought I was showing off my calves. That's probably why in his *Notebooks*, he vengefully calls me "thickset and pretty."

In reality, he was the one who was "thickset and pretty," not me. Predisposed for stoutness, Dovlatov resembled a professional athlete who had happily let himself go. Nevertheless, he wasn't always fat. When his stomach began to jut out like a melon, Sergei grabbed hold of himself and feverishly lost weight. Dovlatov tamed his body with such enthusiasm that it was tiring just to observe him. During one of his dieting periods, he ordered the healthiest thing on McDonalds' menu: some Chicken McNuggets. Seeing that the size (and all other attributes) of these nuggets resembled chicken droppings, Dovlatov flew into a rage and put in eleven more orders.

Any time he was losing weight, Dovlatov exercised. I never saw him do it, but I held the Acme-sized weights he used in my own hands. Sergei would grumble that no member of the intelligentsia could walk by them without taking note—they'd slobber all over them and then not even put them back. Shortly before his death, after buying a small house in the Catskills ("half a hectare of land, with Uncle Tom's cabin not far behind it"), Sergei began to jog along the forest paths. He only went on some three jogs, but he assured me that he had become well-acquainted with a local coyote.

Of course, Sergei liked being strong. As a former boxer, he valued physical strength. He marveled at Muhammad Ali, and he coquettishly wrote about himself: "I was once a prospective heavyweight in the army." The second half of his unpublished novel *Five Corners* is entirely devoted to boxing. It is called "Alone in the Ring." Dovlatov complained that detractors renamed it "Alone at the Market" [*"market" and "ring" sound similar in Russian—A.R.*]. Similarly, one of his early works, *The March of the Lonely*, became *The March of the One-Legged*. I am confident that, as always, Dovlatov himself authored the parodic titles.

Sergei mentions his "boxer text" in his letters: "I want to depict the world of vice as a world of spiritual malaise, joyless and seductive. I want to show how illness follows in our footsteps like a succubus, intermittently reminding us of its existence with flares of baseless anxiety or pain without reward."

Sergei must not have thought this tricky endeavor fulfilled: he showed us the manuscript, but didn't publish it. As far as I recall, the work was energetic à *la* Hemingway, with dramatic subtext, deftly employing professional jargon. One thing in particular stood out: in a scene in a morgue, it turns out that boxers have pink brains.

It's clear why Sergei left the world of boxing. But he retained a nostalgic interest in fighting. Sergei even carried around a club. Because of it, they wouldn't let us into the UN building, which we wanted to show to Aryev, who was visiting New York. Sergei categorically refused to disarm when the metal detector sensed the club's lead lining and started wailing.

Dovlatov's stories about his Leningrad friends—Maramzin, Bitov, Popov—featured as much brawling as *The Magnificent Seven*. Maybe he was just paying his dues to the sixties, a time when body was valued more than spirit. At any rate, the participants of those brawls contradict him.

This is exactly what happened with one of the most popular tales, in which Bitov delivers the following speech at a court of comrades: "Hear me out and make an objective decision. But first, listen to how it all went down . . . Here's what happened. I go inside the 'Continental.' Andrei Voznesensky is standing nearby. So tell me," Bitov cries out, "how could I *not* punch him directly in the mouth?"

Both characters in the story declared that the incident does not resemble what actually happened. Voznesensky even proposed to put it in writing, but they say that Bitov, smart guy that he is, declined.

Bitov was once performing in New York, where he was asked with émigré unceremoniousness how he felt about God.

"I feel about Him the same way He feels about me," Bitov parried.

"And how does He feel about you?" insistently asked the audience member.

"The same way I feel about Him," wearily replied Bitov.

2

Dovlatov was a very strong man. *And* he was enormous. "Great like the harvest," Bakhchanyan would describe him. Sergei was so big that he wouldn't fit in an ordinary coffin. And Dovlatov sacrificed all this physical strength in the name of wordcraft. A certain brutality, which Dovlatov cultivated in himself with a degree of satisfaction, categorically contradicted his literary self-portrait. Every fight he depicted ended the same way: "I took a swing, drawing on the lessons of the heavyweight Sharafutdinov. I swung and fell on my back . . . I saw the sky, so vast, pale, mysterious . . . I gazed at it until I got a heel in the eye."

A troubadour of his own defeats, Sergei reveled in the slights and humiliations he had experienced. As a result, Dovlatov turned out to be not only the strongest author of our generation, but the most beat up as well.

Usually, it's the other way around—we hide our physical shortcomings much more fervently than the spiritual ones. Sergei used to say that a person is more likely to admit to thievery, let alone adultery, than to taking a nap after lunch. If you encounter in a book something like "the bastard crumpled from my hit" or "she began to moan in my arms," you can rest assured that the writer didn't turn out as tall as he would've liked.

Not needing any such consolation, Dovlatov framed his fiasco as his paying his dues to nature for the generous head start it accorded him. But this surface-level motif belied a secret scheme that Dovlatov spent his whole life implementing. Sergei assiduously made sure not to become higher than the reader. Like no one else, he understood the advantage of such a position.

Usually, a text decorates its author. Which is unsurprising: we dedicate our best hours to literature, while everything else gets whatever we have left. Moreover, a writer assumes an inherently advantageous position with regard to the reader. He lets the reader know only the things he deems necessary. The writer knows more than we do, and not because he's holding pocket rockets, but because he snuck a peek at the flop.

This can only aggravate. The more that a writer tries to pass himself off as dressed all in white, the more the reader wants to see him fall flat. Dovlatov met this desire head-on. Unafraid to show himself as laughable and weak, he stands as our equal. And his readers do not forget this.

The strong are loved less than the weak, the smart are feared more than the foolish, the fortunate eat it more often than the unlucky. We prefer a helpless infant to a titan of creation, and the sea conquers the rivers because it is lower than them.

3

By sharing his sins and faults with the reader, Sergei not only satisfied our desire for justice—he evoked our condescension. It was his first, if not his only, commandment. "I was struck by his condescension toward people," Sergei writes tenderly about his father. "My mother spent her whole life loathing the man who fired him from the theater. My father, meanwhile, enjoyed drinks with him a month later..."

Dovlatov built up indiscriminateness—both toward others and toward himself—as principle. Which did not make him at all soft ("Shit," he said, "is also soft"). Sergei's short stories do not have a single unforgiven sinner, but they also do not feature anyone faultlessly moral.

It's not that there is nobody guilty in the world; it's that they shouldn't be judged. Any verdict is dishonorable not because it lowers one cup of the scales of justice, but because it raises the other.

If Bulgakov's Yeshua is absolute good, then what does Voland personify? Absolute evil? No, merely justice.

The idea of "just desserts" disgusted Sergei so much that he once got into an argument with all of Radio Liberty. This was when the Americans responded to Libya's terrorist acts by blowing up Gaddhafi's palace. While his colleagues were excitedly tallying the casualties, Dovlatov, pale from rage, explained to everyone how ignoble it was to rejoice at the news.

Sergei was understanding of crime, but he couldn't stand the idea of punishment. He was governed not by love or kindness or pity, but a sense of deep, consanguineous, unbreakable kinship with everything in the world. There's no need to be like everybody else, Dovlatov wrote, because we already are like everybody else. In his short stories, the author is no different from the characters, because for Dovlatov, all people sprouted from the same soil.

Denying an author the right to judge his own characters means leaving him jobless. And so, Dovlatov really has nothing to do in his prose. He essentially serves as a brake. The author doesn't so much help as inhibit the unfolding events. He resists the impulse to engage in any activity— alter fate, change the world, get up off the couch. The quicker we go in the other direction, the farther we deviate from our own. Resisting adverse circumstances is no different from raising your sail during a storm. Which is why Dovlatov expressed his disagreement with how things stood by not trying to change them. "My whole life," Sergei writes, "I hated activities of any kind . . . it was as if my life was narrated in the passive voice. I passively followed the circumstances. This helped me find a justification for everything."

By becoming a literary position, an author's inaction becomes paradoxical. On the one hand, Dovlatov is the inevitable hero of all his short stories. On the other hand, he's not a hero at all. He doesn't even have a reflection in the mirror. By equalizing himself with the characters, the storyteller steps aside in order to let his surroundings say their piece. Rather than helping them, Dovlatov dedicated all of his strength to not getting in their way.

This is far more difficult than it seems. My wife was once doing an interview in Moscow on a familiar subject: "How did you settle in, you new American?" Since the journalists weren't interested in me, all that was left for me to do was sit quietly nearby. As he was leaving, the pustule of a photographer told me that what he enjoyed the most was watching me: it was like looking at an open bottle of champagne that was shut up again with great difficulty.

Inaction required not only effort, but a natural predisposition—a predisposition for the natural. Respect for something not created by us is the ethical justification for laziness.

Dovlatov considered inaction the only ethical state. "Ideally," he dreamed, "I would be a fisherman. Spend my whole life sitting on a riverside."

I was sure that he wrote this just for the sake of the joke. Imagining Dovlatov fishing is no easier than imagining him starring in *Swan Lake*. But Sergei once showed up with so many goldfish that he himself caught in Queens that there was enough to make a soup.

I find myself recalling those shimmering fish with greater frequency. I imagine that they are coming to me from Dovlatov's nonexistent future. Sergei could have made an excellent old man: a mighty grandfather, surrounded by enamored fans and obstinate members of the household.

4

Dovlatov saw, with himself as the guinea pig, that the author is always the victim of circumstance. He avoided chalking it up to providence and wrote about it directly, though without details: "It would appear that someone very much wanted to make a writer out of me."

Dovlatov didn't believe that people became writers of their own volition. In raising his daughter Katya, Sergei used to say that "artistic professions are to be avoided. But it's another thing altogether if *they* choose *you*."

Sergei believed that a person cannot be in control of their own destiny. But someone else's? That was a different story.

Dovlatov was sooner a plenipotentiary writer in life than in literature. Hence his love for intrigue. Sergei was a brilliant taunter-miniaturist. Where others resorted to a crowbar, he employed such a sharp scalpel that he left no seams in his wake. This is why Sergei was unrivaled in newspaper scuffles.

During *The New American's* enmity with another New York weekly— the *Novaya gazeta*, [*meaning "the new gazette"* —A.R.]—Sergei wrote an editorial either about Americans' spirituality or their soullessness. He described how some woman once got sick on the metro and how he offered her—attention!—a copy of the *Novaya gazeta*. Soon, however, Sergei started writing for that very paper. Which is why when he got to publishing his old editorials independently, he replaced *Novaya gazeta* with *svezhaya gazeta* [*meaning "a fresh gazette"—A.R.*].

Sergei knew how to get anyone involved with his intrigues. He once told the long-suffering Lemkus that "Genis suggests not to read his short stories." I opened my mouth—but I closed it immediately. I never said any such thing, but there wasn't really anything to argue with.

Able to get under anyone's skin, Sergei enthusiastically portrayed himself as a victim too. Every now and then, he would unfold lengthy to-dos about slights that he himself invented.

An experienced director, he didn't instill passions—he focused them so as to observe their flow with genuine engagement. He was a favorite of women who had undergone many misfortunes, and he listened to their convoluted affairs with generous interest. Most appealing to him were those gaudy scenarios that were the result of his "favorite combination—insolence and helplessness." The immigrant community provided more than enough. Sergei dedicated *The Émigrée* to them: "To lonely Russian women in America—with love, sorrow, and hope."

Dovlatov liked being a knight in armor. He loved thunderously quoting *The Captain's Daughter*[1]: "Which of my people dares harm an orphan?" Sergei truly did become frightening when somebody began offending women. He wouldn't even let us make fun of the woman who authored a short story that began: "He sat my naked bum down on the warm washing machine."

Sergei loved intrigue. By becoming hotly involved in his acquaintances' intimate circumstances, he helped them untangle—and re-tangle—them with equal fervor. Sergei was like a Borges character, who, after proposing to take the rook pawn, pens an article about why it's a terrible idea.

Dovlatov wove his web exclusively for the prettiness of the design. Which made it no less dangerous. Sergei didn't try to increase the amount of evil in the world—he wanted to make it more complex. Dovlatov relished

---

1 *The Captain's Daughter* (1936) is a Pushkin novel whose plot takes place during the Pugachev Rebellion, during which Yemelyan Pugachev (1742–1775) led an uprising against Catherine II.

the intricacy of emotions, their contradictions and different hues. In order to be a writer, Dovlatov had to dissolve among others. In order to feel alive, it was imperative for Sergei to exist in a thicket of emotions that he himself evoked.

Sometimes, he reminded me of Pechorin.[2]

---

2   Grigory Pechorin is the Byronic main character of Lermontov's *Hero of Our Time* (1840).

11

A Dotted Novel

1

It is entirely unclear when Dovlatov became a writer. We thought that it happened in Leningrad, while in Leningrad, they thought it happened in America. What's left is to frame as decisive the few weeks he spent in Austria while immigrating. Having wound up in Vienna with his mother and the fox terrier Glasha, Sergei became frantically active. While stuck in a boarding house, he managed to write several excellent short stories, which ultimately wound up in *The Compromise.*

Perhaps his artistic bender was the function of an ordinary one, as was sometimes the case. Before Vienna, Sergei so zealously bid farewell to his homeland that he was taken off the plane in Budapest. Truth be told, I didn't hear this story from Dovlatov, which inspires both confidence and doubt in it. It seems odd that Sergei hid such a vivid detail of his exodus. Then again, it's possible that he considered it heartbreaking.

One way or another, Dovlatov arrived in America with an undeniable degree of renown—and sporting an understated dissident's halo. However, instead of illusions, he entertained only faint hopes. Like all of us, he was prepared to put bread on the table through straightforward physical labor.

Every writer I know started out that way. Limonov became a waiter. The sports journalist Aleksei Orlov guarded lab bunnies. The publicist Grisha Ryskin became a masseur. Friedrich Neznansky, the author of detective novels, had it worse than the others. After word spread that he was a lawyer, the soft and pretty Friedrich began to be cruelly bullied at the factory where he worked—in America, they're so envious of lawyers that they can't stand them. Eduard Topol', Neznansky's co-author, had a different start. After declaring that he had no intention of getting mixed up in the immigrant ghetto, he arrived in America with a preplanned scenario ready to go. The first sentence sounded impressive: "The naked Sara lay on the couch." Pretty soon, Topol' became a taxi driver. When their collaboration ended, Friedrich complained to Dovlatov that Topol' appropriated his typewriter. Sergei was surprised: what sort of a detective is he if he can't even keep track of his own possessions?

Sergei, by the way, was a good judge of typewriters. He was even going to start repairing them. He chose this somewhat exotic specialization as the one that was most closely related to literature. It turned out, however, that they don't repair typewriters in America. So, Sergei signed up for jewelry courses—he knew how to draw and loved little trinkets.

Admittedly, it didn't last long, just like for the rest of us. I, for example, was fired from my first job after a month—for carelessness. I can't think of a more boring four weeks in my entire life. I longed for the work day to end fifteen minutes after it began. And this was despite the fact that I was loading cargo for a company that, as I now understand, didn't so much produce jeans as postmodernism. Here's how things worked: a mound of cheap jeans lay on the ground. A group of quiet Puerto Rican girls sewed fashionable "Sessùn" brand logos onto them. On 5th Ave, the jeans sold for fifty bucks each.

2

I met Dovlatov immediately. Lena worked with us for *The New Russian Word*, and we already knew each other by our publications. As strange as it seems, Sergei and I began using the informal "you" right away. With people from Leningrad, that doesn't happen reflexively at all, which differentiates them from Muscovites. (When Yuz Aleshkovsky went over to visit the Yefimovs, Marina let them in and greeted them. In response, Aleshkovsky screamed "That's enough of your Leningrad nonsense!").

Sergei loved and valued etiquette. He used the formal "you" with many people who were close to him, including Grisha Polyak. Familiarity wasn't so much offensive as puzzling for him. When my wife caught him in some white lie, Sergei replied in surprise: "I didn't think that we were so close."

Our rapidly developing friendship was undoubtedly abetted by a decisiveness in booze. We took Sergei to a strange joint called "Natan," where hot dogs were served alongside frog legs. Drinking it all down with the vodka that we brought with us, we set everything straight right there and then—from Gogol to Venichka Yerofeyev.

This was followed by a story that I've told so often that I've begun to doubt that it actually took place. We were walking along 42nd Street, where Dovlatov towered over everyone—admittedly, like he did everywhere. Disney has now wrested the street from the clutches of vice, but at the time, the street boasted its fair share of pimps and drug dealers. Approaching the most fearsome-looking of them, a black man hung all over in gold chains, Sergei suddenly stooped and kissed him on the top of his head. The man, growing pale from terror, started wheezing something incomprehensible, but then smiled. Dovlatov, meanwhile, imperturbably ambled past him without interrupting our conversation about Faulkner.

It was as if in America, Sergei had come home. Of course, he wasn't at all free from the usual complexes. He spoke English even worse than me. He knew Manhattan approximately. The metro confused him. But he was most concerned, as all immigrants were, about crime. Sergei delightedly dramatized the situation in his letters: "There's practically an ongoing civil war . . . The majority of Americans believe that they might as well capitulate to the Reds so that they could do away with violent crime."

I never got to hear this from his own mouth—either he was embarrassed or else I never asked. I wasn't even thirty yet, and life was in full swing around me, to the point that my wife would fairly often ask the classic question: "Do you know the color of your conscience's eyes at two in the morning?" It's not for nothing that the editor of *The New Russian Word* called me and Vail "those two with the bottle."

But despite everything, nothing dampens my recollections of those New York adventures. For example, not once did I have a run-in with a cop, although it's forbidden to enjoy a brandy while relaxing on a bench even in Central Park. True, we always obeyed if not the spirit of the law, then at least its letter—we never took the bottle out of the brown paper bag. Likewise, I never encountered any serious criminals, though I experienced my fair share of powerful impressions.

One evening, we were sitting on a bench not far from the frightful Harlem, which the wise didn't frequent even during the day. We were so engrossed in our conversation that we didn't notice it had gotten dark. And suddenly, we were surrounded by a group of remarkably tall black men. We jumped up and tried to convey our desperate amiability. But they ran by us without paying us any heed. After taking a closer look, we realized that they were going from church to the gym, where, in New York, basketball is played even in the dead of night.

Another time, there was a group of us taking the subway at night. The cars were half-empty, the light was dim, and our car companions were of a similar cadence. To brighten things up, we were listening to Vysotsky[1] and taking swigs from the familiar brown paper bag. Someone even lit up. Suddenly, a friend of ours took a good look around the night car and exclaimed in dismay: "Good God, we're the worst of them all!" Sergei loved retelling this story, and he found it a spot in his *Notebooks*.

But the most frightening thing happened when I accidentally wound up in a rock club. Lost in the mosh pit, I picked out a dance partner that seemed a tad more condescending than the others. At least, I think I picked her—it was unclear whether she was dancing with me, alone, or in a conga line. In order to find out, I started up a flirtatious conversation. Unfortunately, all I could muster were English phrases that I had prepared for an entirely different situation. With horror, I heard myself yelling over the drum beat: "Sakharov is great. What a nice thing, democracy." And then in Russian: "I chose freedom!"

At first, as relative old-timers, we looked after Sergei. He even took umbrage at it, saying that we took him for an old woman from the province. But Dovlatov soon acclimated to America. He immediately discovered in it something that I couldn't see. Which is how he and I lived in two different countries. I made myself at home in America as I did in any country abroad—I toured the cities, drove out into the countryside, went to museums and restaurants.

Sergei was categorically uninterested in all of this. He had a different M.O. In this foreign country, Dovlatov staked out a zone that he considered his own. Sergei discovered what tied America to his prose—democratism and understatement.

3

In America, Sergei liked translators most of all, closely followed by street musicians and witty beggars. In his homeland, Sergei liked tramps and drunks most of all too. In his short stories, like in "Cipollino," the wealthy are on the receiving end of misfortune more than paupers.

A latecoming *raznochinets*,[2] Dovlatov despised class-based hubris. Sergei claimed that his favorite line in all of American literature was "I stopped to talk with Huckleberry Finn." As is well known, Tom Sawyer says this line in the

---

1   Vladimir Vysotsky (1938–1980) was a wildly popular Soviet musician and actor.
2   Legally, the *raznochintsy* were people who didn't belong to any of the formally established castes in seventeenth- to nineteenth-century Russia.

critical moment when unhappy love desensitizes him toward the thrashing that follows his admission.

Dovlatov was the same. His readiness for dialogue included everyone and excluded only one person—the author. Sergei knew how to listen to his surroundings without disrupting them.

Another line from American prose that Dovlatov loved was "the reachability of moral waypoints." It's not just that American literature demands heroism and holiness from people less often than our own. It didn't demand anything at all—it simply asked: to hold on to one's moralistic verdicts, accepting the world as it is. This isn't to say that they appreciate moral virtue less on one side on the ocean than on the other. It's just that American writers, uninfected with hypermoralism, knew how to pay their dues to temptation. "If I had sold my soul to Satan for a mess of pottage," says the protagonist of *The Reivers*, one of Sergei's favorite Faulkner novels, "at least I would damn well collect the pottage and eat it too."

One American series has a similar scene. The devil proposes to buy the soul of one of the characters.

"How much?" he asks.

"A hundred dollars!"

"Oh! Sounds good!" exclaims the simpleton, unable to contain his delight.

This lack of foresight may be the key to, if not a justification for sin, then condescension toward it. Admittedly, Dovlatov was drawn the most not to the theological exploration of Faulkner's apologia for sin, but its aesthetic sophistry. In the same novel, Faulkner rolls out a thought that Sergei *had* to enjoy:

"Who to the dedicated to Virtue, offer in reward only cold and odorless and tasteless virtue: as compared not only to the bright rewards of sin and pleasure but to the ever watchful unflagging omniprescient skill—that incredible matchless capacity for invention and imagination."

Viewing sin as the source of literature is a very Dovlatov thing to do. And defending sin is essentially American. After all, a democrat is consistent only if he forces virtue to enjoy the same rights as sin. Democracy means tolerance not only of another's thoughts, but another's way of life. It is the ability not to grumble, dividing up the available space between yourself and the other, the foreign, treating it akin to rats or cockroaches. Characteristically, Dovlatov was the sole person in America to stand up for the single most universally loathed creature:

"How is the cockroach at fault? Did a cockroach bite you? Or did he offend your national identity? No ... The cockroach is harmless and elegant in his own way. He has the blistering mobility of a racecar."

4

Dovlatov found in American literature what he couldn't get enough of in Russian literature. Sergei complained that in Turgenev's works, it was impossible to tell whether the protagonist was capable of swimming across a lake in one go. To demonstrate that difference, Dovlatov personally swam across the Mississippi. At any rate, he wrote that he did.

Sergei never forgot about the corporeal aspect of our existence. Especially since it would have been difficult for him to do so. An inebriated Sergei could become physically onerous. On the third day, the usual grace with which he carried his prodigious frame escaped him. More than anything else, his stature was the thing the made him most like Hemingway.

Unlike many, Sergei never disrespected the forgotten idol, but he never quoted him either. Hemingway trampled across the prose of an entire generation like a tank, but he left very few traces in Dovlatov's works. The most awkward were the conclusions of the short stories in *The Zone*: "But most importantly, his wife was asleep. Katya was safe. And she was probably frowning in her sleep . . ."

It's crucial to note that Sergei borrowed not only Hemingway's manly tears, which sometimes grace the pages of Dovlatov's works, but also his renowned narrative gaps. Having appropriated the iceberg theory for his own designs, Sergei invented his own punctuation. An Estonian journalist from *The Compromise* accurately characterized it as "nothing but ellipses."

A period is rarely unnecessary; an ellipsis almost always is. This punctuation mark retains only the appearance of its aristocratic ancestor, and even then, it is thrice diluted. By placing three periods instead of one, the writer hopes that ambiguity will conceal a botched sentence like flowers on a tombstone. An ellipsis, however, crowns not a thought that was unfinished, but one that was aborted.

Sergei understood this better than others. And yet, patiently bearing people's jeers, including his own, he set a record for the use of ellipses. Defending his right to use them, he wrote that "every author invents their own punctuation independently." In his prose, the ellipsis was his authorial mark.

The Dovlatovian ellipsis moreso resembles a road sign than a punctuation mark. It indicates a crossroads of the text and emptiness. Like holes in a head of Swiss cheese, caverns in the text gnawed out by the tri-dots endow the text with an elegant airiness.

The most mysterious Dovlatovian phrase goes like this: "Tomorrow, I'll rent a photographic enlarger." Sergei was very proud of this phrase, even though it has scant significance. Which is actually why he was proud of it.

The phrase masks its own absence. It is a kind of Dovlatovian ellipsis. And he took pride in it not only because an author's craft and daring can be manifested in *what* he writes, but in what he sacrifices too. By not leaving a single phrase in a place where something significant could be said, Dovlatov lets the reader catch their breath.

If prose has no focus, it is no prose, but if the author is happy with a parade of attractions, then the book becomes a variety show sans intermission. Feeling locked in, the reader doesn't want so much to leave as to break free. To avert this, Sergei buffered his most crystalline phrases with cardboard. Colorless sentences refresh the senses, preventing the dulling of one's vision. By thinning out the text, Sergei surreptitiously, but authoritatively imposes his own rhythm of reading. Dovlatov's prose is marked by a very light breath, because it is regulated by the emptiness that saturates it.

Trying to be dazzling but not blinding, Sergei most treasured that sharpness of originality that is known only to the author himself. That one Pasternak quote, "the only one in his life" that Dovlatov wrote down in his youth, speaks of this:

"My whole life, I have strived for the creation of that reserved, unassuming language that allows the reader and the listener to grasp the content without realizing how they are doing so."

In *The Zone*, Sergei contested that we called him "a troubadour of polished banality." In reality, as usual, he was attributing a grievance that he had dealt himself to someone else—thereby immediately turning weakness into dignity. Sergei boldly diluted his secret originality with triviality.

The emptiness of any banal phrase is its own sort of frame. On the one hand, it fences the painting off from the nondescript wall. On the other hand, it unites them into one. Emptiness is the plumbing that connects the text to the surrounding reality. By injecting a text with emptiness, the author mixes fiction with actuality in the exact proportion in which they are typically encountered in real life.

Chinese masters, experts of negotiating emptiness, knew three uses for it. The first is to leave it as is. However, emptiness unnoticed ceases to be itself. It inevitably transforms into something else—the page of a notebook, a dark background, a star-filled night, wallpaper covered in flowers.

The second use is to embellish something with emptiness. Such emptiness becomes decorative. Like the margins of a page, it accentuates the presence of what's there.

And finally, the third, most difficult use involves the injecting of emptiness into a painting, thus granting nonexistence parity with existence. Only the artist who maintains congruence between a thing and its absence depicts the world in all its fullness. Insufficiency is greater than plenty, and when addition is replaced with subtraction, emptiness is able to fill the void.

Like all writers, Dovlatov aimed to recreate the entirety of the world. But unlike many others, he saw a filled-out page rather than the blank one as the obstacle.

5

Dovlatov's American life resembled his prose: a brazenly short, dotted novel filled to bursting with ellipses. And yet, it managed to include everything that others would have dragged out into an epic.

In America, Sergei worked, received medical treatment, went to court, achieved success, made friends with publishers, literary agents, and American "damsels" (his word). He raised his daughter here, had a son, a dog, and real estate. And of course, twelve years in America meant a dozen books published in America: the summary of a writer's life. And he did all of this without leaving the boundaries set by those American authors that Sergei knew long before he moved to their home country.

Dovlatov easily and comfortably lived in the America he had read about, because it was no less real than any other America. Sergei wrote that previously, America used to be like heaven for him—"wonderful, but unbelievable." Hence what surprised him most about America is that it existed. "Could it truly be me?! Drinking Irish coffee in Johnny's Bar?" This is the chief emotion that exhausts his attitude toward the country that he knew, loved, understood, and ignored.

America did not deprive Dovlatov of glory. On the contrary, this is where he found it. Sergei said that he was surprised both when people recognized him in the street and when they didn't. However, the fast pace of American reality is such that it evokes doubt in the value of any admission.

A lovely editor from *The New Yorker* said that they stopped publishing Dovlatov's short stories because he died, and they prefer living authors in America: the dead ones are those who lost. Back in our homeland, the dead seem to be the victors.

In America, Sergei found what he couldn't back in the Soviet Union— indifference, which nurtured such hopeless modesty that it may as well have been called meekness. For a Russian writer, used to the oversight of an envious government, the condescending absentmindedness of democracy poses a difficult trial.

The only person who was brave enough to say this explicitly was Lev Khalif, whom Dovlatov described as "a mix between the toreador and the bull." He settled down so far out in New York's outskirts that he attended parties by phone. Sergei was very complimentary of his biting and funny book "CWH," which, among other things, he lauded in verse:

> Give back my book, dear Sasha and Petya,
> you'd be doing a great deed!
> This same book I praised in the paper
> I would now like to read.

Khalif caused an outcry by publicly complaining that in Russia, at least the KGB paid him some attention.

Dovlatov's excellent track record—many translations, publications in the legendary *New Yorker*, a few hundred reviews, plaudits from Vonnegut and Heller—could have pulled the wool over anyone's eyes but his own. Sergei described his position in America with the same directness with which hopelessness combines with submission: "I am an ethnic writer living 4,000 kilometers away from my audience."

12

All That Jazz

1

Dovlatov owed his success in America to language—or rather, its absence. Without really knowing English, he wrote in it without even realizing it himself. To make everything really muddled, I'd say that Dovlatov wrote American English in Russian. And everyone was happy with "the English Dovlatov," though it didn't surprise many. Sergei was an exception among Russians, not Americans.

Brodsky demonstrated this most decisively. In his memorial sketch of Seryozha (that's how he called him), Brodsky let slip far too profound a thought to let it slide unnoticed: Dovlatov "was relatively easy to translate, because his syntax doesn't put spokes in the translator's wheels."

Indeed, Sergei essentially eliminated syntax. The number of commas he uses in a single work can be counted on the fingers of one hand. It was his way. As everyone now knows, Sergei excluded—even in quotes!—words that began with the same letter. Sergei called it his psychosis. In order to have each word begin with a different letter, in Pushkin's poem *My Monument*, he changed "people's path" to "holy path."

Behind this eccentricity stood the fairly cogent idea of Spartan discipline. As Sergei explained it, a prose writer must come up with his own shackles to replace those that a poet gets along with the territory.

Sergei didn't want writing to be easy. When people tried to convince him to use a computer, saying that it would hasten the artistic process, Dovlatov was aghast. He would say repeatedly that his goal was to write slower, not quicker. In the ideal, he would have etched his words in stone—not for longevity's sake, but because it would take a long time.

Dovlatov wasn't so much afraid of the sleekness of style as much as its spinelessness. An author unfettered from internal restrictions ceases to operate in the world of belles-lettres without even noticing it. To prevent this, a prose writer must answer for his chosen words with the same responsibility that a *zek* defends his tattoos.

A natural function of Dovlatov's "psychosis" is incredibly short sentences, which corresponded perfectly to his entire philosophy.

Because what is syntax? Syntax is connection facilitated by logical ties that bind together thoughts with the shackles of conjunctions. Syntax is an artificial grammatical necessity that constructs its own vision of reality. All it takes is a single "because" for a text to birth a narrative *sua sponte*—completely irrespective of the author's intentions. A neat system that denies us freedom of movement, syntax is the straitjacket of imagination. Tying sentences together in a deathlike grip, conjunctions create grammatical harmony that can easily be mistaken for actual harmony. Syntax is the great organizer, which brings order into chaos even when chaos is the very thing being described.

And yet, however adroitly a grammatical net may be woven, real life always escapes through the finely woven mesh. Preferring explicit capitulation to mock victories, Sergei united his sentences not with conjunctions, but with chasms of ellipses, obliterating the mirage of a meaningful existence.

This is what made Dovlatov stand out from his compatriots, about whom Brodsky noted so precisely: "We are a people of the subordinate clause."

2

I think Brodsky was the only person Sergei was scared of. There's nothing surprising about this—everyone was scared of him. When the need arose for us at the radio to call Brodsky, everyone would look at Sergei, and he, flush with color, would spend a long moment collecting himself before dialing the number.

Sometimes, these calls ended extravagantly. On occasion, Brodsky gave entirely unexpected answers to questions. When asked to comment on Salman Rushdie's sentence, he said that in response to a threat directed at one of his Pen Club's members, he should demand the ayatollah's head—"to see what's there beneath his turban."

Sergei revered Brodsky. Dovlatov said about him: "He's not the first. He is, unfortunately, the only one." Only after his death did Parnassus become crowded. Brodsky was our vindication before time and before ourselves.

"I think," wrote Dovlatov, "that our wretched generation, just like Lermontov's generation, will survive. Because we have artists of Brodsky's caliber."

It's worth mentioning that long before "Brodsky's friend" became a profession, being close to Brodsky was maddening. Sometimes literally. And Brodsky himself had nothing to do with it. Sergei wrote with firsthand knowledge: Iosif is the only influential Russian in the West who clearly, often, and effectively helps people."

Brodsky seemed especially responsive in comparison with Solzhenitsyn, who ignored the diaspora entirely. By my recollection, Alexander Isayevich fostered only a single author—one Oreshkin, who was looking to find Slavic roots in Ancient Egypt. Among other assertions, Oreshkin claimed that the Etruscans themselves declared their own heritage: "these are Russians."[1]

Brodsky reviewed young writers' works with a generosity that can be understood with the help of one of his statements: "I am interested in other people's poetry so very little that I might as well say something nice." It was no better with prose. One time, his terse but well-intentioned words appeared on the cover of a spy novel titled *They Tried to Make Contact*. They say this doomed the author, a respected PhD. Emboldened by the praise, he took up literature with such fervor that he lost his family and his job.

Having read all of Dovlatov's books in one go, Brodsky appreciated Sergei more than others. Which didn't stop Dovlatov from assiduously preparing ahead of each of their meetings. When Brodsky started smoking lighter cigarettes after another one of his heart attacks, Dovlatov brought him a pack of "Parliaments." They had less than 1 milligram of harmful resins, which was proudly emblazoned on the pack: "Less than one." This was title of Brodsky's famous essay in English, which didn't get a suitable equivalent in the Russian translation.

You could've been excused for thinking that Brodsky and Dovlatov didn't have that much in common. And Sergei never compared himself to Brodsky. Brodsky simply didn't pay it any heed. Bringing us the newly published *Winter Eclogue*, Dovlatov grandly declared that it exhausted his ideas about contemporary literature. Whenever Sergei went over somebody's place, Lena determined how engaged he could get based on whether he was declaiming that "a grim Charon is vainly rummaging around in your mouth for his drachma." Responding to the outburst of some crazy person on the

---

1   In Russian, the word for "Etruscans" is *Etruski*, which sounds a lot like *Eto russkie*, which means "These are Russians."

street, Dovlatov wrote: he's "jealous of Brodsky, and he's right. I'm jealous of Brodsky too."

To Dovlatov, Brodsky's character was more precious than his art—Sergei was astounded by his absolute fearlessness. As a witness and a victim of the usual Soviet nastiness, Dovlatov always noted that it was Brodsky who behaved with irreproachable dignity with regard to the regime.

Even more important was valor of another sort. Brodsky intentionally and decisively avoided well-beaten paths, including those that he himself had trod. He said that most of one's life is spent learning how not to bend. Thinking that he was talking about opposition to the regime, I was confused, because those conflicts were in the past. Only with time did I realize that Brodsky was talking about something else. Foreign thought or example bends a person much more powerfully than fear or dogma.

Sergei wasn't envious of Brodsky himself, but of his freedom. Dovlatov dreamed of being himself, and he knew what it cost. Tirelessly, almost like a mantra, he repeated: "I want to be a student of my ideas." "I admire philosophy," Sergei wrote, "and I promise to give it considerable thought one day. But only after I achieve that basic everyday freedom and lack of restraint. Freedom from the opinions of others. Freedom from the stencils enforced by the majority." Dovlatov appreciated more than a lot of other things that in America, "everyone dresses the way they want."

Democracy certainly lets some people unfurl their wings. And it cures each person of what Brodsky called "the complex of exceptionalism." In order to be yourself, you have to be with yourself, usually alone. Autonomy and self-reliance do not exclude, but rather presuppose getting lost in the landscape, in one's surroundings. Like a marsh, democracy equalizes everything with itself.

Dovlatov and Brodsky were alike in the harmonious manner in which they fit into this horizontal landscape. Very close in age, they were of a generation that consciously chose the roadside, the curb as their home address. Brodsky and Dovlatov valued more than anything else freedom from the need for dependency and freedom from the desire to impose it on others. Consequently, they transformed exile into a point of view, estrangement into style, solitude into freedom.

Bakhchanyan, who is accompanying this book like old man Shchukar in *Virgin Soil Upturned*, had something to say on this matter too: "'A superfluous person'—that sounds prideful."

Brodsky and Dovlatov were also drawn together by verse. Brodsky explicitly stated that Dovlatov's short stories "are written like poems." But it's probably more accurate to say that his short stories appeared on the road back from verse to prose.

Poetry, real poetry, contracts reality to the point that it obtains a new set of laws, which undoes time and space, structure and hierarchy. Information space condenses to the point of superconductivity, when everything connects with everything else. There is nothing accidental in such a state. There can be no mistake. It is pointless to ask whether a particular word is correct. If it is uttered, then it is right.

Frost has a poem about why one can encounter bent birches in the forest. He explains that it is because boys swing on them. They clamber up to the very top and bend the trunks to the ground with their weight. Shimmying up the black boughs of the white trunk is the same as crawling down lines of verse on a page. It's not marching toward the sky—it's going in the sky's direction. The thinner the branch-fabric is, the more inescapably it grounds us. In this adventure, the poet and poetry, the poet and language, the poet and reality become allies, as if in a waltz. The poet's art is to take advantage of the material's intractability. Where the fabric thins to the point of symbolism, per Chekhov, space withdraws into itself, it folds. There is nothing beyond it. The distortion of the poetic continuum is an attribute of its physics.

Sooner or later, the birch comes to an end. But the boldness of the poetic game is in climbing as far as possible. The most intelligent efforts combine boldness with calculation, valor with reason, discipline with gambling. Those who climb too high fall without revealing how things are up there. Furthermore, they only made it halfway. The point is to make it there and back again.

Dovlatov didn't condense reality—he rarefied it. In his short stories, the superfluous combines with the indispensable like two sides of a coin. The prototype of Dovlatov's prose wasn't poetry, but music. Sergei could have repeated the words of a composer who once said of his compositions: "The black is the notes, the white is the music."

3

Dovlatov's brother Borya once came to visit him in Leningrad. He asked Nora Sergeyevna where Sergei was. She replied that he was in his room, listening to Shostakovich. "Alcoholics sometimes do that," Boris explained, calmingly.

Dovlatov, who, of course, was the one to tell this story, loved music very much. I once even heard how he sang at some event with his fans. Sergei loved to perform, though he would earnestly get stage fright. At first, sweating and mumbling, he would utter banalities. Gradually, hitting his stride, Sergei would get the situation under control and captivate any audience, answering questions that people didn't ask. For example, in response to the classic immigrant question "How's your English?" Sergei would instead tell the story of how his neighbor explained the speed at which she picked up English with the idiom "live with wolves, and you learn to howl."

When he debuted in New York just after immigrating, Dovlatov was on fire. Demonstrating to the audience all of his talents simultaneously, he read short stories and notes from *Solo on Underwood*, discussed contemporary literature (managing to call Roman Gul' a contemporary of Karamzin), and finally gave an unusually clean performance of a song from his "sentimental detective":

The peony's the dearest flower,
Pretty like a work of art,
I'm afraid I've not the power,
To leave the spy who stole my heart.

So, actually, when he said that Sergei's short stories "were sooner singing than retelling," Brodsky was right: music likened Dovlatov's prose to verse.

Brodsky sometimes said that he wanted to be a pilot instead of a poet. I don't know what Dovlatov wanted to be, but I imagine it was a jazz musician. At any rate, jazz provided the helpful analogies that allowed him to explain his own principles of poetics.

Dovlatov wrote about jazz a lot. He began with a review in the paper about Oscar Peterson's concert in Tallinn, which he somehow managed to attend: "I clapped so hard that my new watch stopped working." His last piece in *The New American* was dedicated to jazz as well.

His article was convolutedly called "A Mini-History of Jazz, Written by an Irresponsible Dunce Who Is Partially Excused by His Unparalleled Enthusiasm for the Subject at Hand." Picking me as his whipping boy, Sergei spruced up his unexpectedly scientific opus with references "to unsophisticated listeners of jazz, such as my friend Alexander Genis." And yet, the piece still turned out boring.

However, he included in the article bits that cannot be interpreted as anything other than an author's confessions. In them, Dovlatov didn't recount the history of jazz, but his own literary utopia:

"Jazz is a way of life . . . A jazz musician isn't a performer. He is a creator, demonstrating the process of creation before the public—a process that is

fragile, instantaneous, and ephemeral like the shadow of falling snowflakes . . .
Jazz is delightful chaos, the base of which is comprised of perfected intuition,
taste, and the sense of collaborative play . . . Jazz is us in our finest hours. That
is to say, when we experience combined inspiration, intrepidity, and candor . . ."

4

It's true, jazz isn't my strong suit, but I did figure out what it meant for Sergei.
It happened in Massachusetts, where we were travelling along with Lyosha
Khvostenko. We wound up in a terrible traffic jam on the highway that dragged
on for hours. The musically inclined Khvostenko saved the day. He opened
the window and started tapping on the roof of the car, singing "summertime,
and the living is easy." Only he replaced the words with Russian homophones,
which translated roughly to "Here and there, they're crushing liver from Izya."
A minute later, everybody else—categorically lacking both ear and voice—
followed suit. Our howling attracted the attention of our languishing neighbors,
and pretty soon, everyone on the road had joined in our revelry. It was an act
of pure creation, a rite that erased the boundary between the performer and
the audience, between the chorus and the soloist, between the melody and
whatever each of us was turning it into.

I've heard that the most important thing in jazz isn't craft, but belief in
yourself, because mistakes are essentially impossible to make. The improviser
is incapable of ruining anything. If the improviser is possessed of enough
courage and daring, an ostensible error can be transformed into extravagance.
By contending only with the rules that he himself spontaneously invents, the
improviser never knows where he'll end up. When doing high jumps, we take
aim at a plank that someone else has set. We make long jumps as each of us
can. This is why the conclusion of true improvisation isn't a scripted finale, but
exhaustion.

Sergei loved jazz, because he created art that involved opening himself
up to chaos; art that doesn't preclude mistakes, but melts them down; art, the
success of which is determined by integrity and audacity.

Sergei tamed his prose by applying his own draconic rules with great
satisfaction. But he loved a bit of advice by Louis Armstrong even more: "Close
your eyes, and blow!"

13

Pushkin

1

Like all Russian writers in the West, Dovlatov was separated from normal America by an antechamber full of Slavicists. Sergei justified his poor English by claiming that the only Americans with whom he had to converse spoke Russian.

I too know people in the Slavic studies world better than other Americans. Which is exactly why they never cease to amaze me. At every single conference, I ask them why they chose such a strange profession. The answer depends on their sex: young women were drawn to Dovlatov, young men to James Bond.

Ever since Russia lost the charm of "an empire of evil," everything changed. Whereas my first ever lecture was frequented by a Slavicist in military garb, my current seminars are mostly attended by young women in glasses. This might be for the best, since Slavic studies in America can only truly be revitalized by a localized nuclear strike.

But Dovlatov arrived in America at the right time. Russian studies weren't academic caprices, but practical affairs realistically determining our entire literary world. The literary process of those years wasn't directed so much by *Novy Mir*, the standard-bearer of door-stopping literary journals, but by the Michigan-based publishing house Ardis. Its founders, Carl and Ellendea Proffer, who crafted the slogan "Russian literature is more interesting than sex," managed to publish an entire library of books that became the foundational literature of our generation. Among these was *The Invisible Book*, which came out in both Russian and English. It was thirty-seven-year-old Sergei's first.

The Proffers looked so little like Slavicists that we can only take pride in the fact that they were seduced by our literature. The tall beauty Ellendea was such a looker that many people didn't buy that she wrote an enormous monograph on Bulgakov by herself. Her work with Ardis earned her the generous and prestigious Genius Grant, the same that Brodsky got a few years before his Nobel Prize. Unlike many Slavicists, who preferred to speak with us in English, Ellendea knows Russian magnificently, including the Russian that gentlemen should not use in the presence of ladies. She is never bothered by it. Once, asking about the works of a particular immigrant writer, she added: "I haven't had that particular cherry popped yet."

Carl looked like a professor even less. A basketball star, he was at least as tall as Dovlatov. And he died early too. He fought his cancer for a long time in order to ensure that his little girl remembered him. A gathering in his memory was held in a New York public library. Everyone recounted how much Carl did for Russian literature. Brodsky concluded the long list with a Frisbee that Proffer himself was the first to bring to Russia.

2

When Andrey Sedykh called Dovlatov "a prison turnkey," Sergei wasn't offended, but it did make him think. At the time, there was no more offensive an accusation than collaboration with the federal organs. Especially in the First Wave of immigration, where they didn't really bother with details or evidence. Even Vail and I, who worked in Riga as firemen, were labelled by polemics as "Interior Ministry flunkies." *The New Russian Word* had a linotypist from the old White Guard, who said that he wouldn't shake the hand of one particular Stalin-era general. The general in question was Pyotr Grigoryevich Grigorenko [*who, of course, was a dissident –A.R.*]. Hence why the "turnkey" accusation caused Dovlatov to explain himself to the public, which had yet to read *The Zone*. In describing why and how he was a prison guard, Sergei wrote that after the army, "he dreamed of philology. An academic career. The cool twilight of libraries."

None of this was true, of course. Sergei wanted to be a writer, not a philologist. As for the "cool twilight of libraries," that was a stock phrase that Sergei used to taunt me after I naively confided in him my own academic ambitions.

Philology didn't really interest Sergei. He loathed literary jargon and loved recalling his one friend who had copied down for his own prefaces intelligent-sounding paragraphs from other books' forewords. I think Sergei simply didn't believe in the existence of such a science.

At the time, I thought this heresy—now, I think it's a hypothesis. Were philology an exact science, its discoveries wouldn't depend on the talent of the researcher—we don't need Newton's genius in order to take advantage of his laws. Unlike nature, literature is comprised of nonrecurring phenomena. If they repeat, it's not literature.

Literature can be parsed only on its own terms. Which is why the best people who write *about* literature are those who write literature. Dovlatov lays this out concisely: "Criticism is a part of literature. Philology is its side effect. A critic examines literature from the inside. A philologist does so from the nearest belfry."

From this follows that good critics are writers. Sinyavsky was considered the best of these. Sergei was going to dedicate to Abram Terts an article about Geychenko, the director of the Pushkin Hills preserve. He wanted to title it "Walks with d'Anthès."

3

A rare patronymic and an artistic attitude toward *zeks* united Dovlatov and Andrei Donatovich. After becoming friends with Sinyavsky, Sergei published a book with Syntax—*The Enthusiasts' Demarche*. Along with Sergei's eccentric short stories, the book featured Naum Sagalovsky's satirical verse and the works of Bakhchanyan, which, as always, defy categorization. Because Marya Vasilyevna can't stand responding to letters, this book accorded Sergei quite a few grey hairs, but even that didn't ruin their affectionate relationship.

After first meeting Sinyavsky at a conference in Los Angeles, Sergei provided an uncannily accurate description of him: "Andrei Sinyavsky nearly disappointed me. I was ready to see a nervous, acrimonious, and ambitious individual. Sinyavsky turned out surprisingly good-natured and approachable. A bit like an average guy from the countryside. Awkward and even funny."

In order to see Sinyavsky in such a way, it's important not to confuse him with Abram Terts. Andrei Donatovich himself was the direct antithesis of his pseudonym, who had a black mustache, was dashing and crafty, and sported a knife, which (Sinyavsky noted with satisfaction) criminals call a "quill." Sinyavsky himself, meanwhile, is small, slouching, and has an enormous grey beard. He didn't laugh—he giggled. He didn't say things—he got them out. His eyes darted in different directions, which created the impression that he could see something invisible to his conversation partner. Smoke was constantly spiraling around him, and he sat on a chair as if on a tree stump. I've only ever seen a kid in a puppet theater do such a thing.

As the years went by, Sinyavsky began more and more to resemble as creature out of Slavic mythology—a *leshy*, a *domovoy*, maybe a *bannik*. He fostered this resemblance, and he enjoyed it immensely. When he gifted me a copy of *Ivan the Fool*, one of his last books, he inscribed it: "The leshy says hi."

It's astounding that a person who was so respected by investigators and beloved by inmates could inspire such hostility. And yet, Sinyavsky was the only person in the history of Soviet dissidence who managed to stir up three separate storms of indignation.

The Soviet regime was the first to take issue with him, as it was under the impression that he was attempting to overturn it. In reality, Sinyavsky was a secret adherent to the Revolution, staying true to its ideals, about which everyone else had forgotten.

In the second instance, it was the diaspora that soured on him, accusing him of "groveling before the West." This too was wide of the mark. With the single possible exception of Vysotsky (whom he was the one to discover), Sinyavsky was the most Russian author of our literary world.

The third time, Sinyavsky landed in hot water as a Russophobe—because of my favorite *Walks with Pushkin*. It was characteristic that the poet was defended from Abram Terts by people who had never managed to write a single grammatical sentence.

Wittily defending himself, Sinyavsky bore his cross with dignity. Bakhchanyan, who used the informal "you" with Andrei Donatovich, depicted the battle as a duel between a fencer and a rhino—an animal that is actually relevant to our last encounter. Andrei Donatovich and I were wandering around the New York Museum of Natural History, and he recalled that he had a burning desire as a child—to live in a stuffed rhino.

4

Although Sergei didn't hold philologists in any particular esteem, in a manner of speaking—a very direct manner—he himself was one. Dovlatov loved words. Not only for the thoughts that they express, but just on their own, for the fact that they were parts of speech. He wrote an editorial about it, an editorial whose publication I opposed out of some ridiculous pedantry. Sergei published the piece as a rebuttal, as a result of which it didn't make it into *The March of the Lonely*. A pity. There was a paragraph in there in which he described his intimate relationship with Russian grammar:

"Industrious little prepositions dragged behind them endless caravans of cases. Sturdy roots united disjointed droves of independent words. Clever suffixes indicated the flow of rapid instances of reconnaissance. On the shoulders of nouns verbs effortlessly executed their maneuvers. Adjectives deftly masked the true heart of things."

In this doll-like grammar I most of all like the role of adjectives, which are considered architecturally superfluous. Brodsky recounted how Rein taught him to cover his verse with a magical tablecloth that erased all adjectives. Dovlatov was more equitable with regard to adjectives.

An adjective is more clever and cunning than other parts of speech. It doesn't decorate a noun—it changes its meaning. Like an experienced karate master, who relies on the strength of his opponent rather than his own, an adjective either turns a sentence around or else makes it fly right past its target. As in karate, adjectives assert their dominance not through pressure but through explosive strength. In the poetic arsenal, they are like grenades without pins.

I have often thought of the outlandish poems that we could have if we could blow up Pushkin's mysterious epithets: "joyful sins," "a mute shadow," "a weary axe," "a triumphant hand," "an instantaneous old man."

5

Dovlatov called his "Tallinn daughter" Sasha in honor of Pushkin: Alexandra Sergeyevna. But he spoke about him rarely, not at all like with Dostoevsky, Faulkner, or even Kuprin. The one exception was *The Captain's Daughter*, whose plot provokes various analogies. If what Nabokov said is true, that the most important thing for a writer is to come up with an author rather a book, then it's tempting to think that Dovlatov wrote *The Zone* as Pyotr Grinyov, who could have made an even better prose writer than Belkin.

I even feel like Dovlatov saw something of himself in Grinyov. Grinyov, much like the overseer in *The Zone*, is always between a rock and a hard place. But it's impossible to say that he is above the fray. Conversely, Grinyov is always in the thick of it, constantly ready to take up arms or face death—but never to hate. Grinyov shares a trait with his creator, a trait to which Tsvetayeva attributes the Decembrists' reticence to accept Pushkin into their number: "insufficient animosity." The drama of Grinyov is that without relinquishing his own point of view, he is capable of understanding—and accepting—the perspective of another.

This isn't Shvabrin's opportunism—this is Pushkin's "omni-acceptance" from Dostoevsky's speech, the omni-acceptance whose limits our schooling, which taught us that Pugachev is a national hero, prevents us from comprehending. Under the real Pugachev, as Tsvetayeva again reminds us, they once flayed a captured officer, "took out all the fat in his body and used it to treat their wounds."

Fully cognizing the character that Pushkin had to deal with, Dovlatov wrote: "Pugachev in *The Captain's Daughter* is depicted with a degree of sympathy. It would be the same as if someone today depicted Beria in a positive light."

Imbuing Grinyov with his own philosophy, Pushkin opened his eyes to the truth of his poetry. In the Pugachev wager, Grinyov experiences poetic ecstasy. The dark beauty of lawlessness evokes a creative impulse: "everything astounded me with some poetic terror."

Was Dovlatov's prose conceived any differently? In *The Zone*, following one of the most brutish episodes, the protagonist is seized by that state of exclusion from life that turned him into a writer: "The world became alive and nonthreatening, as if in a painting. He peered at the overseer without fury or reproach."

6

If *The Captain's Daughter* served as the point of departure for *The Zone*, Dovlatov used Pushkin himself for his best book. *Pushkin Hills* is crafted in Pushkin's image, though it's not obvious. A crafty individual hides a leaf in a forest, a person in a crowd, and Pushkin in the Pushkin Hills preserve.

Dovlatov depicts the Pushkin Hills as a Russian Disneyland. There is not, nor can there be, anything authentic about it. It's a factory that manufactures phantoms. The preserve infects all of its surroundings. It's why the Pskov kremlin that's encountered along the way seems like "an enormous mock-up." As one approaches the epicenter of falsehood, the absurd becomes more pronounced. Sometimes, it manifests itself as mysterious artifacts, like the brochure in the preserve's tourist center titled "The Jewel of Crimea."

The preserve's chief product, of course, is Pushkin himself. The first page features a "waiter with tremendous felted sideburns." These threatening sideburns, like Gogol's nose, will turn into an unshakeable nightmare that haunt the protagonist for the entire book: "An image of Pushkin greeted me everywhere I went. Even near the mysterious little brick booth with the 'Inflammable' sign. The similarity ended with the sideburns." The countless Pushkins flooding the preserve are emblematic of reproduction without an original—in other words, simulacra (good thing Dovlatov will never read that word).

The only place in the *Pushkin Hills* where Pushkin is absent are the Pushkin Hills themselves. Dovlatov's latent, almost fairy tale-like narrative involves a search for the real Pushkin, the discovery of a secret that will help the protagonist come into his own.

The events described in *Pushkin Hills* occurred when Sergei was thirty-six. But the protagonist arrived at the preserve when he was thirty-one, soon after his "thirtieth birthday, which was vehemently celebrated in the Dnieper restaurant." Why did Dovlatov change his age, when he loved to warn the reader that "any resemblance between the characters and any living people is maliciously intentional. But any fictitious speculation is uncalculated and coincidental"? I think it's because Pushkin was thirty-one when he got stuck in Boldino.

This coincidence is intentional and eloquent, since Dovlatov conforms his summer in the preserve to the autumn in Boldino. Carefully but unobtrusively, Sergei builds up the resemblance. A wife who either exists or doesn't. Risky and equivocal attitudes toward the government. Thoughts of flight. A provincial atmosphere. Peasants as if they were from the Gorukhino village. Literature whose narrative essentially retells not only Dovlatov's, but also Pushkin's biography: "Unhappy love, debt, marriage, art, conflict with the government," but most importantly—"life stretched out all around like an immeasurable minefield." The "quarantine"—a kind of meditative pause à la Boldino—ripped the protagonist out of life's usual flow. Which is why when he returns to Leningrad, he feels "like a soccer fan who had run out onto the field."

The tragic events of *Pushkin Hills* are illuminated by the Boldino-esque sensation of an invigorating crisis. By overcoming it, Dovlatov doesn't solve his problems—he rises above them. As he matures, he follows in the tracks of Pushkin's train of thought. In order to experience the Pushkin myth for himself, Dovlatov didn't just have to read Pushkin—he had to live Pushkin.

7

Legend differs from myth as the screenplay differs from the film, the play from the show, the circumference from the circle, the reflection from the original, words from music. Unlike legend, myth cannot be recounted—only lived through. Myth always forces action.

I sensed the power of the literary myth in full when I came to a country that was borne of citations—Israel. The only thing that is considered authentic there is what is mentioned in the Bible. Biblical reference accords names, plants, animals, geographic titles the status of reality. It's not for nothing that Christians call Palestine the fifth gospel.

In Israel, myth folds time in on itself, forcing us to go in circles. It isn't history that is king there—it is eternity. Life engulfed by mythical space is dedicated to its own reproduction.

The most vivid example of this is the Hassidic ghetto in the Jerusalem neighborhood of Mea Shearim. Every single detail of every single local custom—from birth to death, from recipes to tailoring—is strictly prescribed by tradition. Which is why there is not and cannot be anything new here. Every generation digs in deeper rather than trying to break out. The ghetto's walls protect its inhabitants from the drama of change and the whims of fortune. Nobody wants anything, because everybody has everything. By exchanging freedom for tradition, by dissolving life in mundanity, life—unchanging, like a Bible verse—has become a monument to itself. Having transformed word into action and left nothing behind, Jerusalem's Hassids have built a literary utopia. They believe in no other heaven.

It is any book's wont to yearn for expansion. By breaking out of its limits, it strives to alter reality. By provoking us to action, it dreams of becoming the blueprint of legend, which the readers will transform into myth.

Thus, two centuries ago, sensitive Muscovites gathered at the pond where Karamzin's poor Liza drowned herself.

Thus do their equally besotted ancestors take the Moscow-Petushki commuter train, having armed themselves with the arsenal of bottles described in the famous, eponymous poem.[1]

In this sense, the Pushkin Hills aren't a myth—they're a caricature of it: "a grandiose park of culture and rest." Rather than becoming a ritual, literature here has become an amalgam of attractions that is circled by tour guides leading crowds of visitors—from one quote to the next. Pushkin's verse, printed in "Slavic calligraphy" on "decorative boulders" resemble a tombstone more than a living, breathing text.

The governmentally inculcated Pushkin myth is as false as the Komsomol baptisms. Ritual cannot survive abuse. A square myth will not fit in a round hole. But it's equally impossible to disprove a myth—one myth can only be replaced with another, which is exactly what Dovlatov set about doing with some success. I've heard that young people now come to the Pushkin Hills to meander along not only Pushkin's old haunts, but Dovlatov's as well.

---

1 *Moscow-Petushki* (1970) is a poem by Venedikt Yerofeyev (1938–1990). The poem recounts how a man travels by train from Moscow to his childhood town of Petushki.

8

Chesterton believed the best work of detective fiction to be Conan Doyle's short story "Silver," so called in honor of the stallion who killed the stable boy. The point is that we learn the name of the killer in the very beginning—in the title, in fact.

It's the same thing with *Pushkin Hills*—the secret is on the surface. The preserve isn't just a museum that displays dead and even counterfeit things, prepared, as Sergei claimed, by "one Samorodsky." The preserve is just that—a preserve that is bounded by Pushkin's range of vision.

While one Preserve guards the letter of the Pushkin myth, another—the one described by Dovlatov—protects its spirit: the ability to reconcile contradictions without destroying them, but, in fact, highlighting them. In Pushkin's universe, there is no antagonism—only polarities. His world is spherical, like the globe. All paths from the North pole lead to the South pole. After reaching the nadir of baseness, Pushkin's characters—like Pugachev—are condemned to do good, not evil. It isn't amorality, but insight that guides Pushkin's words, which Dovlatov so loved to repeat: "Poetry is above morality."

Only by safeguarding the inevitable and indispensable bipolarity of existence, as with men and women, can a writer recreate the world in its incipient wholeness, not yet partitioned by flat moral judgment.

In *Pushkin Hills*, Dovlatov is endlessly pestered about what he loves about Pushkin. I think it's because Pushkin didn't reject the roles that people forced on him, but accepted them—all of them: "not a monarchist, not a conspirator, not a Christian—he was only a poet, a genius, and he sympathized with life's progression generally." Dovlatov loved Pushkin for the fact that there was enough room in this big person for a little person—Pushkin, in whom "God and the devil easily coexisted," died "the hero of a second-rate romantic novel. Thus giving Bulgarin[2] legitimate grounds to write, 'he was a great man, and he faded away like a rabbit.'"

Dovlatov's book is infused with Pushkin like ashberry-infused cognac. It courses with allusions to Pushkin, but the reader encounters them in blatantly unexpected places. For example, the stale line delivered by the tour guide Natella as she flirts with Dovlatov: "You are a dangerous man"—this is a verbatim quote by Dona Anna in *The Stone Guest*. This play similarly serves as

---

2 Thaddeus Bulgarin (1789–1859) was a Russian writer and agent of the tsar's secret police, in whose service he denigrated Pushkin and generally executed the tsar's will.

the source of Dovlatov's future brother-in-law. The scene in which they meet for the first time parodies the scene where Don Juan meets the commodore: "A brick-brown face towered over a mountain of shoulders . . . The molded arches of his ears were swallowed up by the semi-darkness. . . . The specter of danger lurked in the bottomless, cavernous mouth . . . I nearly cried out when his steel vice gripped my hand."

More important than direct analogies is Pushkin's worldview, which manifests itself not in words, but in images—in *Pushkin Hills'* characters, each of which is comprised of irreconcilable—and therefore natural—contradictions. They are indicated even by such a passing character like the "Russian Man" sculpture sprucing things up in the restaurant called *"Vityaz"*[3]. The retired Major Goldstein's creation resembled "Mephistopheles and Baba Yaga simultaneously."

The symbolic, emblem-like picture that Dovlatov uses to begin describing his preserve speaks of the same mutually augmenting, yin and yang contradictions: "Two heraldic-looking cats—one charcoal-black, the other pinkish-white—sauntered haughtily about the table, weaving past the plates."

The black-and-white pair prepares the reader to meet the book's real heroes, about whom we are ultimately unable to make up our minds in any definitive manner.

The most charming of them is the hopeless drunkard Mikhail Ivanovich Sorokin. Dovlatov describes him like that strapping Russian lad whose very phlegm only adds to his vigor:

"He was a broad-shouldered, well-built man. Even his torn, dirty clothes failed to disfigure him. A weathered face, slender, powerful collarbones beneath an open shirt, a steady, confident stride . . . I couldn't help but admire him."

Mikhail Ivanovich passes through the book like a Frisbee: a mysterious, ultimately unidentifiable object. "Absurd in doing both good and evil," he lives out of turn and speaks accidentally. The best part about him is his backward language, which sometimes gives birth to poetry. About his wife, he says: "She slept tidy. Quiet as a caterpillar."

Mikhail Ivanovich's spontaneous quotes do not function as discourse or self-expression, but as gap-fillers in between trips to get liquor. But Russian wordcraft only benefits from his unwitting mumbo-jumbo, which differs so from the vain, "self-entangling" words of the futurists. Mikhail Ivanovich's

---

3   A *vitzyaz'* was a Slavic warrior-knight.

speech is living language left to its own devices: "Tha' maggot-faggot, God knows wha'..."

Mikhail Ivanovich takes first place in the long line of drunkard-aristocrats who play the same role in Dovlatov's prose that noble bandits play in Pushkin's:

"Vivacious, repulsive, and aggressive, like weeds," they are useless and liberated. True to their nature, they, like flora and fauna, are always equal to themselves. There's nobody else that they *can* be.

In fact, all of Dovlatov's favorite characters are like illustrations for an environmental studies textbook. The spineless erudite Mitrofanov, "a fastidious and vivid flower," belongs to "the plant kingdom." The protagonist's wife Tanya, calm as "the morning dawn," "resembled a force of nature, with her boundless indifference." Into the same category falls the photographer Valera, in whom Sergei took more pride than in others, even though he understood that this irrestrainable chatterbox was what prevented proper translations of his book.

Valera is like an echo. He too is closer to nature than to culture. Speech flows from him freely and irrepressibly, like a river: "You're listening to *The Pioneer Dawn* ... the hairy Yevstikhiev is at the mic ... His words are a worthy rebuff to the hawks in the Pentagon..."

Inquiring about the meaning of that string of words would be as pointless as interpreting the gurgling of a stream. If there is, in fact, any system to this incoherent logorrhea, it is beyond our comprehension, just like the language of nature.

In *Pushkin Hills*, Dovlatov fondly demarcates two types of linguistic absurdity. The haphazard speech of Mikhail Ivanovich is meaningless, the disjointed flood out of Valera is incomprehensible. One excises logic from grammar, the other purges it from life itself.

Admittedly, what's important for us is that neither employs human language, but more of a "bird-like speech." If Mikhail Ivanovich's speech, as Dovlatov says, is like "a goldfinch's song," then Valera resembles a parrot.

Sergei, by the way, owned two little green parrots, but they didn't speak. But a poet I knew did teach his enormous macaw not only to speak, but to taunt the ferret he lived with. Every morning, the poor creature woke up to the Brazilian parrot's mocking cries: "The ferret's a Jew!"

By all appearances, a parrot is a writer's bird. However, Bakhchanyan claimed that they could have a nobler calling. Francis of Assisi, for example, read sermons to birds, especially pigeons. To this day, they frequent his old haunts. Thus, Vagrich believed that if Francis's audience consisted of parrots instead of pigeons, they could have brought to us the Saint's holy word.

9

The gallery of oddballs in *Pushkin Hills* is Dovlatov's best. Sergei's forte was the frontal presentation of his characters. A lack of preemptively determined positions or any established concept of life prepared him for those surprises with which reality inadvertently rewards us.

Dovlatov's prose is thus reminiscent of a rare stone garden, which I was lucky enough to see in Peking. For centuries, they would bring bizarre mounds into the Emperor's Park in the Forbidden City. The beauty of these unpolished stones is that they lack intent. Each stone's beauty is not of our doing, as a result of which the garden does not align neatly with our aesthetics. It is neither realism nor naturalism—it is the art of artlessness. There cannot be an "improperly formed" rock, because any form the rock chooses is its own and proper.

The characters of Dovlatov's prose are like fanciful mounds in a rock garden—each lives independently of the others. The only thing that unites them is our inability to do anything with them—including understand them. This is why Dovlatov's dialogues often resemble a conversation between the deaf.

Interlocutors in Dovlatov's works do not so much ask each other questions as ask each other to repeat themselves. Just about any line evokes misunderstanding, and any attempt to dispel it only make matters worse. Because each person uses their own exclusive language, speech ceases to be a weapon.

Dialogue is not a battlefield, but an arena in which each person speaks without worrying about anything else. There's no one here to listen anyway, aside from the author, who virtuosically recreates the following prison camp *quid pro quo* in *The Zone*:

"'My *kum*[4] would come by to break fast...'

"'*Kum?*' asked Yerokha uneasily. "You mean an agent?'

"'Agent... *You're* an agent. *Kum*, I said... kin...'"

That was a solo by a *zek* from the province. Here's a hardened criminal:

"'Yes, I knew how to move my horns. The girls under me even screamed!...'

"'Why scream for no reason?' Zamarayev asked.

"'Bah, provincial bum. You know sex?'

---

4   A *kum* is either one's godparent or the godparent of one's children. In *zek* slang, a *kum* is an agent of one of the Zone's camps or colonies. His role is to create a network of snitches among the prisoners.

"'What?' Zamarayev clearly did not understand."

In *Pushkin Hills*, even dialogues between very close individuals are devoid of meaning. Every conversation between the protagonist and his future wife only exacerbates their mutual misunderstanding:

"'I have no parents,' Tanya replied sadly.

"I clammed up.

"'Forgive my tactlessness...' I said.

"'They live in Yalta,' Tanya added. 'Daddy is the secretary of the district committee...'"

Or like this:

"'One hanged himself recently. He was called Fish. It was his nickname... So, he hanged himself... Now he works as a proofreader.'

"'Who does?!' I exclaimed.

"'Fish. They saved him. His neighbor came over for a smoke...'"

It would only get worse. The closer two characters grow, the less they understand each other:

"I once put up a photo of the American writer Bellow above my desk.

"'Belov?' asked Tanya. 'From *Novy Mir*?'

"'The very same,' I said..."

This tragicomic mess is interrupted only by Tanya's immigration, which she justifies with words that are clearly not her own. It is the only dialogue that makes any sense, and it is only because Dovlatov simply split in half his own arguments. But even this didn't help them reach an agreement. For *Pushkin Hills*' protagonist, "to go or to stay" isn't a real question. The real question is where to live, and how?

10

Pushkin Hills is a novel of trial and learning, a tale of familiarizing the author with the Pushkin faith, with his "Olympic indifference," which so astounded Sergei. Dovlatov was enthralled by Pushkin's ability to rise above the antagonism of good and evil: "The moon and the stars shone brightly, casting light on the square and the gallows." This sinister scene from *The Captain's Daughter* is recognizable in one of Dovlatov's favorite landscapes—a moon shining on predator and prey alike.

Dovlatov's rare, laconic, attention-eluding landscape is an eloquent declaration of his philosophy, and not just his literary philosophy. Like a watchmaker with his tweezers, Dovlatov excised from the surroundings the necessary parts. Everything else went into the landscapes. They do not aid the narrative. They lack significance, implication, or subtext. Small details of the world, they justify their presence in the text only by the fact that they also exist beyond its limits.

Dovlatov's landscape does not partake in the action—it merely exists. Everything that becomes part of it does not reflect the rays of the author's attention—instead, it emits light on its own, like in Vermeer's paintings. Sergei safeguarded this mysterious luminescence: "A train station-like scene loomed beyond the window. A pre-war building, flat windows, light-filled clocks . . ."

Still in his youth, Dovlatov claimed that "each artistically depicted thing and item carries within itself poetic thought." Obeying his own rule, Sergei carefully depicted the light, form, and texture of each narratively irrelevant thing. In doing so, he restored the equilibrium that is violated by authorial whim. The "unfiring rifles" of Dovlatov's description free nature from an imposed hierarchy. From its perspective, "unnecessary" and "indispensable" are synonyms. They are made antonyms only by our own prejudice, which Sergei dispels with the help of a particular technique. Sinyavsky's Jesuit advice describes it very well: "When you're in a hurry, remember to slow your step."

The climactic moments of Dovlatov's prose are marked by a concentration of details that reveal nothing. Rather, they reveal nothing only to the self-absorbed hero. During thorny moments, Dovlatov departs from his nearly indistinguishable double in order to take a good look around at the exact time when the double is incapable of doing so.

The Zone, for example, has the following paragraph: "The overseer put the bottle in his pocket. He crumpled the poster up and tossed it. It audibly unfolded, rustling as it did." Audible for whom?

In *Pushkin Hills*, the hero approaches the HQ doors, behind which waits the KGB Major, and he presses a "pretty pink button." And here's how a dooming bit of news crashes down on him while he is in the throes of a miserable bender: "The girl looked away embarrassedly. Then she took out of her bra a bluish piece of paper, folded up into the size of a postmark. I unfolded the warm telegram and read: 'Flying out Wednesday night. Tanya, Masha.'"

The "warm telegram" is my favorite Dovlatov heroine. It reminds me of an Auden poem. In it, he praises the old masters, because when they depict an execution, they also show the executioner's horse, scratching itself against a tree.

Despite all the egocentrism of Dovlatov's prose, which essentially lacks any hero other than the Id, Sergei never forgot that the world doesn't care about our problems. By equalizing all elements of creation, his peripheral vision made the fabric of reality whole.

11

Any writer dreams of the same thing: to put into their book the entire world, having removed everything superfluous.

The writer is the last guardian of coherence in a world of disintegrated knowledge. He gathers what others scatter. In putting it together, he winds up with something greater than its parts. Literature pays the surplus value to its readers.

Coherence, however, is a good that is easily counterfeited. Some writers imitate it by hiding any rough edges from themselves and the readers. Thus do bachelors sweep any trash under the rug before a date. Other writers replace coherence with its schema. This is a favorite play of the drunk who searches for his lost watch in places with better lighting. Yet others refuse to search for coherence and expose the eye-popping incoherence of the absurd.

Honest authors have it hardest, since they are, as Beckett said, ready to "admit chaos into the world." They are forced to acknowledge the existence of chaos, suffer because of it, coexist with it, learn to respect it, even love it, and wait patiently for when—and if—it ever reveals an order that is hidden from the unenlightened gaze.

Dovlatov knew the price of the "wondrous power of the absurd," but he dreamed of the norm, which also "evokes the feeling of wonder."

The norm is the beginning and the end of the path. One cannot come to the norm. One can only return to it. And the greater the writer, the longer the circumference that he describes around the chaos on his path back to the banality of the point of origin.

When a Chinese artist began a landscape, he saw only mountains and rivers. For many years, instead of the mountains and rivers themselves, he learned to depict their essence and soul. And then, one fine moment, the shroud fell from his gaze, and he discovered that before him were mountains and rivers. Everything assumed its rightful place in the world, chaos turned out to be the cosmos, and the universe allowed the artist entry, revealing to him the inevitability of their union.

An artist has no subject beyond this. But he is capable of solving it only for himself. He can but invite us to come—not with him, but to the place where he went.

In a letter Dovlatov wrote right when he was working on *Pushkin Hills*, he makes an admission that he called "a metaphorical outburst":

"My whole life, I blew into the spyglass and was surprised that there was no music. Then I carefully gazed into a trombone and was surprised that I couldn't see anything. We dried up rivers and moved mountains, and now it's clear that the mountains need to be returned whence they came, and the rivers too."

In *Pushkin Hills'* conclusion, Dovlatov, having "stepped from paradox to truism," arrives at the point where the coincidental joins with the indispensable: "Suddenly, I saw the world as a single whole. Everything was occurring simultaneously. Everything was happening before my very eyes . . ."

14

A Concert for an Accented Voice

1

The history of Brighton Beach unfolded with such determination that I managed to catch the dawn, the prime, and the twilight of our diaspora's capital. Dovlatov, however, arrived a bit later, so he missed how it all began.

The first businesses in Brighton bore simple, metropolitan names: "The Little Birch," in which, like in a provincial general store, you could find everything— pickles, fish jerky, matryoshkas, and a gastronome named Moscow, which resembled a train station buffet.

The owner of both was a mighty Hercules named Misha, looking at whom made you want to say, "Worry not, you mighty, old oak—there are adventures ahead of you yet." Though he looked like one of Babel's draymen, he was distinguishable by his kind nature and lack of imagination. When business was very good, he opened a branch in Barbados and called it "Red Moscow." They say that once they stopped letting people emigrate, Misha bribed the Soviet authorities to let his grownup daughter leave. The next day, she was standing behind the counter.

Hordes of immigrants circulated between the Birch and Moscow all day long. Everybody wore the same uniform, as if members of some unknown country's army. In the winter, they wore squirrel fur hats they had brought over from Russia and suede overcoats purchased in America. In the summer—sport suits and polos. Everything in between was dominated by leather jackets.

Life in Brighton oozed of the joy of retirement. Not far from the shore, beneath a large poster of Odesa's Chornomorets F. C., sitting at tables covered with Soviet plastic covers, pensioners played dominoes without stopping to remove their ushankas.

This was only the beginning of Brighton. The very first envelopes with photos—our immigrants posing in front of strangers' cars—were en route to Russia. Admittedly, even then, there was already a photographer who roamed the beach, offering to take photos of people with cardboard cutouts of beloved Soviet cartoon characters. He understood far earlier than many others that Mickey Mouse would never be popular here.

Many years have passed, but Brighton is much the same. Not only the black bread and the garlic sausage, but down to the vanilla, the biscuits, the Validol, and the beer. Brighton does not acknowledge American price catalogues. Here—and only here—you can buy Uzbek carpets, four-button bras, cast iron cleavers, calico socks, mouliné thread, and *Zor'ka* toothpaste.

The Brighton entertainment industry is also endemic—it has its own stars, its own competition laureates, its own party rituals, its own humor, and, of course, its own press. Brighton's periodicals continue to host discussions in a language considered appropriate only for private or even erotic dialogues. Only in Brighton will nobody even bat an eyelid after reading in the paper that Zhorik and Beatochka[1] are celebrating their golden jubilee. Brighton's love for diminutive suffixes makes it seem like it is some exotic zoo inhabited by alien avian specimens: Shmulik, Yulik, Zyablik.

After making bank, Brighton kept up with its own peculiar manner of speech even after neon signs began popping up everywhere. Bearing witness to this is the *Opteka* (the "Optipharmacy"), where you can buy either a pair of new glasses or some aspirin. Likewise, there is a restaurant with an English sign that says, "Cappuccino." Beneath it is a curious translation into Russian: "Dumplings."

Americans sometimes visit Brighton. I once met a Woody Allen-like couple in a kebab house. A young man who had probably read his fair share of Dostoevsky ordered a plate of caviar and a cup of vodka. Fifteen minutes later, he was being dragged away from his table: "This isn't a restaurant—it's the Holocaust!"

Our people, meanwhile, are unfazed by alcohol. Only here have I seen my countrymen drink an entire bottle of Courvoisier without even scooting down from the top bench of the steam room in a Russian *banya*.

---

1   The almost unbearably saccharine diminutives of the proper names Georgi and Beata.

But Brighton knows how to surprise its own too. Nowhere else have I ever seen such a concentration of Jews free of complexes. This surprised Dovlatov too: "A confident gaze, wide shoulders, a bulging back pocket . . . In short—a Jew enjoying his freedom. An effective and rather convincing sight. Some people are even a little frightened by it . . ."

In Russia, Jews don't like sticking their necks out. My dad, for example, didn't approve of Kissinger, harboring fears that Jews will have to pay for the high rank of their tribesman. But in Brighton, nobody is afraid of anything, and everyone says whatever they think. We once made the acquaintance of a short fellow who, instead of teeth, had psoriasis across his cheek. After learning what we did professionally, he grabbed his bald head, lamenting: "Oh, what are you doing, Amerhica loves the strong."

2

As I have already said, everything is unique in Brighton. Including, admittedly, Brodksy, the poet, Iosif. Then again, people here like songs more than poetry. Especially one song with a chorus that goes, "Skyscrapers, skyscrapers, but I'm so small." Willy Tokarev wrote it. Ever since his taxi-driving muse crossed the ocean without even getting her dress wet, he's begun claiming that there were no poets in the diaspora before him.

That isn't at all the case. Naum Sagalovsky was the poet of the Third Wave. Dovlatov discovered him, and he took greater pride in him than in all of his colleagues put together. "Twenty years, I worked as an editor," Sergei wrote. "Sagalovsky is the only reward for my efforts." Dovlatov lovingly defended Sagalovsky from accusations of unseemly jokes and antisemitism: "The ability to jest, even to jest cruelly and mockingly about oneself is a beautiful and noble trait of the ineradicable Jewry. I ask you: who came up with the first jokes about Jews? Exactly . . ."

Knowing full well the utility of the art of reprise, Sergei wasn't repelled, but drawn to the vaudeville character of Sagalovsky's verse. "If there existed in the diaspora," he wrote him, "a cultural and decorous musical collective, not vulgar, but vaudeville, then you could make good songs out of some of your poems."

One day, Dovlatov proved this. After Sergei, along with Bakhchanyan and Sagalovsky, published the "eccentric," as he called it, *Demarche of Enthusiasts*,[2] they did a literary evening in New York. Naturally, Dovlatov led it. After

2   This is a pun on a famous song titled "March of the Enthusiasts."

introducing his coauthors, who were sitting to either side, Sergei thoughtfully looked around and noticed that the stage reminded him of Golgotha. Then, he briefly discussed the popularity of Sagalovsky's poetry, after which he unexpectedly sang one of Sagalovsky's poems—which he dedicated to Bakhchanyan—that he arranged to music.

> I'll order a still-life
> That would gaze on me from the wall,
> That would brighten the view,
> That would light up the room.
> Draw me, you artist,
> Four hundred grams of ham,
> Some quick pickles,
> Let's say four of them.

Having accidentally placed his works in *The New American*, Sagalovsky quickly became a darling there. He had the rare and forgotten talent of a songwriter-satirist who reacts instantly to every tiny detail of the little world inhabited by the diaspora. Sergei appreciated this quality very much. He wrote to Sagalovsky: "Without you, a very significant note would be missing from our literature. Imagine *Khovanshchina* without any A's."

A virtuoso of the domestic lyre, Sagalovsky was best at writing parodic lyrics intended for internal consumption:

> Oh, these crazy N. Americans,
> They've no need for poets or verse,
> They just laugh, those petty bastards,
> Mocking them with fist and curse!
> But they're living rather large,
> Can't say it any other way!
> There's the writer, S. Dovlatov,
> Publishing his third book today!
> He uses pretty silverware,
> Drinks Smirnoff, lights up a Kent,
> Then he moonlights in the Underwood,
> Making one more pretty cent.
> Then there's those guys, Vail and Genis—
> Sure, I haven't read them yet,
> But they're simply Marx and Engels!
> Capital really makes them wet! . . .

Sure, all of this resembles a student newspaper, but that's exactly what was missing in our slogan-weary diaspora, in which we had become its carefree, independent faction. *The New American* became the last Communist weekly. "The free labor of freely gathered people" allowed us to exchange debts for hopes. "The situation is still difficult," wrote Sergei, "but it is definitively promising. Even though Vail hasn't paid for his apartment in four months, and Sharymova only eats when over somebody else's home."

In America, the thing that immigrants miss the most is socializing. Our unassuming paper served as a partial substitute. It predisposed people toward it with its familiar tone, which united the Third Wave into a single unit. Everything that happened here was a strictly private affair. Unsurprising, considering how few of us there were. You could have invited all the immigrant writers to a single wedding. The readers too, but then it would have had to be a Georgian wedding. Under such conditions, literature returned to its roots—an unprofessional, private activity. Books printed in tiny numbers were written for our own—both friends and enemies. Having done away with responsibility for a hot second, literature breathed a sigh of relief.

Salinger advised artists to use brown wrapping paper: "Many serious masters used it, especially when they didn't have any serious design."

3

After publishing *The Compromise*, Sergei wrote on the back cover an excerpt from our article, which began: "Dovlatov is like a ten-dollar bill—everybody likes him." In response to which Dovlatov immediately wrote *The Price Catalogue*, putting forth the bottom line for all immigrant literature. The verse, written in the then-beloved style of friendly dunking, had a bit about us too:

> . . . there's nothing to be done,
> nobody out there cares . . .
> they've forgotten Vail and Genis,
> three roubles for the pair.
> They are, quite sadly, critics,
> and though to me, they're dear,
> they will not write about me,
> they're ignoring all my tears.
> I mess around with muses,
> enjoying some small release,

and the things that I keep writing
are worth twenty kopeks at least . . .

Sagalovsky's first collection—*A Vityaz' in a Jewish Skin*—came out in the specially created publishing house "Dovlatov's Publishing." When inscribing his book to me, Naum carefully wrote: "From someone who costs twenty kopeks to someone who costs one and a half roubles."

Naturally, Sagalovsky was starkly different from his poems. A courteous, deeply honorable engineer from Kyiv, he spoke in a beautiful baritone. He had assumed the mask of an easily offended smartass. He wrote his satirical feuilletons as the "ethnically Jewish, Russian poet" Motl Leshchiner. It was impossible to miss this practical lyricist with his unparalleled common sense in the Brighton crowds:

Yesterday, my grandson David
came home from school, picked up his spoon,
wiped off his mouth, and then he said
that he descended from baboons.
I said: "You stupid or you crazy?
I don't know about the others,
But don't you scratch this table—
You descended from your father and your mother."

Sagalovsky's hero, seized with the idea of staking out a spot in the New World that he didn't even have in the Old World, represented the immigrant version of the "little guy" who had made his way to America from his small, but homey apartment for unclear reasons:

It wasn't very large, our place—
I grew up on the doorstep.
They circumcised me,
so that I'd take up less space.

Living in Chicago, Sagalovsky didn't like Brighton and wasn't afraid of letting Brighton know it. Thus, in response to our article comparing Brighton to Babel's Odesa, we got an anonymous response, whose author it really wasn't all that difficult to identify:

I'm being told it's like Odesa,
Oh, Aunt Khaya, oh, the fish market!

But Brighton Beach isn't worth a mass,
or a good word, or your tears.
It's demeaned and robbed you,
and don't start yelling that
we need a new Babel
to praise Brighton Beach.
To give you your due!
Personally, I think one thing—
Babel's not the one who's needed, but Denikin!
Or at the very least, Makhno . . .

4

Brighton could be despised but not ignored. Our readers lived there. And we wanted them to like us. Sergei managed this effortlessly. Thoroughly devoid of intellectual snobbery, Sergei was more tolerant of his readers' boorishness and ignorance.

In order to get their attention today, all you need to do is reprint the criminal reports from Russian papers. Nothing makes your "new" homeland seem prettier than bad news from your "old" homeland. But while the Soviet regime was alive, readers had access to a far less vivid dissident news source. Which is why, in entertaining our immigrant audience, we told them either about the intimately familiar or the utterly unknown. In the latter case, we put out things under the general title "Woman Embraced by Crocodile." In the case of the former, we would do an interview under a heading invented by the same caustic Sagalovsky: "How Have You Settled In, You New American?"

Sergei eagerly took part in it, describing the successes of his many buddies. In his rendition, they all seemed like writers. In a conversation with Dovlatov ornately titled "Leisurely Reflections on the Curb of the Gastrointestinal Tract," one of our mutual acquaintances, a doctor who had served many years in a submarine and who rarely made do without swearing, seemingly sings a paean to that same tract:

"Internal organs are extraordinarily harmonious. Any illness is a disruption of this harmony. A healthy organism functions in an intricate and strict rhythm. It is constantly in motion and constantly switching colors. Any abstractionist would be envious. It's a shame that I'm not a director, like Solya Shapiro. I'd have made a brilliant film about internal organs. For example, take the dramatic interplay between the stomach and the intestine . . ."

Sergei inserted his friends into every one of his texts, not just the ones in the paper. It is difficult to find an acquaintance of his about whom he didn't write anything. He tried to make the immigration intimate by making it his home. Purposefully framing the myth of the Third Wave as a family narrative, Dovlatov employed phantoms. He came up with a particular newspaper genre: "Instances." These tiny, unsigned notes were published as real-life events. There was nothing interesting about the episodes other than the dramatis personae—always immigrants.

For example, there was one instance in which a gym teacher from Lviv, Garry Pivovarov, beat up three black hooligans in the subway. And one of them "lightly wounded him with a carpet cutter." Only this last detail betrays the author of this unremarkable story. With the typical improvisation of an artist, Sergei spruced up reality, meeting the violent crime-fearing immigrants halfway. Admittedly, I did know one Ukrainian Jew who fought off some muggers with a vacuum that he had just got at a yard sale. Usually, though, encounters with muggers typically went in the muggers' favor, of course. In the span of a month and a half, my brother had his TV stolen twice.

One time, after reading his fair share of Dovlatov's "instances," Zavalishin came to our office and asked us to publish that his apartment had also been robbed. An art critic and a Malevich expert, Vyacheslav Klavdiyevich was a legendary personality. An exceptional skier, a hero of the Winter War, he was captured by the Germans. In the D. P. camps, Zavalishin managed to publish a four-tome collection of Gumilyov's works. When I met him, he was a destitute old man with bad handwriting. His reviews in *The New Russian Word*, which were gobbled up by the likes of Tselkov and Shchemyakin and Neizvestny, paid out seven dollars each. Five of them would go to the typists for reprints. Unsurprisingly, Zavalishin was constantly loaning small—and, as is the wont of heavy drinkers, uneven—sums. Knowing this, everyone became interested in what the bandits that had broken into his apartment had taken. Clamming up, Vyacheslav Klavdiyevich said that they hadn't taken anything. In fact, they may have left something—he found a knife and a hammer next to the broken-down door.

5

Treating the paper as his sandbox, Dovlatov often came up with a fictitious conversation partner, trying to pass off the rough draft of a short story as a special report. Sometimes, Sergei, who rarely left his home, would take advantage of another's experiences.

In this way, he retold a sequence of events that had happened to us when the Soviets had only just invaded Afghanistan. We had gotten the bright idea to go to a billiard room, where we quickly learned the American rules. However, when we suggested playing a few rounds according to our rules, one tall fellow venomously retorted: "You can play by your rules in Afghanistan." We left without a fuss.

Russians were so uncomfortable at the time that our taxi drivers pretended they were Bulgarian. Sergei wrote a frustrated article on the subject: *The Unavoidable Percentage of Morons.*

Another time, he recounted our adventure in Harlem. In a letter, he even tried to pass it off as if it happened to him: "Some two years ago, at night, I was writing a report from Harlem; we had taken a gallon of vodka (I still drank then) and armed ourselves with guns . . ." In reality, it was Vail and I who had meandered the streets of Harlem, sober and unarmed. As I remember, we had made our way along every single street. Some hadn't seen a white face in three generations. Seeing our camera and therefore taking us for tourists who had taken leave of their wits, the only thing we heard thrown our way was an errant "welcome." All in all, it was a peaceful affair. The most powerful impression I got was from a portrait I saw in a book shop's window display: it was a portrait of Pushkin that depicted him black as a boot. We became truly scared only when our politically incorrect report titled "White on Black" caught the attention of a black State Department employee who knew Russian. After he explained that we could be deported for something like this, we spent a long time repenting in print, with Sergei's help.

Unlike us, Sergei was more interested in how America saw us than how we saw America. In one of his pseudo-reports, an American woman complains that her Russian neighbors presented her with an entire "flotilla of wooden spoons." "But we don't eat with them," she explained. "We used to, maybe 200 years ago."

Another time, Dovlatov asks his conversation partner: "Do you know where Russia is?" "Sure," he allegedly replies. "In Poland."

But the silliest of all these characters was a street sweeper from Barcelona named Chico Diasma. "We saw lots of things under Franco," he consoles Dovlatov. "But when Franco died, lots of things changed. When Stalin dies, things will change too."

Sergei responds by explaining what's what until the newly enlightened street sweeper admits, "Chico said something stupid."

This was simply too much, and we mocked Sergei with that phrase to the point that it entered public discourse. Whenever someone blurted something out at a strategy session, everyone would happily proclaim: "Chico said something stupid!"

Of course, Sergei didn't take his journalistic mischief seriously. These stories were just etudes. He was intently searching for the American narrative. As his search grew warmer, he discovered a familiar set of characters—lowlifes, idlers, drunkards, and hooligans. Our diaspora saw the myriad Puerto Rican immigrants as such. They said that the only contribution Puerto Ricans made to New York culture was cockroaches. Dovlatov, meanwhile, treated both sides without prejudice.

15

Halfway to the Homeland

1

If we ignore the parrot, then the Puerto Rican Rafael Jose Belinda Chicorillo Gonzalez is the only positive character in *The Émigrée*. This romantic loafer, revolutionary, and Casanova has much in common with Dovlatov's favorite characters. And his Latin American heritage only abets this fact. It exacerbates the North-South duality that was so important for Sergei. If jokes searching for categorical opposites force together a Ukrainian and a black guy, then in Dovlatov's rendition, immigrants can achieve such a point of absurdity all on their own:

"We don't have a lot of black people. More Latin Americans. In our minds, these are mysterious people with transistors. We do not know them. But we despise and fear them just in case. Cross-eyed Frida expresses her discontent the following way:

"'Go back to your godforsaken Africa!'

"Frida herself is from Shklov."[1]

As a whole, *The Émigrée*, Dovlatov's most immigrant-focused book, doesn't work—it resembles a comedy screenplay too much. Like all writers in America, Sergei would size up Hollywood every now and then, since Hollywood is an author's only way out of the literary ghetto. *The Émigrée* may have been the side effect of such a size-up. It's no coincidence that Americans that use it to learn Russian like it at a lot. But *The Émigrée* doesn't make for a good book. It tries to pass off a bland retrospective and a chaotic mess of action for a narrative.

---

1 Shklov is a tiny town in Belarus.

What it does do well is offer a gallery of immigrant types, drawn bitingly in black and white. Absent the Soviet authorities, everyone assumed their natural places. Inflated reputations burst, foolishness became more obvious, lack of talent was more easily seen, people's outlooks narrowed, and the world grew smaller, because there was nowhere to run.

Dovlatov was infuriated by immigrants' boorishness. Though he readily forgave sins and crimes, Sergei couldn't stand self-righteousness, avarice, philistine superciliousness, confidence in the impregnability of one's ideals, the presumption of one's own incorruptibility, intolerance for another's way of life, cowardly narrowmindedness, and the inability to go outside the wan borders of one's own flightless life.

In other words, he despised the norm. The very norm for which he yearned and of which he was frightened.

2

The unique feature of our immigration was that we brought with us an enormous amount of experience that was almost foreign to the first two Waves. Unlike them, we arrived in America as authoritative representatives of Soviet civilization in its most vivid, characteristic, and concentrated manifestation. Consequently, we had nothing in common with the old diaspora.

I think it's a shame now, but back then, they all seemed like fossils akin to Kisa Vorobyaninov. True, I did like Andrei Sedykh. His Siberian pseudonym led to amusing situations every now and then. Once, we received an aggrieved visitor at our office for *The New Russian Word*. After disgustedly taking in the whole room, he declared that he wanted to speak with a real Russian— Andrei Sedykh. "Yakov Moiseyevich!" called out the secretary, and the visitor disappeared instantly.

Yakov Moiseyevich Tsvibak resembled Abazh—[*the backwards spelling the Russian word zhaba, meaning "toad"*—A.R.]—from *The Kingdom of Crooked Mirrors*. After spending his youth in Paris, he behaved like a typical Frenchman: he was stingy, but he never attended dinner without female companionship. Sedykh took pride in his early books, asserting that they made a name for him, but when I asked for a few when I was preparing to go to Paris, the decaying little tomes turned out to be overly wordy guidebooks. The chief achievement of his literary life was the Nobel Prize received by Bunin, who brought Yakov Moiseyevich with him when he went to Stockholm.

Sedykh was best at writing obituaries. Having outlived everybody he knew, he responded to every death with a cheerful article. A conversation with him resembled a spiritual séance. Sedykh knew everyone: Mandelstam, Rachmaninov, Conan Doyle. He was deeply and earnestly uninterested in us. He tolerated Solzhenitsyn. He neither understood nor published Brodsky. Especially since—as explained by his deputy—Brodsky didn't write ads. When I asked Yakov Moiseyevich if he liked Tarkovsky films, he replied, yawning, that he hadn't attended "the cinema" since 1954.

Despite a difficult youth, he was rewarded with a lengthy old age. Bakhchanyan claimed that Sedykh decided to enter history not as a writer, but as a long-liver. Before his death, Yakov Moiseyevich fell into senility and was perfectly content. Energetic and elegant, he would sit in the surrounding of old ladies, informing them how hard Trotsky had it living in Brooklyn on immigrant welfare.

But Sedykh retained his characteristic tenacity to the very end. When he visited our editorial office for old time's sake, he asked whether we had hired any lefties; Yakov Moiseyevich had managed to notice that right side of the urinal had been bespattered.

Out of Sedykh's peers in *The New Russian Word*, I only met Gerenrot. He introduced himself as a cadet, as a result of which I thought he was an officer before I realized that he meant the Constitutional Democrats. Gerenrot's posture was a function of horseback riding, and his liberal convictions were caused by his old party. After the war, Gerenrot went to vacation in Florida. At the train station, he had to use the restroom, but seeing the "Whites only" sign on the door, he immediately boarded the return train without relieving himself.

Gerenrot believed the Soviet Union is to Russia as Turkey is to the Byzantine Empire. He wouldn't acknowledge Soviet language, and since there was no other, Abram Solomonovich invented his own words. In his rendition, armored corps became panzer divisions. A young translator once invited Abram Solomonovich over his place to "relax with the guys." "There will be peasants there?" asked a surprised Gerenrot.

It's worth saying that Dovlatov didn't give a fig about any of this. He felt no deference to the old-timers, and he was probably right. When *The New American* was born, Sedykh fired the endlessly hard-working Lena, who had been working as a typist.

Frightened of the new rival paper, *The New Russian Word* waged a ruthless war against us: they scared off potential writers, bribed whomever could provide ads, and told everyone else that we had sold out to the KGB.

Sergei entered the fray with relish. In an open letter to Andrei Sedykh, he defended the Third Wave's right to be unlike the previous two: "People are divided by the most different of attributes. Which doesn't prevent them from being people. Only a flock of sheep is indivisible . . ."

When Glasha died, Sergei got himself a dachshund and called her in honor Andrei Sedykh—Yasha. He loved her no less than he did his famous fox terrier.

3

We all considered America a well-edited homeland, so we thought to find in the New World a fixed version of the Old. In America, we searched for our—rather than its—ideal. Like Columbus, we made for one country and wound up in another.

Disappointed by this discovery, Dovlatov began doing something to which immigration always consigns a writer. He had two ways out—to live in the past, like Solzhenitsyn, or in the future, like Brodsky. Since the most notable thing about the future is our absence, most preferred to write about what was rather than what was to be. Having arrived in the West, writers opted to finish saying what they weren't allowed to say at home rather than say something new.

This is natural, but not inevitable. Immigrant literature doesn't have its own theme, but it does have its own place—on the fields of a strange, other reality. Sinyavsky, an immigrant par excellence, had passed through this school of marginalization while still in prison. There, deprived of paper, he would write in the margins of the *Izvestiya* newspaper. After arriving in the West, Sinyavsky accepted immigration as a challenge: by becoming a foreigner in both his own and a foreign country, a writer "ceases to recognize reality and attempts to depict it and cognize it anew, drawing simultaneously on two points of his estranged, foreign position."

Émigré wordcraft consists of a dialogue with one's past, which the writer pulls out of a present that is now foreign to him. This dialogue takes place in a fantasy zone, a realm of myth. All Russian writers left the same country, but in the West, each of them discovered their own country of origin that was starkly different from those of the others. Bunin and Nabokov couldn't find a common language to discuss the Russia that they had left at the same time. Even less like each other were the "homes" of two *zeks*—Solzhenitsyn and Sinyavsky. All of these private homelands are united in their illusory nature. They exist only in memory. Each writer carries his home with him like a snail.

The danger is that the immigrant situation threatens to morph into a metaphysical one, with which every single writer will have to contend. Brodsky said that exile gives a writer an invaluable lesson in humility. Lost amidst the books of others, he is like a needle in a haystack—it's great if anyone is searching for it at all.

Exile provides an author with a short window of time in which to cognize something that he would otherwise need almost an entire lifetime to understand: at some point, every writer is left alone with language. But if Brodsky is correct, then the phrase "literature in exile" is tautological. Literature *is* exile. A writer is always an exception—he is always on the curb. Only from the curb can he look at life without partaking in it.

4

In Russia, they quickly found a justification for Dovlatov's premature death: "loneliness, longing, nostalgia." This triad, much like other universal banalities—the "three little stars" or "brains, brawn, and beauty"—is applicable in any situation. But what to make of loneliness, if on this side of Yevtushenko, Sergei was the most popular guest at any party? And nostalgia doesn't fit all too neatly either. Nostalgia failed to do Nabokov in until he was seventy-eight, and Bunin made it all the way to eighty-three. For Russian writers, nostalgia is probably safer than living in the homeland.

Besides, nostalgia is an aristocratic illness. Whence are we supposed to get it? In this, like Bazarov, I would sooner trust the body than the soul. I think that one's homeland is a physical, carnal concept. A function of metabolism, a homeland forms in the cells of an organism and the atoms consumed in one's country of origin. We feast on the homeland, we breathe it in, because it becomes us. Like arsenic, a homeland comes to rest in the tissue of an organism, condemning us to a feeling of physical belonging in a specific longitude, latitude, and climate zone.

Love for one's homeland is a reflex, a physiological cognition, the resonance of external nature with the nature that is dissolved within us. This is why patriotism births the strongest and most resilient attachments: it is more difficult to stop liking borsch than Dostoevsky, to say nothing of Solzhenitsyn.

Patriotism is incurable, because it is inseparable from the soil in a far more literal sense than that imagined by the Pochvenniks themselves. Love for one's homeland, circumventing one's consciousness, doesn't even return us to an animal state, but a plant state. The only genuine nostalgia is that which we share with daisies or mushrooms. A foreign country isn't distinguished from a homeland by its language and customs, but by a collection of amino acids in the soil, the angle at which the sun hits the earth, a few hundred molecules that endow the air with the impalpable, inexplicable, but unforgettable aroma of childhood.

5

Failing to make the diaspora his home, Sergei rebuilt it in his "nostalgic" books. Unlike *The Zone* and *Pushkin Hills*, *Ours* and *The Suitcase* are the fruit of artistic design rather than organic necessity. They aren't untamed—they're domesticated. It's the difference between a garden and a vegetable patch. The merit of the former is determined not only by the gardener's mastery, but also by his trust in nature. The latter boasts great utility. Sergei's later books are more orderly than his prior works. This is the fault of discipline—not the author's discipline, but that of the genre.

Memory requires systematization exactly because it neglects it. Destroying the past in favor of the present, memory creates history, which retains from the past only those things that have entered history. Memory masks the selectivity of its whims with encyclopedic aspirations. Any whim needs justification—a change in formation, inflexible laws, historical necessity, autobiography. Obsessed with memory, an émigré book more often than others resembles a catalogue, a registry, a dictionary, or a crossword.

That was the plan for *The Refrigerator*, which yielded Sergei only two short stories. This was also the style of Sergei's best American books—*Ours* and *The Suitcase*. In them, Dovlatov didn't so much discover the new as cultivate the old so well that it continued to bear fruit.

A perfectionist and a miniaturist, he derived enjoyment from the non-linearity of art: microscopic changes in timbre and tonality result in catastrophically far-reaching aftereffects. Sergei thus told the story of his marriage three separate times, and each rendition yielded a completely different wedded couple, each of which only vaguely resembled the one that I knew in real life. If Dovlatov were a composer, he wouldn't have composed symphonies and songs—he would have come up with variations on a theme.

In *The Suitcase*, the theme was determined by the suitcase. Lapidary like a verdict and capacious like an ark, this image morphed into a symbol of immigrant life without shedding its essence as a suitcase.

Everyone had a suitcase. We carried out of the Soviet Union all of our idiosyncratic belongings, which nobody else had any need for. My suitcase, for example, had a metalworker's kit: some joker claimed that they valued Soviet instruments in Italy—sell one there, and you'll have enough for a ticket to Venice.

In America, suitcases stowed away in closets served as a reminder of immigration far longer than most everything else. Huge, creased, and cheap, they haunted us like Russian dreams.

Dovlatov turned *The Suitcase* into an immigrant fairy tale: each item in the suitcase tells its own convoluted story. Or rather, it tries to, as it is constantly interrupted by virtuosic cadences—tangents. Just think of the writer Danchkovsky, who somehow ended up in the book and who titled a book on Lenin "Stand Up, You Who Are Branded by the Curse!"[2]

But still, the contents of Dovlatov's suitcase aren't merely a trigger for storytelling. All of these poplin shirts, crêpe socks, and establishment shoes envelop the protagonist like bandages cover the Invisible Man—thanks to them, he becomes visible.

We knew him earlier, of course, but he was different. Once again writing his life script, Dovlatov imperceptibly changed the point of view. In *The Emigrée*, Sergei is far more venomous toward immigrants than he is toward Party functionaries in *The Suitcase*.

In America, time turned into space, which used the Atlantic Ocean to partition us off from the past. Our view of it was justified by Dovlatov's sentiment—Blok's words, which he put in the epigraph: "But even such, my Russia, you are dearer to me than any other land."

As the years of immigration, the Soviet regime never got any better, but it did become more amusing.

6

If *The Suitcase* resembles a crossword, then *Ours* is like a chainword. By substituting his own relatives into the vacant cells of the text, the author knows the answer ahead of time—his own.

By creating his personal "blood and soil" myth, Dovlatov began his family tree with rather epic characters. His towering grandpas—all seven feet

---

2   The first line of "The Internationale," which the author used to address Lenin specifically.

tall—straddle the boundary between portrait and allegory with some difficulty. Raucous like forces of nature, they are both mighty, but in different ways.

The beer-stand-drinker and food-cart-eater Isaac is a carnival mask, a circus strongman, a living black hole of a stomach: "He would fold pieces of bread in half. He drank vodka out of a cream soda cup. When desert was served, he asked not to take away the aspic..."

The surly old man Stepan is powerful in his constancy, like a cliff. Even death struggled to wipe him off the face of the earth: "At home, it took them some time to notice his disappearance. The same time it would take you to note the disappearance of a tree, a stone, a river..."

These two mighty warriors supplement each other like water and mountains, laughter and tears, life and death. If one accepts the world with no questions asked, the other refuses to dignify it with his approval via his inexplicable silence:

"Perhaps he was dissatisfied with the world as it was? In its entirety or in small details? Maybe the change in seasons? The uninterruptible sequence of life and death? Gravity? The contradiction of the sea and dry land? I don't know..."

Each of his legendary ancestors reflects Sergei himself, of course. From one grandpa, he inherited an ambivalent relationship with the universe, and another passed down his appetite. "Dombrovsky invited us over today," the author's wife reminds him. "You should eat in advance."

In the version published in the paper, the abstract Dombrovsky is replaced with a concrete Vail. But in the book, Sergei followed the complex twisting of his emotional attachments and switched the last name. I had it worse. *Solo on Underwood* has the following note: "Genis and evil are incompatible with each other." In the second edition, Sergei resignedly made the following amendment: "How wrong I was." The third edition dropped the comment entirely, and now, only bibliophiles can track the rise and fall of my reputation.

Resisting both the Revolution and nature itself, Sergei's stalwart grand-dads put roots down into their homeland, roots that stretched all the way to America and turned into the Dovlatov family tree. In examining each of its branches, Sergei transformed each chapter of his "family album" into a didactic parable: the one about the Honest Party Man, another about the Force-of-Nature Existentialist, about the Healthy Body and Unhealthy Soul, the Prosperous Loser, the Grammatical Errors, the Nightmare of Imperturbability.

Without sacrificing their miraculous individuality, Dovlatov's characters are manifestations of archetypal traits. This means that Sergei described his extravagant family so juicily that it stopped being his own. You want to rent out Dovlatov's family—you could role-play each of his relatives.

Like Dovlatov's other works, *Ours* is an egocentric book. But if Sergei previously depicted others through himself, here, he showed himself through others. I think that in *Ours*, Sergei was searching for proof of the genetic inevitability of his fate. Without trying to avoid it, he hoped to accept it not as a possibility, but as his due. Earlier, Dovlatov was interested in the genesis of a writer; now—just genesis: "God gave me what I have asked him for my entire life. He made me a regular writer. After becoming one, I realized that I can aim higher, but it was too late. You don't ask God for seconds."

After achieving renown, Sergei won the freedom to live like he wanted. But he wanted to like how he lived.

16

A Matryoshka with Genitals

1

"To be dependent on the tsar, to be dependent on the people—does it make any difference to me?" It didn't matter to Pushkin, but it sure matters to us. We knew that depending on the people is worse. Tsars come in different flavors. They can be deceived and they can be used to deceive. The public, however, rarely defies expectations. Especially in the diaspora, where it is so small that for many writers, trial by market can be fatal.

In the end, the market is what doomed all of our publishing enterprises. None of us truly learned how to exchange words for money. It may be that it is simply impossible. Any spiritual value is illusory. It only pretends to be a commodity. Words are worthless, and like an echo, they belong to all whom they reach.

Admittedly, Mark Twain had a character who collected echoes. The businessmen with whom we had to negotiate tried to deal in echoes. They frightened me more than anyone I've ever met in my life. Thinking about them, I forget to smile.

Naturally, our fault is greater than theirs. Having come from a country where cronyism-favoritism replaced the market, we imagined businessmen as depicted by Soviet children's writer Gaidar—armed with a barrel of jam and a basket of cookies. Believing that the rich like money, we hoped that we would be exploited. Proletariat of intellectual labor, we feverishly searched for such masters that would have allowed us to keep our wheelbarrows.

Maybe they exist too. Sulzberger, the owner of *The New York Times*, was so afraid of interfering with the paper's affairs that he tried to influence the editors by mailing letters signed under a pseudonym. And only until he was discovered and mocked by the editor—his own granddaughter.

Immigrant businessmen were too complex to be interested only in business. We dreamed of Chichikov, but we got only Nozdryovs.

Our paper attracted myriad unsuccessful artists posing as businessmen, brandishing newly purchased briefcases. All of them wanted to be coauthors rather than business owners. They appreciated our work—not enough to pay for it, but enough to divide it with us. They always spoke "for the people" and always knew better than us what we should do. They were interested not in profit, but their own creative passions. They had cupidity enough only to shortchange us.

At the sight of our owners, I would lock myself in the restroom. And I was right to do so, because their complaints were like the whims of the gods—inexplicable and indescribable. One wanted us to sing praises to Jewish heroism, another really liked the pictures we used, and a third demanded that our articles "make the Young Communists hard."

Our businessmen discussed our finances haughtily. One, for example, declared, while hitching up his sweatpants, that he was only interested in sums featuring nine zeroes. "A billion?" we exclaimed. The businessman faltered—and with good reason, because when they locked him up, his case featured much smaller numbers.

Another, trying to appear more refined, expressed himself allegorically: "My ass is clean," he introduced himself. "If only he could be deported to Mexico," Sergei said wistfully.

2

I reacted to the thought of business with a panicked sense of terror, but Sergei was attracted to it, like a young woman to a grenadier. Maybe Dovlatov was attracted to the flavor of moral taboo—after all, "in our neck of the woods," he wrote, "it's better to steal than to trade." Spurred on by material necessity and spiritual need, Sergei looked for a way to transpose business into the artistic arena.

It's true, a businessman has much in common with an artist. They are both preoccupied with what Berdiayev called "creation from nothing"—something wasn't, and then it was. Spirit acquires form, thought is given flesh. A thing intangibly sublime obtains the weighty solidity of existence.

At the same time, business is the straightforward organization of life, unfiltered by artistic method. Business creates its own reality without the interference of art. By "ascertaining harmony via algebra," business fulfills each author's dream of his works' indisputability. The bottom line endows his art with the round persuasiveness of a mathematical example that is not subject to interpretation.

As for money—money is for a businessman what a book is for a writer: not the end, but a step towards the realization of the project that concludes with the full incarnation of a person into life. As with any craft, the problem isn't making money, but in spending—everything that you have in you.

"I am confident," wrote Dovlatov, "that money cannot be the goal in itself. Especially here, in America. How much does a person need for his welfare? A hundred, two hundred thousand a year. Meanwhile, people here turn over billions. It would appear that money has achieved par with other, much more significant values…Sums have transformed into numbers. Numbers have transformed into heraldic symbols."

This may be true when you have money. We didn't. The first editorial office of *The New American* was located in a room the size of a closet. Before any women worked there, we had strategy sessions in the restroom a level down.

Sixteen full-time employees had to divide among themselves one proper salary. The food at editorial parties would run out before we could uncork the first bottle. We would steal sugar from the local café. Grisha Ryskin once ate a lemon for lunch, and another time, he had mint candies. But nobody complained. On the contrary, our president, Borya Metter, said that when you're hungry, at least you're not bored.

Sergei determinedly tried to change things. He would bring in shady managers, pestered the administration constantly, and got his hands on the finances that none of the others wanted anything to do with. Nothing helped, and the paper was headed for ruin. And then, despairing at our inability to fix one job, we started a completely different one, the wildest one in which I have ever participated.

The idea was an obvious one. Since two of the three forbidden topics in the USSR—dissidents and Jews—had already populated the immigrant press, all we had left was sex. Thus was born a project extravagantly christened *"Russian Playboy."*

Deciding first to familiarize ourselves with our competition, we set off for a sex shop. We had more experience than Dovlatov. By the point, we had already written the article *Simpletons in the World of Sex*, and Sergei had already—completely justifiably—tore it to shreds. He especially let me have it—for sanctimoniousness. "If Genis is Aramis," pondered Dovlatov, "then Vail is Porthos. And both write like Dumas—ably, quickly, carelessly."

However, the shop, chock full of sexual paraphernalia, laid bare the extent of Dovlatov's prudishness. After scrutinizing a sleek center spread, he reproachfully cried out: "She's probably a student!" Though we tried our best to express a professional interest in our surroundings rather than an ordinary one, Sergei, unable to withstand the shop owner's suspicious gaze, quickly fled the battlefield.

In light of the task we faced, bashfulness wasn't the most useful of traits, but we quickly overcame it by erecting a barrage dam of Jewish pseudonyms. We came up with a fictitious editor from Lithuania. As we all knew from firsthand experience, the Baltics were more laidback about such things.

Things got easier from there. Vail compiled an Anglo-Russian dictionary of bedroom terminology. I wrote an expansive article about the erotic arts. Sergei wrote a lyrical short story about oral sex.

We got our relatives and close friends involved with the new enterprise. Lena typed the text, my brother wrote letters to the editor, my wife ran a column titled "Through the Keyhole." Obviously, we had neither a photographer nor models, so we simply cut out raunchy images from American journals.

But the design was our own. Sergei's involvement was particularly impactful. The page numbers were situated on plaques, each of which hung from a male member. Sergei took it on himself to endow each with its own characteristic individuality, depicting them in varying degrees of erection. But the cover turned out best of all. On an *art nouveau*-style ornament, Dovlatov drew a pair of matryoshka dolls with genitals. The original still hangs above Dovlatov's desk, like the steering wheel of the *Titanic*.

The cover is all that's left of our *Playboy*. When the time came to sell the journal, Sergei dug up another couple of businessmen. One had a print shop in Philadelphia, the other had a car. One rainy evening, we took the car to Pennsylvania. The ride itself was captivating enough. The car didn't have any windshield wipers, and our new boss would intermittently remove his suede cap and use it to wipe off the windshield, resignedly stretching out the window.

In Philadelphia, the *Russian Playboy* was met with genuine excitement. In exchange for our promise to mail a new issue each month, we got a check for a thousand dollars, armed with which we began our difficult journey back.

Thankfully, we never saw these people again. The first Russian language pornographic journal disappeared with them.

Most shockingly, despite three spelling errors in the word "thousand," we managed to cash the check. With our share, Vail and I published our first book, which boasted a far less graphic title than the aborted journal—*Contemporary Russian Prose.*

3

The generation that Dovlatov abutted valued women more than family or work. Partly because in Russia, flirting was a faintly dissident thing to do. Since both love and politics were secretive affairs, masculine gallantry partially supplemented its political analogue. At least among writers, many of whom lead busier lives than they would like. On the other hand, they have something to say, like one writer I know, who disappointed one fussy lady with the words, "I'll still bang you, but don't expect any love."

As in life, literature has exceptions, like the author of the "immoral" Terts, who once asked his young countryman with a hint of sorrow what a "whorepath" was. But as a whole, a surplus of love is a trait inherent to writers. In their enkindled minds, every written letter is a spermatozoa, aiming to burrow somewhere else and take root there as if it owned the place.

Authors are simpler, directly correlating their success among the ladies with success generally—they consider it proportional to circulation. I witnessed how one incredibly popular Jewish writer whose *parrot* even spoke Yiddish seduced women by showing off his books. And he did so while avoiding the need to lug great loads around, so he only carried the covers with him. Books were his secondary sexual characteristics. Musing on the subject, Dovlatov writes, "One has money. Another has humor. A third is courteous. A fourth is pretty. A fifth has a soul. And only the most careless have but a phallus. Nothing beyond a member."

Sergei assuredly didn't suffer from carelessness, and I can't really speak to everything else. I recall only that when he described his turbulent youth, Sergei, as always, savored misfortune. Often, it was related to his stylistic strictness. Thus, one romance never came about because at the crucial moment, his lady-friend noted that she liked starchy foods. Sergei believed that the only "starchy" thing that existed was "starch worms."

Having finally tasted freedom in a new country, immigrant writers also acquired the freedom to call things by their name earlier than their colleagues back in the motherland. That's when it turned out that these things don't *have* names. You had to invent them.

Truth-seekers like Limonov honestly copied the names down from the fences on which they were scrawled. Lyricists committed themselves to graphic details. Surrealists built a system of transparent analogues. In America, even moralists like Solzhenitsyn became excited: "he thrust his bearded face into her womb."

Dovlatov took another path that he himself had worn out. He did away with contradictions. This time, the duality comprised of chastity and carnality.

In literature, to say nothing of real life, Sergei didn't avoid risqué situations. Far from it—because of them, the prissy *New Yorker* even rejected one of his short stories—"Up the Mountain."

It's another story that Dovlatov always depicted sex indirectly. Sergei was frightened not by the indecency, but by the banality of the self-evident. The level of erotic charge is inversely proportional to the directness of the depiction: minimum details with maximum clarity.

A gay friend of mine found *Robinson Crusoe* to be rather piquant, because he discovered in it the phrase: "Friday bent over." Sergei bragged about how he once managed to set the post-coital stage merely by describing the chill of the ashtray balancing on the protagonist's stomach.

In his quest for illustrative clarity, Dovlatov would create erotic outlines, which would suggest how to fill in the missing bodies in the allotted space: "The enormous amber brooch scratched his face." Raising the temperature, Dovlatov leads onto the stage an invisible eavesdropper: "I hear: 'Mishka, I'm going to die!' And a barely audible rattling. That's Marina using her distant, free, invisible, extra hand to steady the wine glass."

Sergei forced the reader to cognize the scene without describing it. And the clinically precise details—"spots of wet grass on the knees"—recreate what had occurred more vividly than any gynecological pedantry.

Dovlatov managed to endow even innocent things with sexual attributes: "A hole in the wall, full of pastries and clamps. Artistically designed diagrams, showing us meat, eggs, fur, and other intimate goods."

4

We're accustomed to thinking that the boundary between the animate and the inanimate is inviolable. Per the *Buratino* quote, "the patient is either alive or dead." Language does not permit us to amend either the living or the dead with the murky "more or less." But the second you tear yourself away from conventional grammatical necessity in favor of straightforward physiological reality, you discover that something *can* be "deader" than something else. Inanimateness may serve as a mask that hides away a passion-filled life. Are inner and outerwear equally lifeless? Are stockings and an overcoat? A bra and a swimsuit?

As could have been expected, the latter became the hero of one of Nabokov's Russian novels. He dresses his favorite heroine in it—the teenage seductress from *Laughter in the Dark*: "Within the darkness of the leotard shown even darker nipples—and her whole, tight costume with its deceptive catches and gaps, with the straps atop her glossy shoulders, held together on a whim and a prayer—make one cut here or here, and it would all come apart."

We do not see the bare body. It is hidden, like gold bars in the bank safe. But the very fabric of the bathing suit becomes charged with the mystery that it hides. The power of this description, inspired by burning, ruthless, and inarguably genuine emotion, is exceptional in its elision.

The farther away you stretch out passion, the greater the distance between its source and the depicted subject, the higher the art. It is what differentiates scatological paintings from the depraved lechery of an "empty kimono." By substituting an object for a body, the artist transforms the sexual question into a theological one. After all, the observer's passion is directed not at the object itself, but at the mystery that lurks within.

In a world where everything is as blatant as on a nudist beach, there are no fetishes. Fetishes are inhabitants of that twilight zone of audacious ideas and timid hopes, a zone that is equally strange to both the believer and the atheist, but is quite familiar to the agnostic.

The first short story about *The Zone's* protagonist Alikhanov begins with a swimsuit. In recalling this rather out-of-place vestment during a winter in the Komi Republic, he provides the first lines: "The young woman wears a wet swimsuit. Her skin is hot, slightly rough from the sun." Dovlatov himself then writes: "Alikhanov felt a quiet joy. He tenderly erased two words and wrote: 'In the summer . . . it isn't easy to seem in love.' Life became pliant: it could be changed with a single motion of the pencil with its cold, hard edges . . ."

It is doubtful that the short story's Freudian subtext, begotten with the "motion of the pencil" in the "pliant life," got here intentionally. Though, Dovlatov's attitude toward psychoanalytical interpretations was utterly devoid of the condescension that people who never read Freud radiate when talking about him.

Sergei liked to recall one party in Leningrad, when Paramonov interpreted dreams in accordance with his idol's teachings. Neither managed to convince the hostess. "It's all nonsense," she said. "What does Freud have to do with anything if my dream is about my husband thrusting a bottle of champagne into a bucket of ice?"

Sex is a universal metaphor. It is the lowest point of our life's trajectory. A single kernel that you throw into a saucer will roll in circles unpredictably, but sooner or later, it will make its way to the bottom, which in chaos theory is called the "attractor." In literature, the role of the attractor is played by talent. In the end, everything that we know and understand comes down to talent. Talent itself, though, is blind, deaf, and inexplicable, like desire. "Talent," wrote Sergei, "is like lust. It is difficult to hide away. It is even more difficult to simulate." We can judge its strength only by the degree to which it resonates with us. Similarly, we can judge the strength of the wind by looking at the bent trees outside the window.

The animalistic nature of artistic talent seemed indisputable to all of us. The question is whether it is exhausted by frequent use. Pessimists said that nature had allotted each of us a finite amount of sperm. Optimists believed: "use it or lose it."

In my opinion, the more decorous echoes of these eternal masculine debates can be heard in one of Dovlatov's final maxims: "God's gift is like a treasure . . . Hence the fear of losing it. The fear that it will be stolen. The worry that it will depreciate with time. And one more thing—that you'll die without spending it all."

5

Sergei was more worried about the secrets of marriage than the great mysteries of sex. Not every reader will note that Dovlatov's most popular characters are his wives.

Endlessly retelling the story of his marriage, Sergei would always return to its point of origin. "How is it that you can . . . an entirely strange person—with your hands! . . ." Sergei would exclaim, at a loss. He wrote on this same subject in *Pushkin Hills*: "A thousand times I will fall into this hole. And a thousand times I will die of fear. The only consolation is that this fear takes less time than a cigarette. The butt is still smoking, but you're already a hero . . ."

Enraptured by the quantum leap from two to one, Sergei never tired of describing that magical second that changes the past and determines the future.

One of the strange things about love is its ability to alter the quality of time. The brevity of the act excises us from time's linear flow. Translating this into numbers is impossible, because we would need units of measurement that evade the imagination, like geological epochs or the lifespan of a moth. Love knows no yesterday or tomorrow. If it finds them, love turns into family or separation.

I am a bad skier, but I occasionally manage to go down the slope without falling. This happens only when I am wholly consumed by an uncompromisingly indivisible instant. The second you imagine yourself from the side, or feel any fear or pride, or start thinking about something, you instantly plow into the snow, embarrassingly losing your skis in the process.

Dovlatov depicts such a catastrophe in *The Branch Office*. This novella, begun in the hopes of an honorarium, quickly lost its narrative spark—it was yet another portrait of the diaspora, this time pretending to be the government in exile. To give the book some weight, Sergei injected it with parts of the unpublished novel *Five Corners*, which was dedicated to his first love.

I once briefly saw *The Branch Office's* Tasya, who was "capricious, awkward, and immoral like a child." A lively face, a boyish figure—it was reminiscent of those about which humorists in the 60s wrote, "Buddy, did you breastfeed Alyoshka?" Her elegant beret evoked a phonetic association with the idol of an entire generation: Brett Ashley.

Admittedly, *The Branch Office's* heroine interests me less than its hero, who spent his life fixing the mistakes of youth. As it turned out, it is most difficult to fix the one that tempts us to stop time:

"You would think: love, and that's it. Be proud that God did you an unasked kindness . . . But I kept complaining and grumbling. I was like a gardener who pulls the flower from the ground every day to check if it has taken root."

"The most important thing in life," he thinks simplemindedly a quarter of a century later, "is that there's only one of it. A minute goes by, and it's over. There won't be another."

He forgot to say that this should only cause us joy.

17

The Unwilling Son of the Ether

1

For me, the most important of all arts is the radio. This surprised me until I realized that it could be no other way. Radio is in my blood. My father was a radio major in university. As long as I can remember, he was never separated from his transistor. At the time, Spidola was a member of the family. Someone even sent me a poem about it once:

> In the air or on the ground,
> Inside, outside, all around,
> In seconds lost and moments found,
> Never for want of better sound,
> To Spidola we are bound.

Only inhabitants of Riga called it correctly—with the stress on the first syllable—but everyone loved the little radio. I grew up with Goldberg's voice in the background. I don't remember the names of my own school teachers, but I remember Goldberg: Anatoly Maksimovich. Those who listened to him need no explanation, and an explanation wouldn't do the others any good.

What's amusing is that immigration didn't change anything. My father continues to live not in America, but on the radio waves. Now he listens to Moscow. And I myself, like all New York writers whose profession predisposes them to a sedentary life, am constantly listening to the Manhattan station that plays classical music and the news with terse, ironic commentary. My connection to the radio has turned out to be the most lasting. I write books, I go to the movies, I watch TV, I read the papers, but the radio accompanies me from dawn 'til dusk. When buying a car, I'm more interested in the dynamics than the horsepower.

McLuhan wrote that by providing humanity with a common nervous system, the radio destroyed our old concepts of time and space. The world's reaction to the invention of radio was hysterical—it enabled the rise of Stalin and Hitler.

Today, radio seems old-fashioned, but it, like gossip, can never go out of fashion. The radio washes over us with a soft, almost imperceptible informational wave. It can remain unnoticed, as air, which we remember only when there's none to breathe. We hear four fifths of all news via the radio, often without even recognizing from what source we derive both our knowledge of the latest events and our attitude toward them.

Radio is a creeping media. Like a voice from off-screen, it is neither within, nor without—it is nowhere, it is in the spiritual bore, in the ethereal emptiness of the airwaves. Even a TV is intended for a whole family, but everyone has their own radio. It is an instrument of intimate conversation. Like a prompter, the unnoticeable and inimitable voice of the radio finds its way only to the individual it is addressing. This ethereal *tête-à-tête* is capable of recreating the intonation of that inaudible conversation that we all conduct with ourselves.

2

Dovlatov had a voice that was uncommonly well-suited for radio. Whereas Paramonov—another ace of the airwaves—confidently growls into the mic, Sergei's voice, like Bernes's, was a husky whisper in the mic. Every time I heard Sergei's dull baritone from the studio, I recalled Ward Stradlater from *Catcher in the Rye*, who kept trying to convince a girl to take off her bra "in this Abraham Lincoln, sincere voice."

By the way, Salinger had a greater and more acute effect on Dovlatov than many others. Especially his short story "For Esmé—With Love and Squalor." First and foremost, the likeness of their situations: the army, beastly surroundings, a soldier who happens to be a member of the *intelligentsia* and whose drama we understand with the help of his accidentally meeting orphans of the war. But the most important thing for Dovlatov was the fastidious vocalization. In the short story about Esmé, almost nobody speaks with their own voice. Even the ten-year-old Esmeralda uses a cliché she overheard: "I'm training myself to be more compassionate. My aunt says I'm a terribly cold person." But in contrast to her, who has already mastered adult speech, we hear the voice of the underlying human nature. Salinger rarely makes this person older than five. Exactly the age of Esmé's brother, who is willing to speak only about the things that genuinely interest him. For example, "Why do people in films kiss sideways?"

Salinger strove for nonverbal wordcraft. He wove language into nets that caught verbally inexpressible content about whose existence we can know only by the weight of the tautly wound sentences.

While in Hong Kong, I was once served a sea critter that looked like a louse under a microscope. When it was lowered into boiling water, it became completely transparent, which admittedly didn't ruin the invisible dinner.

In literature, a similar focus occurs when the writer uses words in a manner contrary to their purpose. Not to tell a story, but to hide it under perfectly meaningless utterances. Stripping them away one after another, the reader discovers a concentrated emptiness swathed in alien words.

Ever since Salinger retired to New Hampshire, nobody knows anything about him other than that he likes bagels—because they have holes in them.

Like Salinger, Dovlatov suffered from the uselessness of the material that was available to him: "The word has been flipped upside down. Its contents have poured out. Or rather, it *had* no contents. The amassing words were intangible, like the shadow of an empty bottle."

But Sergei learned from Salinger to respect words that shone, like water colors. They helped Dovlatov listen to his characters' voices, which cut through the word salad like a hidden knife:

"The captain offered him the pack of cigarettes, signaling that the talk would be unofficial. He said, 'The New Year is coming. This is, unfortunately, unavoidable.'"

3

In Dovlatov's prose, the voice that is best heard is the one that breaks through the interfering noise. It is unsurprising that Sergei wound up at Radio Liberty. Especially considering that it paid well.

Sergei considered work in radio to be an odd job, and in *The Branch Office*, he depicted our editorial team as a pile-up of monsters. Like everything of Dovlatov's, this is only partially true. Admittedly, Sergei settled in at the radio as soon as he immigrated, and he saw more than us there. I also witnessed quite a few oddities, which repelled me from Radio Liberty for many years.

Especially since in Russia, unlike the BBC, it wasn't respected, because it was considered "one of our own."

Truth be told, it was at Radio Liberty that I heard something that both complicated and enriched my life. One time at the beach, I turned on the Spidola and heard a voice saying things about literature that I, to this day, dream of saying. They were doing readings from *Walks with Pushkin*. Sinyavsky, however, lived in Paris. In New York, the office was run by immigrants from the Second Wave. They were even more difficult to understand than the old men from *The New Russian Word*. The war had made their past completely impossible to untangle.

Yurasov's past was indisputably heroic. The book in which he described his tempestuous fate became a bestseller. Eyewitnesses said that when the Americans liberated him from the German concentration camps, Yurasov drove the nurses crazy. Later, at Radio Liberty, he bet big on horse races. When the Perestroika began, Yurasov went to the embassy to ask whether they cancelled his death sentence, which was decreed *in absentia* in Moscow. This mighty old man with his unruly eyebrows had a condescending view of us—like the merchant Kalashnikov.[1]

The quiet Adamovich, who had worked in a Minsk newspaper under the Germans, preferred to stay silent about his past. The Jewish Defense League was searching for him. Adamovich felt safe only at the radio, where he spent his days sitting behind a table full of cans with baby food. He was over ninety, and the unceremonious would borrow money from him.

The most mysterious character at Radio Liberty was Riurik Dudin. He spent the war in Germany, where he studied Heidegger.[2] After meeting him at an editorial party, I assiduously began talking about existential dread and reality's horizon. Dudin ignored me—he was showing off his dagger, without which he claimed he never left the house. Taken aback, I felt the edge, but Dudin hastily took the weapon back. "Sweat leaves spots on the blade," he said, and then added: "Blood never does."

Ryurik hosted a harmless program called "Far from Big Cities." "My people live in villages," he explained the title. Dudin asked me if I wanted to take part in the program, but he asked to give him a heads-up about any benders. After learning that I drink in moderation, he grimaced again. An

---

1   This is a reference to a character from a Lermontov poem.
2   Martin Heidegger (1889–1976) was an existentialist philosopher and supporter of the Third Reich.

expert in all things Mexican, a manuscript collector, a large, hospitable man, Dudin got on famously with Dovlatov, even though he didn't like Jews. He defended his antisemitism by explaining that it was instinctual rather than intellectual: Jews simply made him sick to his soul.

We truly became involved with Radio Liberty when Yuri Gendler ran things. Though Sergei asked us not to jump to conclusions, we thought Gendler was insane. He didn't like literature, and he liked everything else: baseball, Hollywood, fishing, gardening, aviation. Which makes it all the more astounding that Gendler did time for disseminating illegal books. He would spend hours telling the story, and it was always interesting. In his rendition, the labor camps were funny, much like war was for Švejk. Gendler, for example, recalled that in Leningrad, his cell neighbored the most opulent cell in Kresty Prison—it once held Lenin. In honor of his birthday, they would give it a new paint job and populate it with fresh flowers, readying it for a TV special about the atrocities of the tsarist regime.

Having assembled a pretty good team, Gendler commanded us with an iron fist, while simultaneously managing not to hinder any of our work. The New York Radio Liberty—like *The New American* before it—turned into a club that hosted more guests than members. I, however, was still the one who had to do store runs: I was still the youngest. Pretty soon, it became so festive at the radio that Bakhchanyan asked us to hire him as an artist.

4

In the meantime, the Perestroika began. And a stream of guests made for our radio station. Usually, these were Soviet writers. They differed from ordinary writers in that they rarely used the word "I." Understandable. Back home, they all thought themselves dissidents. In the West, they were representatives of, as some Congressmembers characterized it, a nation with the power to destroy America. The shadow of the atom bomb allowed them to put on airs of pacifism and discuss politics.

At the time, it was still believed that Russia was treading a unique path, living off the fruit of a special economy that our guests prettily called "nontrivial." Radicals proposed replacing the economy with a Swedish one, while conservatives had their doubts, as they didn't believe that there were enough Swedes in Russia. Neither they nor onlookers abroad ever ceased keeping track of the saplings of Russian liberty.

Once, a group of democrats from the "Nationwide Front for Battling the Bureaucracy" got stuck in Helsinki on May 1st. The situation was very touch-and-go: nobody knew what had been said in Moscow in honor of the holiday. Frightened out of their wits, the activists began reading Gorbachev's speech in Finnish. Struggling through the thicket of non-Indo-European words, they found a familiar name—"Bukharin"—and sighed in relief: they could safely go home.

When our guests tore themselves away from the mic, they turned out to be nice people. Like everyone after a few drinks, they liked to talk about the intrigues of the top brass. None of them ever asked any questions: they never came over to meet us—they came to make us meet them. Our guests weren't even really interested in New York, though they often asked me to show them around.

Typically, I began tours with the Twin Towers. There was something writerly about them: one skyscraper is a skyscraper, but two skyscrapers are an ode to circulation. Once, when I took a Moscow-based critic up to the 110th floor, I gestured customarily at the Manhattan skyline. My guest raised his head, beamed, and, concluding his internal monologue, declared, "Yevtushenko really is a piece of shit after all."

Radio Liberty's guests were mostly liberal writers who had made a name for themselves in the battle for glasnost. But every now and then, we would get a few nationalists. As happens all too often, the most set in his ways was a Jewish publicist. When we were discussing the viability of establishing a cement factory in the Azov Sea, he said that Russia, thank God, isn't the Ivory Coast, having to build resorts for foreigners. Having been tempered by the Young Guard, he stood out for his decisiveness and judgments.

There was another Jewish writer in the same company—Izya Shamir. The son of Novosibirsk, an inhabitant of Israel, and a citizen of the world, Izya served as a paratrooper, married a Swedish girl, wrote in Japanese, translated Joyce, and was friends with Arabs. He travelled across his "new homeland" on the back of a donkey. I sometimes see him in New York. Once, we were having coffees outside the Borgia, and a Ragulin-sized, blue-eyed stranger ran up to our table. He lifted Izya up from behind the table and pressed him to his chest, Izya's feet dangling above the ground. "He served under me in Lebanon," sheepishly explained the crumpled Shamir. In peace time, he worked in the Knesset, where he fought against discrimination—there was nowhere to tie up Izya's donkey outside the parliament building. Since there was nobody in Israel farther to the left than Izya, as soon as the Perestroika began, he moved to Moscow, where he made friends even in *Nash sovremennik*.[3]

Because I didn't know Soviet literature very well, I had to look up our guests in the encyclopedia, where nearly every single one of them had a book to their name that said "consider me a Communist." The music scholar Solomon Volkov wasn't surprised by this. He asserted that in Russia, as in Florence, there was an eternal struggle between the Guelphs and the Ghibellines. Whoever won, power would stay within a closed circle that did not admit outsiders.

Dovlatov also believed that "class barriers are mighty and indestructible," but he was more receptive of Soviet writers than many others. At a conference of Russian writers from both West and East, he made a generous gift to the Soviet delegation—forty bucks per head. At the time, I shrunk back from the gesture. Now I think back to how Sergei never had enough money.

It must be said that meetings between the diaspora and the metropole rarely went smoothly. At the very first, I sat in the front row, so I didn't miss a thing. On one side sat Soviet UN diplomats, on the other—an immigrant writer who was known for his eccentricity and flawless English.

Alexander Yanov was invited as another representative of the Third Wave. At the time, he had yet to make the discovery that made him famous: the secret copper cable that Stalin allegedly ordered buried for a rainy day between Moscow and Gorky. By the Perestroika, Yanov had written an array of serious books solving "the Russia problem." He invited us over to celebrate the release of one of them. Unfortunately, a thunderstorm knocked out the power, and Yanov didn't know where the breakers were, so we had to identify what we were eating by touch.

The televised discussion was led by the resourceful Grigory Vinnikov. He began by introducing the participants. When Grisha got to Dr. Yanov, a writer who was sitting right next to him remarked in clear Russian: "Some poor excuse for a professor *he* is." Vinnikov amiably noted that people can have different opinions. In response to which the writer, again in Russian, called the host "a Soviet flunky" and hit his mic against his head. The Soviet delegation didn't utter a single word.

---

3   A literary magazine whose name means "our contemporary" and that was renowned for its unfiltered nationalism and antisemitism.

5

As I've already said, Dovlatov considered the radio an odd job and didn't really care for his scripts. If he had to print them, Sergei indifferently signed them "Semyon Grachev." However, writing things half-assedly isn't all that easy, which is why Sergei came up with a particular genre for the radio. He didn't speak of Russia's past and certainly not of its future—he covered its present.

History allows us to solve riddles, while politics poses them: the future will make everything clear. As for the present, all that's left to tell is what everybody already knows. That's exactly what Dovlatov did. Leaving dissidents, Jews, and Politburo intrigues to others, Sergei talked about the motherland's tramps:

"Drunks are filled to bursting with agonizing impatience. Drunks are mobile, twitchy, restless. Drunks are governed by a concrete, if despised goal. But our drunks are full of serenity and calm . . . I remember, I once asked a bum I knew:

'Volodya, where are you living now?' He stayed silent. Then he threw out his hands and exclaimed:

'Me? Everywhere! . . .'"

The Soviet regime didn't interest him—the Soviet person did. Knowing him by himself, Sergei didn't pass judgment on his hero, but neither did he fawn over him. He saw in him a natural phenomenon that had the right to exist no less than the sunset or an autumnal leaf fall.

For Dovlatov, political views were replaced by what he called "worldview": the opposite of the Soviet regime wasn't an anti-Soviet regime—it was *life* in all its complexity, depth, and unpredictability. Rather than arguing with the authorities on their terms, he proposed his own—to discuss life without ideas and concepts.

Dovlatov was neither the progenitor of this practice, nor even its most eloquent champion, but he voiced it more successfully than others. The radio was responsive to the acoustic nature of Dovlatov's talent. Sergei wrote aloud and released a sentence only when it sounded beyond reproach. In this, he was aided by language that Brodksy called "malleable."

The beauty of Russian speech lies in its freedom. Liberated from a rigid word order, it vibrates with microscopic inversions. Thus, standing still, like Debussy's music or a cork in the midst of ocean waves, language conveys *voice* rather than thoughts.

Dovlatov valued no less than poets the ability of sound to retain what is lost in written form. Sergei always thought it important not what was said, but who said it. Truth was replaced by identity. Voice comprised his handwriting. This is why, in his condescension toward Radio Liberty, Sergei declared that if he ever got rich, he still wouldn't abandon the mic. It was impossible to tear him away even from the telephone. Then again, Dovlatov loved writing letters even more.

6

They didn't publish Dovlatov's works for such a long time that they functionally *were* letters. As a result, Sergei became accustomed to treating his prose as his own private affair, but his correspondence he made public. He would make carbon copies of his letters. He sent the most important ones to his acquaintances, "so that there were," as he wrote Nekrasov, "respectable witnesses of our correspondence."

Lots of things in Sergei's letters are funny, and even more are malicious and unequivocal. However, you can't trust them any more than Dovlatov's short stories. Letters played the role of the subconscious, which is much less aware of its surroundings than it is of itself.

After all, the subconscious isn't any more truthful than consciousness. It is simply capable of seeing things inside out. In Eisenstein's first *Ivan the Terrible*, he created two parallel, but time-shifted video tracks. All of the film's characters are accompanied by their shadows, which not only demarcate their personalities, but predict their actions.

These shadows resemble Dovlatov's letters. They served Sergei as rough drafts of emotions. By sharing them with his correspondents, he transformed witnesses into conspirators.

I used to not have a phone book, but because of Dovlatov, I even came to love the mail. My correspondence became so fecund that the mailmen call me by name. They think that I am in communication with aliens, because there cannot possibly be a country on this planet called "EESTI."

The post makes me think of Dovlatov's characters. It owes its charm to ineffectiveness—in this case, its tardiness. An oasis of deliberateness in a world of dangerous acceleration, the post does not require an instantaneous response. A phone call catches us unawares, but a letter patiently waits to be opened or even forgotten. They say that the Chinese actually preferred "matured" letters. They quite reasonably believed that the month it took a letter to arrive wouldn't in any way diminish good news, and it would only defang any bad news. The mail combines traits of two different literary genres: first, like a detective novel, it slows the action down before the denouement, and then, like an epistolary novel, it promises further narrative knots.

I always respond to every letter, first and foremost those sent from Russia. It's just a shame that normal people write so seldom. The most sound of mind was the gentleman who suggested that I borrow money from him. He asked me to call him "Lyolik Knut" on the radio. At any rate, most people offered to lend their ideas, not their money. Some know how to save humanity, others—how to sterilize it.

They were all of them outdone by one Viktor Mikhailovich Golovko, who sends me a notebook every month. Golovko grew up so deep in the backcountry that he went to the village library for the first time as a fifth grader. When he saw all the books, he began to cry, thinking that everything in the world had already been written. After the army, his wife bought him a typewriter to keep him from drinking, and he began to write about everything under the sun—like an encyclopedia. Unlike graphomaniacs who look to publish their works, Viktor Mikhailovich lacks any and all ambition. Like a Platonov character, he is simply incapable of not thinking about the speculative. For example, Golovko came up with a use for the American navy, sitting without use after the Cold War. An aircraft carrier, he reasoned, is an engine with an enormous deck that's just perfect for dry-curing fish in the tropics. Once, Golovko's place was invaded by robbers, but they didn't find anything, because the money was hidden in the third tome of Dovlatov's collected works. Ever since, Viktor Mikhailovich admires Sergei more than other writers.

The listeners always liked Dovlatov, and he got more letters than everyone else put together. Sergei complained that they all ended the same way—with a request to mail a pair of jeans.

18

Death and Other Concerns

1

I rang in 1972 at the place I was stationed at the time: the fire depot of Riga's minivan factory. Since then, I've been to forty countries across four continents, but I haven't seen a single place stranger than that depot. My coworkers reminded me of characters from the theater of the absurd. Their past was multifaceted, their present—indistinguishable. They were all united by an indisputable alcoholism and absolute satisfaction in their positions. Having hit rock bottom, they cast off all their fears and hopes, and they seemed the most content people in the city.

They led their own way of life, and their morality departed into the mysterious realms of boundless patience. The Old Ritualist Razumeyev relieved himself without removing his breeches. Colonel Kolosentsev slept with his daughter. Chief Political Officer Brustsov was never separated from the Lācis novel *The Fisher's Son*, and he dried himself off with my towel. The sea captain Strogov played chess—twenty-two hours a day—and he drank three times a year, but everything, from glue to brake fluid.

This was my company as I rang in the New Year. There wasn't a whole lot to eat. The firemen bore their way through the snow to rip up some wild grass and boiled it in a company-owned pot until the broth took on a vivid green hue. Then, they took the plastic cover off the kitchen table and shook off all the leftover crumbs into the brew. It wasn't as easy with the booze: each of us had his own bottle of Birch Water-brand skin freshener (which also had a verdant shade to it).

The leader of our watch, former KGB major Vaclav Mejrans, famous for drinking away his mother's coffin, looked over the celebration in satisfaction and said a toast: may we ring in every New Year at a table no worse than this one. His wish probably came true.

It was difficult to avoid being the black sheep in this group of firemen. They thought that I, like anyone who watered down his cellulosic ethanol, didn't really drink. Which would be hyperbolic today, to say nothing of then. Few things in my life have I loved quite so devotedly as drinking. Vodka has taken both friends and relatives from me, but I won't say a bad word about it. It rescued me from the life of a tzadik.[1] I've never even worn glasses in my life, because I exchanged the nearsightedness that I was due for an alcohol-induced ulcer.

Debauchery is a rare art. It is devoid of its own object. Like Wagner's Gesamtkunstwerk, vodka unites all forms of life to transform them into an ideal method of existence. Like that same opera, vodka lifts us up beyond the borders of verisimilitude into a world that rejects our common perceptions of time, space, and the hierarchy of things in nature.

The banality of this state does not in the least make it any less sacred. "People don't drink out of need or sorrow," wrote Sinyavsky. "They drink out of a desire for the wondrous and the extraordinary." "Reality," echoes the internet's youth, "is an illusion caused by a deficit of alcohol in the blood." The ability to go beyond oneself and mundanity is too rare a gift of nature to return it unused. Even in Dante's hell, where there is space aplenty for harmless gluttons, there wasn't any room for drunks.

The problem is that there is no way to describe vodka. Lacking its own dictionary, booze retains its secrets no less than the Eleusinian Mysteries. Many times, I have tried to explain what goes on around a bottle. And every time, I would go into the weeds—I would describe the surroundings and the accompanying food: the sweetness of the apple eaten off the slightly powdered down slab in an ancient graveyard or a bit of tinfoil that stuck to a piece of melting cheese. Many times, I tried to explain all this before coming to terms with failure. The imperfection—or maybe, actually, the perfection—of language is that in circumventing a zone that is linguistically impenetrable, it demarcates something indescribable. It's how I speak with my cat: you can't call it silence, and it certainly doesn't qualify as a conversation.

The closest analogy to booze that I can come up with is related to another nonverbal experience—a tea ceremony. From the perspective of an onlooker,

---

1   A tzadik is a Jewish spiritual leader and carrier of the divine presence.

during a tea ceremony, nothing happens, and from the perspective of a participant, even less happens.

The point of ritual tea-drinking is in limiting our life, narrowing it as much as possible by concentrating entirely on the slice of the present that is unraveling in front you, devoid of both past and future. This hour isn't made beautiful by the drink—macha, thick like sour cream—or the handcrafted cup, or the exceptional cleanliness of the floor, or the natural feel of the ikebana, or the tokonama scroll in the red corner emphasizing the time of year, or the fish-eye-size bubbles in the cast iron pot, or the smoothness of the master's long, measured movements, or the appropriateness of a relevant quote, or the subsequent silence, or the semi-darkness heralding a pre-evening warmth—it is made beautiful by the absence of everything else.

A teahouse's amplified crampedness and bareness protects it from the complexities and variety of life. The beauty of the ceremony isn't in what we do, but in the fact that while it lasts, we do nothing else. Instead of remaking the world, the Japanese narrow it, while we water it down—with everything that can be poured.

2

The epistemological question posed by vodka used to be simplified by the fact that I used to not have any non-drinking friends. Because life isn't a bed of roses, I got some with time.

Dovlatov was one of them, rarely drinking with us. In another life, of course, much earlier, he drank like everyone—with his relatives, with friends, colleagues, passers-by. But when we met, vodka was no longer Sergei's friend, but an enemy.

Just as words circumscribe silence, so does heavy drinking circumscribe alcoholism. Two paths lead there. One road, flat like the Gobi, is full of chronic drinkers who walk along the road with fierce indifference to their surroundings. You can pick them out by their gait. Elbows apart, feet scraping against the ground, and hunched over, these are people who are never in a rush. Wherever they go, they can turn around at the drop of a hat. Learning to walk like that requires an unyielding faith in happenstance and the ability to wake up not at home, but wherever you fell asleep. I know just about nothing about the other, even more irreversible path.

In my youth, as is often the case, I was attracted to extremes. With some envy, I read about Gilyarovsky's friends, who could drink away all their furniture up to the window bars. But this too is nothing more than an adventure. The true mystery begins when a person is left alone with a bottle. I have never understood what this person does with this bottle on his own—day after day!—and do not understand it today. This is a boundary beyond which begins another state of existence, foreign like the great beyond. Those who haven't been there can only hypothesize. Their fruitlessness is fueled by the inexpressibility of the post-boundary experience—a type of drinking that our language calls (more accurately than one might like) "dead man's drinking."

Sergei despised his benders and fought them fiercely. He would go years without drinking, but vodka, like a midday shadow, patiently waited its turn. Acknowledging its power, Sergei wrote not long before his death: "Even if I spend years without drinking, I still remember Her, damned, from dawn 'til dusk." That big, capital letter in the middle of the sentence stands out like a stake in a vampire's heart. And it is just as frightening.

3

In Dovlatov's prose, boozing plays an enormous role, but it is the opposite of the one it played in life. In his short stories, vodka has a sobering effect on the author rather than an inebriating one. This is a familial trait of the school to which Sergei belonged by birthright. I would call it "Leningrad baroque." Baroque art tames an artist's typical attraction to the supernatural with a monastery-like discipline: the more frivolous the content, the stricter the form.

In Leningrad, they solved for x in that equation more often than anywhere else. Leningradites—from Maramzin and Bitov to Popov and Tolstaya—are too exacting toward fiction to write a novel. A novel, like snow boots, must have some wiggle room. This group, meanwhile, writes in ballet shoes. Which is why the Leningradite Dovlatov's vodka is starkly different from the one drunk by the Muscovite Yerofeyev, whom Sergei appreciated more than all his contemporaries.

In Yerofeyev's rendition, alcohol is concentrated nonexistence. Inebriation is a way to break free, to become—literally—not of this world. Venichka's drunkenness is the apotheosis of asceticism. By heralding the rejection of the terrestrial in favor of the celestial, Yerofeyev compares himself to a pine tree: "Like me, it regards the heavens, and it does not—nor does it want to—notice what is beneath its feet."

Vodka is the midwife of a new reality. Each gulp melts away the rusted structures of our world, returning it to that amorphousness, that fruitful, primeval chaos were things and phenomena exist only potentially. Bathed in vodka, the world is reborn anew, and Yerofeyev calls us to join him for the christening. This is the source of the sensation of life's fullness and freshness that infects the reader with an ecstatic joy. However tragic Yerofeyev's poem may be, it fills us with joy: we are at a celebratory feast, not a funereal one.

Venichka's debauchery opens a path to a new world. This path, like the steps of Mount Athos's monks, leads to the liberation of the spirit, which is held hostage by the body. This is why it is so important for Yerofeyev to track each step—from the first sip of the morning to the sequence of train stations approaching Petushki with greater and greater pathos.

Anyway, in Yerofeyev's world, drinking is done on the go. In Dovlatov's world—it is done sitting down. Maybe because in Leningrad, as Uflyand explained to me, there's always a draft, and there's nowhere to drink.

4

Speaking of vodka, Dovlatov replaces the word itself with a virtuosic gesture. Literature is wont to scorn clarity, because it isn't easy to achieve. Try to paraphrase the user manual for your alarm clock. It isn't surprising that if there's a deficit of writers in America, then it's only of those who are capable of writing coherent memos for using the phone. Think about it: it's more difficult to write down the rules for a card game than describe a landscape.

Speaking of landscapes. My son, whom my wife and I forced to read in Russian out of pedagogical considerations, decidedly preferred Dovlatov to *Fathers and Sons*. When reading Turgenev, he said he'd read a paragraph, then look out the window, and then he'd have to start everything over. Dovlatov, meanwhile, he read without complaint—something must have hooked him. That's how I imagine it: there you are, flying down the page until you come across something that sticks out. And this architectural excess is so well camouflaged that you can identify it only by touch. Back in my school, we had railings like that, with little bumps. They look smooth from afar, but God forbid you try sliding down them.

In Dovlatov's works, a loving clarity accompanies every detail related to vodka. For example, the hot-water bottle filled with hooch that, "changing its contours, floundered in his hands like a pike fish." Contrary to logic, the refined expressivity of Sergei's gestures grows in direct

proportion with the amount imbibed. Thus, in my favorite scene, the
protagonist is drinking from the bottle in the back of a taxi. The driver says:

"'At least crouch down.'

'Then it won't pour.'"

The elegance of this meaningless line reveals the mystery of
Dovlatov's boozing: vodka made his world maximally straightforward.
Releasing things from the weight of our gaze, it helps them become
themselves. And here is where we get a division in the metaphysics of
Russian boozing: Venichka seeks to escape this world, Dovlatov seeks to
dissolve in it. For his protagonist, vodka doesn't reveal some other world—
it brings into sharp relief this one.

In *Pushkin Hills*, Dovlatov complains that no one has written about the
benefits of alcohol. But in that same part, Sergei fills in this gap:

"The world didn't change for the better right away. At first, I was
tormented by mosquitos. Something sticky crawled into my pant leg. And
the grass itself seemed damp. Then everything changed. The forest parted,
enveloped me, and accepted me into its sultry folds. For a time, I became
part of the universal harmony. The ashberries' bitterness seemed indivisible
from the damp smell of the grass. The leaves above my head vibrated ever so
slightly from the buzzing of the gnats. Clouds swam by as if on a TV screen.
Even the cobwebs seemed decorative . . . I was ready to cry, even though I still
understood that it was the alcohol at work. Clearly, the harmony lurked at the
bottom of the bottle . . ."

5

Dovlatov's drinking passed by without leaving a trace in his literature. Which
can't be said for the hangovers. The morning's remembrance of the previous
night's harmony endows the physical suffering with a spiritual dimension.
Yerofeyev again knew more about this than most. His proximity to Dovlatov
wasn't through his prose, but through his *Notebooks*, in which he explained
through prose his Biblical poetry: "A hard hangover teaches us humaneness,
for example, the inability to throw a punch in any respect and the inability to
respond to a punch . . . we could have avoided a lot if, say, in April of 1917, Ilyich
was in such a state that he couldn't even crawl onto one of the armored cars."

Yerofeyev didn't consider vodka a ball and chain—he viewed it as a
sackcloth. As for hangovers—the justification for hangovers lies in their
preventing people's heads from swelling. The alcoholic equivalent of

submission, a hangover doesn't set you on the path of truth, but it does turn you away from false paths. In a daze, blotted out of our surroundings, denied the will to change our fate, we can finally hear it loud and clear. Yerofeyev believed that before comprehending God's plan for humanity, we have to offer up ourselves as uncompromisingly passive collateral. And this was very close to what Dovlatov believed.

Vodka did not bring Sergei any joy. It exhausted him, like lust exhausts bull deer in heat. Release was brought about not by inebriation, but by liberation from it. The difference between this and the sobriety of a non-drinker is the same as the difference between a divorcee and an old maid.

Returning to the fold, Sergei would set about fixing what had been broken. He repaid loans, asked forgiveness, and patched up familial and professional fault lines, and he kept it up until, writhing and grimacing, life settled down on the tracks that he had laid down. There was, however, a ray of light between debauchery and sobriety that Sergei discussed so stingily that I suspect that it was in those brief hours that his best short stories were born.

By subtracting one's personality, vodka aids it in coming to terms with death, while the subsequent hangover brings it to terms with resurrection. After the plunge into nothingness, everything becomes equally near and equally far. The panorama, unfurling out of nowhere, is unlimitedly broad, for it accounts for any point of view other than the one that makes the world commensurate with a person. Before everything was back in its place, things took on an extreme definition and clarity that are accessible only to the impartial point of view.

Doctors say that people die from vodka not when they drink, but when they sober up.

6

Sergei entered his final drinking spree slowly and unwillingly, like a tanker enters the mouth of a river.

It was hot out. His renown was growing. For the first time ever, Dovlatov was enjoying a decent income. After an agonizing break, he had begun some short stories for *The Refrigerator*. In Russia, a Dovlatovian canon was developing, and it required the author's scrupulous attention. With an experienced hand, Sergei crossed out the unnecessary, assembled the best, and rejected the superfluous. Joyfully sensing his responsibility not to the readers but to literature itself, he carefully conducted his works, which had finally made their way to his motherland.

"Only those who are ready will die," Sergei once wrote. In August of 1990, he wasn't ready. During his last summer, Dovlatov seemed content, and if he wasn't, it wasn't for any reason outside of the ordinary. Sergei very much did not want to die.

As it happened, we spent those days together. He was drinking then, but he continued to work at night. Gradually drifting apart from everyone, Sergei latched on to his responsibilities, setting aside his last hours of sobriety for them. Everyone was scared for him, but also angry.

Things soon got worse, however. Sergei disappeared, then he began ringing people up, as he always did when exiting a period of heavy drinking. Listening to his labored, but still precise speech, peppered with jokes and descriptions of his hallucinations, was awful, but not hopeless. I thought that he had gone too far. That since he was frightened, everything would work out, the nightmare would end once and for all, and a new life would begin. This is why I didn't believe it when he died.

It's true, though it sounds foolish. I wanted to wave away the news as if it were a poorly thought-out bit of gossip. It seemed either exaggerated or misquoted. And a strange bargaining started up in my head—let him be in the hospital, let him be hanging on to life, this can't be happening. But it was, and I'm ashamed to remember it, because more than sorrow, I felt a deep, tear-wrenching bitterness at his death. For many years, it seemed like I would never forgive Sergei for it.

The funeral didn't fit him. A coffin that was too small. Some tie, even though he never wore ties. His swarthy, Armenian face.

Then it started raining. I had never seen anything like it; it was as it someone tipped the sky over. Everything became soaked in seconds—to my underwear, to the money in my pocket. I had never carried a coffin before, and I didn't know that it would be so heavy. Right before the grave itself, the storm cloud passed, but everything was slippery. Stepping along the narrow plank lying in the sticky clay, I nearly plunged into the damp hole before him. It was so large that the coffin seemed almost imperceptible in it.

We stood woodenly around the filled-in grave for a bit, and I went home to write the obituary that I managed to finish only today.

—New York
March 13, 1998; November 19, 2020

19

Without Dovlatov

When I finished this book on March 13, 1998, I felt like I had finished an obituary that I began the day Sergei died. But many years and multiple publications later, I no longer think that I said everything about Dovlatov that I could have. It's his own fault, since he died halfway through the journey that continued after his death.

Shortly before he died, after that creative hiatus that every author finds so agonizing, Sergei finally started writing new short stories, which he wanted to turn into an anthology titled *The Refrigerator*. He wanted to structure it as he had *The Suitcase*, which had turned out so well. In *The Refrigerator*—which, by the way, he intentionally emptied of all alcohol—it seemed that Sergei was using tried and true material. But the last two stories, "Grapes" and "An Old Rooster Baked in Clay," featured a new theme. Dovlatov took his Russian characters, put them in America, and watched what happened. The result was interesting, fresh, and unexpectedly thoughtful. For instance, "The Rooster" used prison slang as a lens through which to examine a motif from *King Lear*: "Allow not nature more than nature needs,/ Man's life is cheap as beast's." It's not by accident that Dovlatov preferred "The Extra" to all his other stories.

It might be because of this creative surge that Dovlatov looked focused and almost happy in his last summer. He absolutely did not want to die—especially not, as they wrote in Soviet obituaries, from a heart aching for his homeland.

Nothing has changed. Dovlatov is still beloved by all—from the plumber to the academic, from left to right, from unpretentious fans to fastidious bibliophiles. Not too many names are left from the bloated Perestroika years, which accompanied Sergei to the metropole's literary sphere. The icons of glasnost, for whose books their fans were ready to level fields and forests, stayed in the old subscriptions of thick journals. But Dovlatov's thin books still stand, not as memorials to an epoch, but on the shelf for contemporary reading. They say that when Solzhenitsyn returned to Russia, he asked whether anything good had been written while he was away. They brought him the first tome of Dovlatov's collected works, then the second, and finally the third. And, mind you, in America, Solzhenitsyn didn't pay Dovlatov any heed whatsoever, much like he ignored our entire Third Wave.

Today, many are searching for the secret to Dovlatov's enduring success. Films are shot, articles are written, conferences and festivals are organized. But I think that the secret of his writing lies on the surface, where, as in a good detective novel, it is most difficult to notice. As a master of prose, Sergei created a nobly restrained style that contrasted surreptitiously with the careless and damaged but endlessly charming character of the author himself.

In doing so, Dovlatov entered the halls of Russian wordcraft and avoided an avant-garde scandal to boot, unlike many of his St. Petersburg colleagues. Sergei had never wanted to change Russian literature—he would have been satisfied merely by leaving a trace of himself in it. By nature, Dovlatov wasn't a revolutionary, but a guardian. He always saw the most important thing as becoming regarded as a classic. Which he accomplished.

In the years that have passed since Dovlatov's criminally premature death, everything has been attempted in Russian literature: Sots Art, postmodernism, distortion, joke-telling, *styob*.[1] And the more experiments there are, the quicker the reader grows weary. Against such a backdrop, Dovlatov's works have become irresistible, because he is a normal writer for normal readers. Sergei always defended common sense, the truth of the banal, and the strength of the mundane, among whose number he counted ordinary people, knowing full well that there was nothing ordinary about them.

He loved books like that, he wrote books like that, and nobody will ever forget it.

---

1   *Styob* is a style of mocking one's conversation partner or something else. *Styob* features elements of irony and sarcasm.

20

A Brief History of *The New American*

1

The New American began with business cards, because the paper's founder Borya Metter had been told that most important thing about a business is its address.

"Location, location, location," explained the businessman next door while they were taking the elevator together. "Remember this, you putz: in America, the location makes the man."

It was impossible not to trust the neighbor. He owned one quarter of a little shop that sold squash spread, sprats, and *The New Russian Word*. Dreaming of starting up some competition and tearing down its monopoly on the freedom of speech, Metter reread Dreiser and prepared to be unbending, like the "Financier," the "Titan," and the "Stoic."

In his past life, Borya was an overseas sailor, which was unusual for a Jew, and the relative of a famous Leningrad writer, which is far less unusual. No match for any of us, Metter, before setting out for his historical homeland and finding it in New Jersey, spent time in some other exotic ports. The story I liked most from his travelogue was about the ship chief political officer. He had gotten lost in Hong Kong and was late to his post, so he hired a rickshaw. Afraid of being mistaken for a sahib, rather than getting into the rickshaw, the officer told the driver to get in and forced him to give directions while he himself pedaled all the way to the dock.

Despite his sea tales, Metter was the only one of his coworkers who didn't have literary intentions. He wanted to publish the paper, not write it. Putting his faith in his neighbor from the elevator, Metter chose the second-most prestigious address in America—after the White House—and rented an office there. On the business card, it said: "One Times Square."

This was where neon section of Broadway stretched toward the heavens. The legendary 42nd Street was just around the corner. The triangular skyscraper itself—boasting a modest height but immodest ambitions—served as a window display for capitalism. Ads flickered by on the façade, calling on passers-by to buy beer and a car and join the army. The scrolling text showed the market indexes and shared the latest news from 1980: Iran, Carter, hostages, a rescued cat. On December 31st, the glowing ball was lowered from the roof, marking the passage of a new year.

Like every American, I believed this landmark to be nothing more than an ad column, and I didn't even know that it was hollow inside until I joined the *The New American's* first editorial team. We worked out of a windowless storage closet. Dovlatov could fit only sitting down. The tightness didn't prevent us from drinking, smoking, and fighting. In fact, Vail and I were invited specifically to lighten things up. The first issues of the weekly paper didn't meet expectations, for which the founding fathers blamed each other.

"You're unprincipled cynics," they said in an attempt to persuade us to join them. "Completely airheaded, you're just in it for shits and giggles, and our paper simply can't do without someone like you."

"True, all true," we agreed—and went to Andrei Sedykh to hand in our resignations.

He took the news of our betrayal in a panic. Nobody ever left *The New Russian Word*—not alive, not of their own volition. He turned grey in his umbrage, then pulled himself together and asked us to find him a spot working for the competition's team as well.

Excited, not even thinking about exchanging a full-time job for rarely compensated work, we got a taste of freedom and found ourselves without a penny to our name. Granted, we had enough to celebrate our first free Monday at 11:30 in the morning. We poured out the bottle right there on the Broadway sidewalk and clinked plastic cups in honor of that American freedom we had finally found. It differed from the typical Russian loafing in that it held the promise of work you loved without pay. This chaste utopia was headier than the bubbly, and we spent the whole day putting together dazzling plans for the future—right up until our wives came home from work.

I rarely jump ahead, but I must, with a degree of gratitude, acknowledge that Monday as foundational. Since that day, I have only ever done what I loved how I wanted to—or rather, as I could. I was fortunate enough not to betray the freedom that was mentioned in *The New American's* exuberant slogan, which was printed in the same place where Soviet newspapers called on the proletariat to unite.

"We chose freedom," the slogan's inventor—Dovlatov—convinced the reader, "and now our fortune is in our hands."

A little below that was the self-identification of the organization where Vail and I would have to work: "A Jewish paper in Russian." Nobody knew what it meant.

2

The Third Wave's very first newspaper was in crisis after having barely taken its first steps. It differed from *The New Russian Word* only in its format, as it still preferred the adventures of the "Kremlin's old men" to any other subject. In order to get someone else to pull their chestnuts out of the fire, they pulled us away from the enemy's ranks and offered us any positions we desired. We liked the sound of editor-in-chief—for Dovlatov.

It took three tries to break Sergei, but after he agreed, he decisively took up the reins—and handed them to us so that he wouldn't have to worry about the details. Other than the editorials, he left for himself various ceremonial functions: he would make peace and start feuds between coworkers, he would have exhausting negotiations with everyone about everything, and most importantly, he represented the paper in dealings with the outside world— chiefly Brighton Beach, where he was immeasurably respected for his virtuosic use of *zek* slang.

The moment of truth would occur once a week at our strategy session, where Dovlatov would go over the latest issue. After coyly declaring himself— the only one of our number who didn't have a diploma—not competent enough to discuss the content of our material, he passed judgment only on the style, but he did so in a way that made everyone's ears burn up.

"So actually, what did you mean," Sergei sweetly asked the poet, pedagogue, and masseur Grisha Ryskin, "when you wrote that 'the bloody hand of crime is choking New York, where bums are loafing around dressed all in tussore?'"

We got it as bad as the others, but no one dared take offense, because our team thrived on mutual roasting, which we carefully cultivated. Nothing was holy, and we were most afraid of what Aksyonov called "beastly seriousness." We would cross many lines, thinking that laughter was appropriate in all situations;

we didn't yet know that jokes could become a nervous tic and turn into *styob*. Sergei foresaw this. He loathed professional humorists and was afraid of being considered one.

In general, he didn't care what anyone wrote about in *The New American*, as long as it was clean, clear, appropriate, sympathetic toward everyone involved, and skeptical of the author himself. By doing away with anti-Soviet rhetoric—no less predictable than Soviet rhetoric—eschewing all back-slapping, avoiding pathos, joking with restraint, and seeing the reader as an equal, the liberated *New American* blossomed. It turned out that freedom lay in style, could be found in the dictionary, and could be dressed up in simple syntax. Nobody had ever considered that spoken language could become written language without the use of swear words.

I feel like Dovlatov, having discovered Lomonosov's "middle style" anew, didn't even notice the revolution that he had brought about. Sergei *physically* couldn't bear it when someone wrote "casted" instead of "cast," and something like "could care less" would make him hound you for weeks, as I myself learned. Taming and weeding our grammatical garden, Dovlatov cleared out the soil for everyone. At *The New American*, everyone became demanding readers of others and cautious writers for themselves. We were afraid of embarrassment, and we were ready to own every extra, imprecise, or bland word—we wrote constantly on alert, as if we were behind enemy lines.

The basketball-loving Lyosha Orlov wrote more than anyone else—three pages at a time. Unfortunately, the two-meter-tall Dovlatov wasn't interested in basketball and considered sports articles ad space, which didn't stop Lyosha. Sinewy and skinny, he resembled the toy bunny from those Duracell commercials. While everyone worked themselves to their breaking points, Lyosha moonlit as a taxi driver, wrote about politics, seduced the ladies, and filled random silences by clapping his hands as if at a stadium, chanting the name of a beloved soccer club: "Spar-tak!"

A couple of enthusiasts wrote about film. Batchan was learned, Sharymova was older and more experienced.

"You can't be jealous of her," said Dovlatov once, "because we were together before you were born."

The same much-suffering Ryskin wrote about life. An expert in German philosophy, a poet at heart and on the job, he thrice attended programming courses and came to despise computers without ever learning how to turn one on. Grisha was terrified of poverty, ate more than he had to, and for a rainy day, he bought two houses in the slums at a buck a pop. When he discovered that you have to pay the city property taxes, Ryskin got rid of the properties with great difficulty, and finally achieved plenty by becoming a professional masseur. The job rewarded him with a new perspective on America, about which Grisha wrote an interesting book. I wrote a laudatory review. It was called "Below the Belt."

The most amiable fellow in our team was the artist Dlugy. A disciple of the nonconformist Nemukhin, who drew playing cards, Vitaly limited himself to drawing dominoes out of respect for his teacher. When he was invited to an exhibit in Latin America, my brother—who, by the way, wrote to the paper under the pseudonym "Aunt Sarra"—advised Dlugy to send the images by telegraph rather than by plane—double twos, five-one, four-blank.

Next to Dovlatov, the pocket-sized Vitaly seemed like a puppy—and he was just as scrappy.

"I'm not Rembrandt," he responded to any criticism. "I'm Dlugy."

That didn't help, and Sergei nearly choked him to death when, at the height of the battle for the Solidarity labor union's freedom, Dlugy colored the Polish flag with green and brown paint.

"Why is the flag on our cover not red and white?" asked a still-in-control Sergei.

"These are conditional colors," replied Dlugy haughtily. "True art doesn't abase itself by copying reality."

He hadn't even finished before Petya and I started holding Dovlatov back, knowing full well his attitude toward the avant-garde.

Thankfully, neither of them held a grudge. We redid the cover, and Sergei gave Dlugy an autographed copy of his book as an offering of peace.

"Vitaly, I love you," Dovlatov wrote, "from your balls to your hairdo."

3

The New American was a success: people read us, loved us, invited us over, and many even subscribed. Bathing in our success, we lived on loans, half-starving, because the better things were, the less money we had. Sergei, who had been working free of charge since his first day, decided to solve the paradox: he decided that we could be saved by a professional manager.

"Our paper," declared Dovlatov at an emergency meeting, "has enough journalists, artists, critics, poets, and photographers, but nobody knows how to count money."

"What is there to count?" asked Ryskin, but everyone shushed him.

"We are children of socialism," lamented Sergei. "In our view, it's better to steal than to sell. The paper needs a true, bloodsucking predator who could grow fat off our talent."

Each of us had his own image of this predator. Dovlatov preemptively worshipped him—I loathed him.

The first one came to the editorial office on his own. Portly, sporting a then-fashionable sandy mustache à la Lech Wałęsa, he had experience managing the affairs of a large American business and had no need for more income, so he agreed to help us out of pity.

"I will sell penknives, and the paper will get 5% off each sale almost for free—in return for two ad pages. Can you imagine how much will add up in a year?"

We couldn't imagine, but we were afraid to ask so as to avoid sounding like idiots. Unable to bear the lengthy silence, I changed the subject.

"Have you read Joyce in the original?"

"What do *you* think?" he asked, smiling condescendingly.

A week later, the mustachioed businessman disappeared, and we would, for a long time, get letters asking us to refund purchased but never delivered knives. Sergei courteously replied to each letter, however, and this didn't stop him for searching for a rich benefactor.

The next manager was a youthful American who had just finished Dartmouth with a major in macroeconomics.

"They say he's a good football player," said Professor Losev, who had recommended him in the first place. "A shame that it's American football."

The youth immediately grasped the situation and found a solution:

"Per the economic analysis, the cause of your deficit is that your income is smaller than your expenses, which means that you should simply cut down on the latter," he said and stopped all payments to the print shop.

When the paper missed its deadline, this manager also disappeared.

The third manager was introduced to Borya Metter by his neighbor—the one from the elevator. A scrawny young man in sweatpants, he immediately took the bull by the horns.

"I'll save the paper," he said. "There needs to be a place for Bunin to publish his stuff."

"But Bunin died," we said.

"Oh, no!" exclaimed the manager.

This one didn't cause any harm, because our ad agent Misha Blank threw him down the stairs when he recognized him as the dealer who sold him a car with no engine.

Dovlatov, however, didn't lose faith in big business and brought a new fat cat to every strategy session.

One guy with psoriasis suggested that we write "zestfully," another demanded that we fire Bakhchanyan, a third advised us to sell the paper to the Hassids, a fourth—to the Baptists, a fifth promised that he would shoulder all the costs personally, then asked us for a metro token for his return trip. They all looked down on us from on high, seeing that we were willing to work free of charge—like inmates, afraid that someone would take away their wheelbarrow.

4

When the paper gave up on growing rich, we agreed to grow poor and implemented a moratorium on personal expenses, learning to eat only when going over someone's place, including my parents'. But even sitting at a set table, our team continued to strategize.

"In order to arouse the reader's interest," said Dovlatov, "the paper needs to get into a squabble."

"Polemic?" I asked.

"That works too," approved Sergei, "but a squabble would be better."

He was essentially right. Every paper is as strong as its opposition, even Soviet papers, which we used to peruse jealously for the "Other Customs" section. That was where, long before Komar and Melamed's experiments in which they painted together with animals, I read that an American abstract art exhibit featured a painting made by a one-eyed parrot. That stayed with me, because I sympathized with the bird—my mom also only had one eye, and she would often miss the teapot when she tried to put on the lid.

"The article's author is implying," I decided then, "that if the bird had both eyes, it would paint as well as Repin."

We needed a "parrot" of our own, and Solzhenitsyn became that parrot. We were all fans of his, of course. It was, after all, Solzhenitsyn, whose *Archipelago* brought us to America, having convinced us of the irreparability of our homeland. However, in the New World, he despised us and refused to acknowledge our existence.

"While we revel in America's fertile fields," his silence said, "he, Solzhenitsyn, gnawed on the bitter bread of exile."

It's unsurprising that the picture of Solzhenitsyn in a pair of shorts, playing tennis on his court in Vermont, evoked a curiosity that bordered on and engendered schadenfreude. Nevertheless, everyone was in awe of Solzhenitsyn—the liberal part of the diaspora with some reservations, Bakhchanyan without any reservations whatsoever.

"Come hell or high water," he said, "you have to live without lying."

Simultaneously both poet and tsar, Solzhenitsyn functioned as the diaspora's Brezhnev, which also spawned myriad anecdotes. When Brodsky was awarded the Nobel, Solzhenitsyn reservedly approved of Stockholm, but he advised the poet to safeguard the sacred purity of the Russian language.

"Look who's talking," Brodsky allegedly replied.

Hiding away in Vermont, Solzhenitsyn intrigued us all with his inaccessibility. The only Russian writer whom nobody but Boris Paramonov ever saw inflamed the imagination and provoked our paper to publish sacrilegious articles. Solzhenitsyn apologists wrote to us complaining, dithering notes in response: "Dear misguided gentlemen . . ."

We would hand-wave everything away, the polemic would smolder, the scandal would grow, and at our strategy meetings, I would quote *Three Men in a Boat*: "The big dogs fought each other indiscriminately; and the little dogs fought among themselves, and filled up their spare time by biting the legs of the big dogs."

Dovlatov was thrilled by all this, and the paper gleefully published all aspersions sent its way, thereby evoking admiration at its tolerance.

"A shining example in democracy," our friends said.

"A liberal cesspit," our enemies corrected them.

"What's important," Dovlatov mollified everyone hypocritically, "is that nobody is indifferent."

Truly nobody was. *The New American* incensed the old diaspora because it employed Bolshevik language ("are frankfurters little sardines?"). Jews were angry that there was too little written about them, others—that there was too much. And everyone condemned us for our unforgivable levity when our homelands (old, new, ancestral) were drowning in blood.

"How, how are we supposed to feed Poland?!" Borya Metter's renowned elevator-riding acquaintance asked him, complaining about *The New American's* insensitivity right up to the point when, at another one of our meetings, we forbade Borya to use the elevator ever again.

Drunk on impudence, inflamed by hunger, we delighted in the freedom of speech, unaware of how easily it became the as-of-yet uninvented *styob*. Readers enjoyed keeping track of the newspaper fights in which we would engage each other, publicly settling scores—with Dovlatov too.

"Do you really think it wise," we asked Dovlatov ingratiatingly, "to deport all Iranian students from the US in response to the American diplomats' being taken hostage in Tehran?"

"Of course, but it would be better to put them behind bars," replied Dovlatov without hesitation, and we published this in the paper as proof of its chief editor's backward sense of justice.

Dovlatov would respond in kind, and the readers, seeing from week to week how we goofed off, came to consider the paper dear and necessary. We became certain of this when *The New American* had been around for a year. Celebrating our anniversary, we rented a hangar in Brooklyn, where we hosted more than a thousand of our fans. Drinking and eating, they watched as Dovlatov led a strategy session onstage. This was a cut above even *Tom Sawyer*: people weren't paying for the honor painting the fence—they were paying for the opportunity to watch others paint it.

The singular commercial success of that event spurred the idea that maybe we should replace the physical paper with an oral one, thereby saving on printing and distribution. But by that point, there were too many writers working for the paper, and they weren't looking for a change of profession.

5

Spurred on by need, *The New American* has long since left its prestigious crypt on Times Square, searching for something cheap with all its might. Our vagrancy began in a joyless office on Fashion Avenue, where there once used to be sewing shops, but now—in memorial to them—there sits a bronze Jew with his sewing machine. The light was always on in the office because the sun couldn't penetrate the windows, which hadn't been cleaned since the times of *Sister Carrie*. Things, however, did not become any roomier after the move. The office was constantly crowded with strangers sneaking peaks at how our atmosphere of indiscriminate love and envy begat and birthed the paper. We never shooed anyone away, but when businessmen came, Dovlatov made me sit in the bathroom.

"If you grimace like that," he complained, "then you can forget about ad revenue."

Nevertheless, *I* was right. Businessmen were no different from anyone else. They wanted to invest talent, not money, in the paper. Sometimes it was verse, sometimes prose, and always useful advice. None of it helped, and, unable to pay the Manhattan rent, we crossed over the Hudson into New Jersey, where a group of Ukrainians housed us in their printing shop, where they printed an old and serious paper called *Svoboda* ("Freedom"). They were the only ones who took *The New American's* ethnic persuasion seriously, and they gave each of us an ornate album and wished us all "a happy New Year" (in Ukrainian) in accordance with the Jewish calendar. None of us could figure out how it worked.

American Ukrainians had nothing in common with the ones we used to know. They didn't speak Russian at all, and they had only a vague understanding of Soviet realities. They called their wondrous rye bread "kolkhoz" bread, thinking it meant "peasant" bread. However, the Ukrainians knew the Kremlin's warlords, and they loathed them as much as we did. This helped my one acquaintance who directed Kharkiv's amateur art scene make his way to America. Together with a local folk ensemble, he staged an anti-Soviet hopak titled "Zaporizhians Write a Letter to Andropov."[2]

New York assigned the Ukrainians to the eastern part of downtown, which they shared with the punks. Despite the warlike mohawks, the youths peacefully ate borsch at a place called "Veselka." Other than restaurants, the East Side harbored the Church of Saint Yura, the Shevchenko Institute, and a museum that truly began to prosper when they thought to augment the list of Ukrainian artists with everyone who had ever visited Crimea, Odesa, or Kyiv: Malevich, Chagall, Arkhipenko, and the rest of the avant-garde.

Other than art, I was also interested in Ukrainian sausage. Twisting into a thick ring, like a firehose, it gave off a generous aroma and promised to be the star of any feast. Preparing for one such, I once loaded a sausage ring into my trunk, along with black loaf and a bottle of then-popular Absolut. When I went back outside after spending longer than wise in the museum, I discovered that my car had been stolen. Even now, I fill up with emotion at the thought of what those thieves did with the sausage. It's no secret that guileless Americans (nobody else would jack old cars) are suspicious of garlic and alien cuisine. At any rate, when the police returned the car a month later, the only thing in the otherwise empty trunk was a box from McDonald's.

Our alliance with the Ukrainians didn't save the paper. From the wrong side of the Hudson, Manhattan looked like Kitezh. The setting New Jersey sun was reflected in the glass skyscrapers and bathed the city in an almost Baltic amber light. Having failed to subdue New York straight away, we decided to

---

2   This is a play on the famous Repin painting *Zaporozhians Write a Letter to the Turkish Sultan.*

wage a war of attrition—if not against it, then against ourselves. Vail stopped paying for his apartment, I was ashamed to look at my working wife, Ryskin ate a whole lemon, and for lunch, Metter enjoyed packets of sugar that he stole from cafes.

Our poverty began to cause actual fights. We accused management—that is to say, Metter—of inaction. He accused us of carelessness. Unable to deal even with himself, Borya took to fixing our problems, and he appointed the mighty Popovsky to look after Dovlatov. He lived across the street from me, and I often came over for various materials.

"My father," said Mark Aleksandrovich when we only just met, pointing at the portrait of a man who looked much younger than Popovsky himself.

"I don't see the resemblance," I said, surprised.

"My spiritual father," he explained. "Aleksandr Men'."

As any neophyte, Popovsky fiercely loved Christianity, and he managed to destroy the only functioning organization of the Third Wave—the Veterans' Union. He was condescending toward me and Vail, as if we were mutts. Trying to purge everything from the paper for which its readers loved it, Mark Aleksandrovich tried to make us see reason and replace us with prisoners of conscience.

Our strategy sessions became louder, the food disappeared entirely, and the end was imminent, but I was indisputably happy, because I only did what I loved, and every day, I spoke about what mattered most.

6

Dovlatov didn't hold on to books for long. He knew his favorites—like Dostoevsky, "Master and Man," and, of course, Faulkner—by heart, and he easily parted with others, passing off to me and Vail everything from Lev Khalif to Sasha Sokolov. His relationship with literature shocked me to the point of hiccups, as did mine him, especially when I let slip my thesis about Menippean satire.

Sergei fundamentally eradicated any respect I had for the silliness of literary studies, and I zealously learned from him how to make do without them. I eagerly listened to him while suppressing my internal protests—after all, like any straight-A philology major, I revered the word "poetics," and I dreamed of discovering its secret rules and applying them to some literary object.

Furthermore, we were very different: I wanted to know everything, while Dovlatov wanted to forget everything in order to discover it anew. It's not that Sergei despised erudition—he tolerated it, waiting it out like somebody else's drinking, firm in his belief that it's impossible to learn anything useful by reading. Frightened by this demonstrative ignorance, I sensed Dovlatov's rightness, but I didn't dare share his views. Maybe because I drank less.

Rejecting schools of thought and philosophical directions, Sergei was interested not in different authors' similarities, but in their inimitable differences. To hear him tell it, each author was a literary unicorn. He didn't value books' themes or narratives, but the clarity of their portraits and the tone of the dialogue; not the path to the finale, but the moment of truth; not beauty, but precision; not width or depth, but accidental diagonals, surreptitious like an outstretched leg and irrevocable like a slap. Infected with Lotman and a youthful impetuousness, I loudly argued and quietly took it all in, realizing that the truth lies where no one had been before.

Chats with Dovlatov didn't develop your intellect or your taste (though it did that too), but your tactile relationship with words. Sergei probed the text, noting where the superfluous jutted out and where the missing yawned. I did roughly the same thing when I worked as a *metteur en pages*.

And yet, if we ignore the Menippean satire, Dovlatov rewarded our experiments. Categorically refusing to differentiate fiction from any other literature, he considered criticism an equal genre, convincing us of the same. Moreover, Sergei demanded that we publish a book, and he didn't understand why we weren't in a rush. Personally, he waited too long to put off this decisive event in an author's biography.

"A writer," preached Dovlatov, "begins with his second book, because anyone—even if it turns out good—can write a first one."

Once Sergei persuaded us, we gathered and mangled everything we had written and brought it to Dovlatov's wife Lena so that she could type it up on a computer. To pass the book off, we met with Sergei at a McDonald's. We celebrated our hard work with some brandy we brought with us, stayed late, and left pleased with one another. Only in the morning did we realize that none of the three participants of the festivities had the manuscript of our first book. As with the sausage before, I grieved for the thief who would find in his new suitcase—specially purchased for the occasion—nothing but pages lined with strange letters.

We had to compile the book again, which didn't make it any worse than it could have been if we consider the wan, publisher-enforced title: *Contemporary Russian Prose*.

Dovlatov as an Editor

1

I always believed in communism more than the regime that preached it. Ignoring the dogmas of its own religion, it lost sight of the mystery of hard work and savagely punished anyone who wanted to work well. For example, Dovlatov. His homeland inhibited his ability to do what would have been beneficial for both sides. In fact, that's the only reason why we crossed the ocean. Our American dream, however, wasn't a house with a lawn, but a community cleanup.

And we achieved what we wanted. We built communism in one independent paper, which lasted longer than the Paris Commune and made us all happy.

As in another—bigger—world, capitalism naturally emerged victorious over communism, but not before we ran out of money. In one year, *The New American* made 240,000 dollars and spent 250,000. And nobody managed to figure out how to make these guileless numbers switch places.

Now, a quarter of a century later, historians of the Third Wave count their chickens in the fall and eviscerate *The New American's* very lining in their attempts to discover its secret. I think it's all for naught. A paper is like a rainbow—it leaves no trace. It is all process rather than result, nonstop, stimulating commotion, memory that requires no documentation. It happened—and thank God for that.

2

Dovlatov didn't fit in at the paper, but he liked it. It couldn't have been any other way. The paper was a portal of Soviet literature, its propylaeum and courtyard.

No other path led to official wordcraft, and Sergei accepted that. In his search for a little money on the side, Dovlatov worked for the most exotic publications. Judging by his stories, he was the king of newspapers of general circulation. This was quite believable, because Sergei could spruce up any junk with a clever artistic detail. For example, the following.

When by some miracle, the famous jazz pianist Oscar Peterson wound up in Tallinn and even played a concert, Sergei wrote a review of the concert that ended on a high, Hemingway-esque note: "I clapped so hard that my new watch stopped working."

Thirty years later, my colleague and big jazz enthusiast Andrei Zagdansky brought to the studio a recording of that same Oscar Peterson concert—November 17, 1974. We put the recording on the air, warning our listeners that the applause that intermittently interrupted the music included Dovlatov's own clapping.

Sergei's handiwork, which he prudently shared with the press, gratified editors. Like all people, including Party members, they wanted to be taken seriously even when the organ directing them advocated victories of labor. Dovlatov bragged that there wasn't a single editor in all of Russia who wouldn't forgive him his drinking sprees.

Having amassed a multitude of stories from his time toiling for various papers, Dovlatov arrived in America with a vengeful scheme, which he carried out in *The Compromise*. I've heard that many have tried to find the quotes in the book in the bowels of the party press, but I doubt that they'll find them there. Sergei loved falsification, deftly parodying the primary sources—even if he himself was the source. He was a virtuoso when it came to that special, romantically elevated journalistic style that was necessary to write about ordinary—rather than communist—life. When reaching the part of the paper that covered this—typically the last page—the author, compensating ideological congestion with heightened metaphoricity, soared above the text. Without pausing for breath, Dovlatov could come up with a lengthy, lyrical sketch with the universal (as he claimed) title "The Caravan Leaves for the Heavens."

The thing is that a Soviet paper, utterly devoid of any informational utility, was a *literary* paper. It stayed that way when it again found itself in the rearguard. But we didn't even think about that then. The paper was our community cleanup, and Dovlatov—its chief decoration.

3

When Sergei appeared in New York, the immigrant press was dominated by *The New Russian Word*, an outfit that differed from Soviet papers only in that it was their anti-Soviet supplement. Perhaps I wouldn't be as critical of a paper that hosted veterans of the Silver Age—the critic Weidlé or the philosopher Levitsky. But in our youth, we couldn't care less about them. We didn't want to read—we wanted to *write*. And there was nowhere to print what was written.

Grasping the situation, Dovlatov quickly became ready for his own paper. After forming an unstable and, as it turned out, accidental alliance with three buddies, Sergei plunged into newspaper life. For the first thirteen weeks, we watched *The New American* from the outside—with apprehension and envy. But pretty soon, Dovlatov enticed me and Vail to join the paper that he considered his own, even though it had yet to become his. We set one condition—name Dovlatov editor-in-chief. This step seemed natural and inevitable. Sergei hadn't yet become the Third Wave's favorite author, but as his enthusiastic fans, we were sure that we wouldn't have to wait long.

At first, Dovlatov hypocritically refused, like Boris Godunov. Then he agreed and took the helm with great satisfaction. The thing he liked most was signing his name: the reader of any individual page knew who the editor-in-chief of *The New American* was. Dovlatov always loved pro forma, he loved meetings, and he never begrudged anyone time for business—or casual—conversations.

Only much later did I realize what the position meant for Sergei. Having become accustomed to being an unofficial writer and accepting the role's accompanying limited popularity and unlimited carelessness, Dovlatov finally worked his way up to become an editor-in-chief. He dearly valued his newly attained position and took it seriously. When, during the vicissitudes of newspaper battles, the publishers tried to formally remove Sergei from his post but have him retain all his power, Dovlatov said that he prefers form to content, and everything stayed as it was.

At the paper, Sergei implemented a constitutional monarchy of the most liberal order, demonstrating a phenomenal finesse. He reveled in democratic formulae and always left the last word for himself at strategy sessions. But even then, Dovlatov reserved the right to criticize only style and language, declaring that everything else was outside his competence. Despite the narrowness of his set task, his reviews were entertaining—and elucidating. Sergei grandly flaunted his ignorance all while boasting unconventional knowledge. I, for example, had no idea that tussore was an expensive silk. Grisha Ryskin didn't know that either, which is why he dressed the bums from his temperamental sketch in tussore—and burlap. In essence, carousing at the paper, we were the same.

Most interestingly, at *The New American*, Dovlatov truly was concerned only about form—clarity of language, rhythmic variance, organic tone. And he turned out to be absolutely right. Without saying anything particularly new, *The New American* spoke differently. It won the readers' love only because it spoke to them as a friend. The paper shook off the idiotic torpor that used to grip us at the sight of a press sheet. It is why people loved us. Now, there's no need to mince words about the nature of that affection. The best thing about the paper was the atmosphere, but it is the first thing to be aired out, and it is the most difficult thing to convey.

4

At the center of the magnetic field that pulled in grateful readers was Dovlatov himself, of course. His authorial contribution was the weightiest. Beginning with the fact that each issue began with an editor's column that fulfilled the difficult role of both tuning fork and epigraph.

Sergei wrote these measured, weight-like texts with the same fastidiousness as his short stories. This is why it's unimportant what the columns were about. Liberated from justification, they easily entered the Dovlatovian canon. These light opuses were grounded in a secret, but strict, almost poetic meter, and they demanded extraordinary skill.

Nevertheless, the columns often infuriated the readers, who were irritated by the principled flippancy of the compositions. Today, in the era of absolute *styob*, it's too late to argue with that, and foolish besides, but at the time, Dovlatov had to constantly bat away complaints. He suffered for it, but he didn't let up, even though the toll it took on him was obvious to the naked eye. When he once opened a letter with a dose of uncivil (read: boorishly rude) criticism, Sergei tore it to shreds and bounded from the room, at which point we cheerfully reminded him of democracy and glasnost.

Overall, however, Sergei was a yielding editor, and he didn't despise his readers. Which wasn't easy, especially when they addressed him with the informal "you" and condescendingly gave advice. Sergei knew how to mildly bear any such address. He took offense only at his own people—which he did often and heatedly.

It must be said that misunderstandings never inhibited our merry work, which *The New American* transformed into the highest form of recreation.

Our open editorial meetings would gather crowds of observers. When Sergei wanted to punish his young daughter Katya, who translated TV programs for the paper, he forbade her to come to work. When he took stock of each issue, Sergei noted the best material and rewarded its author with an enormous bottle of cheap wine, which was immediately poured into sixteen paper cups—one for each of us.

5

Dovlatov loved all the technical minutiae of newspaper work: printing jargon, line gauges, mockups. He swooned over the massive and complicated magnifier that everyone was afraid of, he heatedly discussed various projects' cover pages, and he drew amusing pictures for each issue. Furthermore, Sergei kept a hawk-like watch over the work of our artist—the amiable and forgiving Vitaly Dlugy, whom he lovingly and mercilessly criticized for his indefatigable avant-gardism. This rarely happened, because Sergei eschewed anger in favor of such a keenly honed and biting sarcasm that it delighted even his victims. This talent he also brought to bear for the paper.

Where the paper was concerned, Dovlatov knew how to do everything, of course, except for the crosswords. He could take care of any issue—from a problematic sketch to image attribution, from fake letters to the editor to lyrical sketches of life in a Russian grocery store, from a clever anecdote to an inventive caricature. Under the headline "ROY MEDVEDEV,"[1] he drew little bears flying around the Kremlin's spire.

Dovlatov struggled most when it came to pseudonyms. His style was so recognizable that it was impossible to hide it behind a fake name. When he had no other choice, Sergei signed "S.D." [or C.D. if using Cyrillic letters—A.R.] He liked the initials because they were the same as the Christian Dior brand, which figured in one of Dovlatov's short stories.

Strange as it may seem, Dovlatov's authorial egocentrism didn't prevent him from standing out in an unexpected role. Sergei published excellent interviews. The first was with an elderly immigrant who had only just come to America. It had a noteworthy ending: "S. Dovlatov conducted the interview with the father."

---

1 Aside from being the name of a famous dissident, this also literally means "a swarm of bears."

Transitioning from his close ones to less familiar faces, Sergei went into a rage and published interviews with all of his acquaintances, including, it must be said, imaginary acquaintances. Coming up not only with the questions, but the answers, Sergei used these "interviews" to hone his unparalleled dialogues, that art of the quip when each one seems not only pithy, but—something that is much harder to pull off—organic.

Settling in at *The New American*, Sergei felt at home at the paper—in a bathrobe and slippers.

6

Dovlatov loathed abstractions, and he became bored when he heard expressions like "general trend" or "duty to the reader." He was more interested in genres. For example, Sergei grew livid from the fact that any printed opus by a journalist was called the same thing: they were all "articles." Even more important to him were words—words independently of anything else, divorced from context, subject, or purpose. He took joy in any stylistic discovery, but even then, he preferred phraseological neatness, regardless of where he found it—in a sports article, a horoscope, or a reader's letter.

However, what truly concerned Dovlatov in *The New American* was the computer.

"It's smarter than Popovsky," Dovlatov said reverentially.

At the time, the machine cost so much that nobody argued with him— even Popovsky.

Though he respected technology, Dovlatov, like all of us, was a little afraid of it. He entrusted his own thoughts only to an old typewriter, shooting down any suggestion that he get a computer of his own.

Sergei was a big proponent of manual labor. He especially liked watching others work, and he never missed an opportunity to watch how Vail and I composed the paper. Sergei fit in the windowless little alcove with two flatbeds only sitting down, but even then, it was impossible not to trip over him. This didn't bother us. Accompanied by his snide comments, we dexterously did our work and merrily bantered with each other. Gradually, the laughter would attract our other coworkers, then our guests, and finally, complete strangers. It was as if we were working in an overcrowded subway, but we could never kick anyone out, even when we turned off the light to print the latest issue's photographs.

Dovlatov liked publicity and became fired up from the audience, but the paper became a club all on its own. People came to *The New American* to witness a rare spectacle: people genuinely enjoying their work. For us, our work was a privilege, hence why nobody made any money off it. Dovlatov, at any rate, refused a paycheck. The paper's owners did too.

As always—and certainly as before—poverty didn't prevent us from enjoying ourselves—the work itself was the reward. Which is essentially what Marx said, Lenin practiced, and Brezhnev promised. I still don't believe that there is a better way to be friends than to work together—especially to *create* together, though if the company's good, then even moving furniture can be a hoot.

In our team, Sergei wasn't a generator of ideas—rather, he fostered an environment in which ideas couldn't *but* be generated. It was incisively interesting to share space, thoughts, and bread with him (but not booze). Sergei electrified those who were within arm's reach, he infected everyone with a thirst for friendly competition: each person excitedly rushed to contribute, desperately hoping that his input would be accepted into the fold. After locking steps, the paper created a resonance that brought down now-useless bridges and raised the level of expectations. Every phrase was in rhythm, every word became hilarious, every thought became topical.

Like a bender or an orgasm, something like this cannot last forever, or even for all that long. But to his last day, Dovlatov considered the year of *The New American* the best in his life.

22

Dovlatov on the Screen

It so happened that the interval between Dovlatov's date of death and date of birth (August 24, 1990–September 3, 1941) came to be known as the Dovlatov days and is celebrated with festivals in St. Petersburg and Tallinn or just with a drink at an appropriate watering hole. Gradually, these rituals fused into one, through which we understand the writer who became the darling of two generations—ours and the one that is coming to replace it.

Everything makes sense about the former, but not about the latter, because it never knew the context that birthed Dovlatov and his first readers. After Dovlatov himself, the best way to learn about that time is Aleksei German Jr.'s film. The film isn't so much about Dovlatov as his environment, i.e. it is about all of us, the invalids of the Stagnation, we who wintered and survived and are now looking back at the past without sparing it an iota of nostalgia.

Disregarding narrative, transitions, internal logic, and compositional wholeness, the director goes alongside reality, bringing with him a magic mirror. Reflected in this mirror, the accidental takes on the noble traits of the authentic, inevitable, and characteristic. The muted, almost inaudible quips, semi-dark apartments and poorly lit streets, song lyrics, excerpts of jazz compositions that cannot be finished, landmark quotes, and cult figures (typically Iosif Brodsky and Jackson Pollock). The viewer is steeped in a raw reality unfiltered by scheme or purpose, where nothing really means anything, which is precisely why every shard neatly fits into the overall picture of hopeless grey.

Only, there's no need to pity anyone. This gaggle of unrecognized geniuses, shuffling around on the edge of drunkenness, prison, and death, comprised that artistic environment that birthed honest thought, indisputable talent, and boundless dedication to one's calling. The grimmer an era, the greater its need for bohemia, which guards the spark of culture in conditions not intended for its survival. It's worth recalling that at that time, what passed for prose were Georgy Markov's novels, Yegor Isayev's poems for verse, and socialist realist Cézannism on the topic of "The Fraternity of Peoples" for painting.

On the other side of the front, the film shows servants of the regime—the ones who choke and suppress. But as in Dovlatov's own works, they are depicted neither angrily nor scornfully.

"They are not letting us into literature," said Dovlatov, "we wouldn't let them onto the tram."

On the screen, everyone is waiting for a holiday—November 7th—and everyone wants only the best for the protagonist, for the homeland, for the regime. "In order for life to become better and more exciting, it needs to have room enough for heroic deeds," they harp, not even suspecting that this very chronic shmuck in his invariably black coat will write books that will make their lives funnier and therefore better, that this quiet man will be the one to do the heroic deed, writing—as he often recounted—400 short stories with no publication prospects.

23

Dovlatov and Death

1

Russian America pays more attention to anniversaries of its favorite authors'
deaths rather than their births. This is understandable: they were born in their
language's homeland and died in the homeland of another. This is why in
the dead of winter, January 28th (usually in a restaurant named Samovar),
people remember Brodsky, while at the end of the summer—August 24th—
people raise a glass in the Armenian corner of the Jewish cemetery in Queens,
next to Dovlatov's monument.

I met Sergei when he wasn't even forty, but even then, he already liked
talking about death. Admittedly, he couldn't really do that with me. I was only
twenty-five, and I earnestly didn't understand his alarm. I'd heard about death,
sure, and I even thought about it sometimes when I was little. I'd argue that it's
the most important discovery kids can make—everyone will die, even grandma,
but only Mandelstam ever really remembered this:

Oh how we love to hold our breath,
And then forget that—free from fear—
The closest we ever are to death
Is in childhood, our early years.

Coming quite a ways since his "early years" and spending three years as a
prison guard, Sergei always remembered what lies in wait—not for him or for
us, but for the works he had written. A stranger to any metaphysical perspective
but the one Brodsky espoused in his poems, Dovlatov worried about the
posthumous life of his works. He knew for a fact that they were destined to
stand on a bookshelf—by Sergei's estimation, somewhere next to Kuprin.

Feeling a duty to his future readers, he fastidiously guarded his compositions and categorically forbade publishing the occasional compromise that saw the light of day in the Soviet Union. So as not to forget, Dovlatov kept a memento mori in his desk—a large, sealed envelope with the inscription, "Open after my death." All of his frequent guests saw it, but nobody ever took it seriously. Last wills weren't our genre, and neither were obituaries. I wrote my first one about Sergei. He introduced the topic of death into my life and literature, but I needed many years to come to terms with the former and figure things out with the latter.

2

The eleventh compromise of the eponymous book was a standalone short story titled "Someone's Death and Other Concerns." The title itself contains the central idea, underlying narrative, and main image.

However, Dovlatov sacrificed the title when he was assembling short stories for the book, but this opus is still prominently distinguishable, notable for its unusual finale.

As in the other "compromises," an anecdote forms the crux of the novella. At the morgue, they mixed up the bodies of the party functionary Ilves and the bookkeeper of the fishermen's kolkhoz Gaspl. So as not to ruin the official event, they buried one, pretending he was the other. That's the whole story. But against this simple literary backdrop, there is a complex knot of motifs and meanings that envelops and develops the topic of death.

First and foremost, it is a drama of language. The short story's tuning fork is an epigraph from the Party press: "... Hubert Ilves's whole life was an example of selfless service to communism." This text is composed entirely of clichés and is utterly devoid of content. The Party language is so faded that it could be resuscitated only by a mistake, which trips up one interlocutor and proves lethal for the other: "'Tallinn is on the line,' said Bykover ... In response, he heard: 'My dear Comrade Stalin!' Those freedom-loving Bulgarians ..."

Informational perdition, the underbelly of language serves as the point of conflict between inauthenticity and earnestness. Dovlatov so deftly depicts each shade of every falsehood that it takes us a while to notice how he spares no one—not even himself. It isn't only the editor Turonok's clichéd speech that is false—the author's dissident rhetoric is no exception (albeit in a slightly different manner), as it explains things that do not need to be explained, such as: "The newsman is earnestly saying something he doesn't believe in."

Throughout all this, the author keeps a close watch on himself, boasting with effective comparisons: "I felt awkward, like a dead whale in a pool. A horse in a dog kennel. I paused, writing down these metaphors."

Equally false are his relations with Marina, who embodies different, but similarly conventional clichés, like the author's jumper (Hemingway says hi): "She turned on the record player. Vivaldi—of course. Long associated with booze."

Characteristically, the culmination of inauthenticity, which concludes with vomit, occurs when the author proclaims his funeral speech: "Comrades! How I envy Ilves . . ." And then, when Marina shows him an excerpt from her diary: "He was a celebration for my body and a guest for my soul." This is that quintessential, vulgar banality that—to avoid Nabokov's creeping definitions—forms the connection between triviality and pretentiousness in an unbearable ratio.

Constant falsehood causes permanent double-think, which results in doubles. Characters double and get mixed up. Everyone, including his lover, believe the protagonist to be the missing Shablinsky. Ilves Jr. is mixed up with Ilves Sr., one corpse is confused with another ("It really isn't Ilves, but they look so alike").

The accumulation of the absurd leads the short story to its denouement, which—as with the best literary finales—is simultaneously inevitable and surprising. Death appears in the text virtually unnoticeably. It imperceptibly shadows the characters on their path to the end: "'We've reached our goal,' said Bykover. Life's transience could be heard in his quivering voice." Dovlatov depicts the graveyard romantically, like Böcklin's *Island of the Dead*: "Everything here responded to the idea of immortality and peace. The hills stood as ruins of ancient fortresses. An invisible sea rumbled in the distance."

The shift in tone readies us for the tale's turning point, about which the author warned us in the beginning: "When faced with someone's death, movement of any kind seems amoral." This means that the presence of death can dissipate falsehoods too. As Bakhtin said, when standing at the side of a coffin, you can ask only the final questions. But inside the coffin itself, he added, "is always someone else." Which is why the protagonist, in order to escape from the shroud of inauthenticity, had to equate himself with the dead man in the coffin: "I felt the fragrant smell of flowers and pine needles. The sides of the uncomfortable bed squeezed my shoulders. Fallen petals tickled my hands, folded on my chest."

Only now, having put himself in the dead man's place, could he accept "someone else's death" as his own and finally ask the real questions that are unrelated to the elemental conflict between truth and lies, to which the short story was seemingly dedicated. The inauthentic world of our mundanity isn't juxtaposed with the truth hidden away by the authorities, but the essential truth that has nothing to do with them whatsoever. We know nothing about it, but standing at a coffin's edge, we have the right to ask "about overcoming death and anguish. About the laws of existence that were born in the depths of millennia and will live on until the sun is extinguished."

These words sound helpless—it is as if they are demonstrating any language's inability to communicate with death and address it. But Dovlatov was never going to reveal anything new about this eternal subject. He merely wanted to bring the narrator to the Party funeral and tear him out of the web of predetermination, say something inappropriate, and cause a scandal—not with the higher-ups, but with reality, which is assuredly on nobody's side.

To use a fashionable word, death *nullifies* life, and it would be criminal of the author not to take advantage of that.

3

And now, I must admit to some maladroitness. When we read this short story in draft form (Sergei showed me and Vail everything before it went to print), we acted foolishly. The literary fabric was certainly delightful. The humor hid elegantly inside the text, which doesn't even hear itself: "His father and grandfather fought against Estonian absolutism." Each character was portrayed using hasty details, like Dovlatov's own caricatures ("The editor had a beige, child-like face, a wide waist, and a childish last name—Turonok").

In short, this was the same Dovlatov that everybody went nuts for—from Brodsky to Brighton Beach. But the ending horrified us. It seemed cut and pasted out of somebody else's book. We neither understood nor accepted the last page, and we implored Sergei simply to throw it out, to excise what we perceived as an inappropriate and pitiful part of the story. Dovlatov took no offense, didn't listen to us, and explained nothing.

I finally got it, but only when I came to be in the same spot as the protagonist—at the edge of a coffin. The day of Dovlatov's funeral—the first in my life—I recalled the details in the short story. A tie, though Dovlatov never wore ties. The heavy load, which the six of us barely managed to carry. The grave, where "water stood and the whites of chopped tree roots could be seen."

A. Genis. Doodle by S. Dovlatov.

Dovlatov's funeral in New York.

About the Translator

Alexander Rojavin is a multilingual intelligence, media, and policy analyst specializing in information warfare. He is currently editing a book on modern Russian cinema as a key battlefield in the Kremlin's information war (forthcoming Routledge). At the same time, literary translation has always been one of his first loves.

www.ingramcontent.com/pod-product-compliance
Lightning Source LLC
Chambersburg PA
CBHW031949010726
47493CB00007B/2142